Lone Star Christmas

HOLY NIGHT

ISBN: 978-1-68313-042-0
First Edition
Printed and bound in the USA

Cover and interior design by Kelsey Rice

Lone Star Christmas

HOLY NIGHT

BOOK III IN THE SACRED JOURNEY SERIES

KAREN HULENE BARTELL

𝑃

Pen-L Publishing
Fayetteville, Arkansas
Pen-L.com

BOOKS BY KAREN HULENE BARTELL, PHD

THE SACRED MESSENGER SERIES
Angels from Ashes – Book I

THE SACRED JOURNEY SERIES
Sacred Choices – Book I
Sacred Gift – Book II
Lone Star Christmas: Holy Night – Book III

Belize Navidad
Christmas in Catalonia
Sovereignty of the Dragons

Fine Filipino Food
The Best of Korean Cuisine
The Best of Taiwanese Cuisine
The Best of Polish Cooking
American Business English

With all my love to my husband, Peter William Bartell

With special thanks to the speakers at the 2015 San Antonio Catholic Women's Conference

Chapter 1

"The soul is healed by being with Children."
— ENGLISH PROVERB

Three minutes. She replaced the cap, laid down the test stick with the result window facing up, and read the directions yet again. *Three minutes.*

Staring at herself in the mirror, Maria looked at the dark, curly hair framing her oval face. She saw the pinched lips, the pucker between her brown, almond-shaped eyes. *How will Mal take the news?*

I didn't test positive last month, but I know I'm pregnant. I can feel it. I can smell it. Inhaling, she turned up her nose. The restroom's air freshener did nothing to mask the pizzeria's reek of oregano, greasy sausage, stale beer, and urine.

With a sigh, she checked the time. *Two minutes.* The sounds of 'You Belong To the City' wafted from the speakers. She remembered the first night she and Mal had heard Glenn Frey's song. *Our song.* Recalling the magical moment, Maria gave her reflection a wistful smile. *May first . . . nine weeks ago yesterday.*

She checked the time. A minute to go. How will he take it? She watched her reflection as her creased brow dissolved into smile lines. What am I worried about? Today's the Fourth of July and his birthday. This will be his best gift ever.

Maria focused on the test stick's result window. *One pink line.* She remembered the stories of home pregnancy tests giving false readings. *I tested negative last month, but* . . . A second bar faintly appeared in the result window. *Is it? Am I?*

Yes! Test stick in hand, she stared at the two bars. Then she glanced at the mirror, saw her beaming smile, and squealed with delight. Too excited to keep it to herself, she joined Mal at the table.

He glanced at her and drew back his head, scrutinizing her. "You look like the cat that swallowed the canary. What's up?"

Others were seated at the table, so she whispered in his ear. "Happy birthday, Mal. You're going to be a daddy."

Chapter 2

*"You never soar so high as when you stoop down
to help a child or an animal."*

– JEWISH PROVERB

"Focus on the mother's needs first." Develyn turned toward Angela with a smile. "It's like the airlines' safety demo." Develyn stood up straight, mimicking a flight attendant's spiel. "If you're traveling with children, make sure your own oxygen mask is on before helping others."

"Mother first. Got it." Angela nodded as she caught sight of her reflection in a car window: shoulder-length, dark hair, high cheek bones, and a creamy complexion.

"She's in crunch mode, often struggling for her own survival." Develyn grimaced. "I ought to know."

Comparing Develyn's black postulate jumper to her own tee-shirt and jeans, Angela studied her friend and former roommate. *Goth girl to postulate, she's still wearing black, but that's the only thing that hasn't changed since our freshman year.* "What then?"

"Keep brochures from local health centers in hand, so you can offer them to women entering the clinic."

"Check." Angela held up a handful of pamphlets. "Then what?"

"Remember, it's not so much what you say as how you say it."

Angela cocked her head. "Meaning?"

"You have sixty seconds to communicate, from the moment she steps out of her car to the instant she enters the clinic's doors." Develyn's eyes met Angela's. "You have to engage her. Not only with words, but through your body language, your tone of voice. To connect with you, the mother has to believe you'll help her."

"One minute to earn her trust, convince her you're her best hope." Angela took a deep breath. "That's not much time."

Develyn started to speak, but a parking car caught her attention. "Watch."

While Angela stayed on the sidelines with the prayer group, she saw her friend leap into action. Smiling as she approached a young woman, Develyn cradled a tiny replica of a baby in her palm. "This is a life-sized model of a baby at twelve weeks."

A clinic escort met the woman and accompanied her, engaging her in a loud conversation meant to drown out Develyn's words.

Develyn held up a brochure within easy reach for the woman. "You have alternatives. Would you like to discuss them?"

Both women ignored her as the orange-vested escort hurried the mother inside the clinic.

When Develyn returned to their group, Angela gave her a sympathetic smile. "You didn't have a minute. It was closer to twenty seconds."

"That's why it's called counseling on the fly." Taking a deep breath, Develyn shrugged her shoulders. "You have to reach out to women in crisis. No matter how some view it, we're their front line of defense."

Angela looked at the people gathered. Several were praying, creating an umbrella of spiritual protection about them. Two were kneeling in front of lit candles. Hands in pockets, clinic escorts milled about like shop-keepers keeping sharp eyes for incoming customers. Another 'angel' like Develyn watched the parking lot, waiting to approach abortion-minded mothers as they drove up.

"Is it just because this is San Antonio," asked Angela, "or are most of the women coming here Hispanic?"

"In Texas, the highest number of people using Parentage Incorporated are Hispanic. At first, they come for the low-cost contraceptives, which makes them easy targets later, when they come back for the abortions."

A woman walked out of the clinic. Pale, looking neither left nor right, she stumbled past their prayer group as if in a daze. Angela watched her get into her car, momentarily slump over the steering wheel, then start the engine and drive away. She turned to Develyn.

"How often is that scene repeated each day?"

"Twenty, twenty-five times."

Angela gave a low whistle. "You mean, this clinic aborts that many babies a day, every day?"

"That's just this facility."

"It's like," Angela searched for an analogy, "a terrorist shooting a classroom of school children."

Develyn nodded. "Multiply it by the number of abortion clinics around the country."

Angela took a deep breath. "That puts it in perspective."

They stopped talking as a woman got off a bus, crossed the street, and started walking toward them.

Angela studied her, trying to place her. *She looks familiar.*

Develyn hopped into action. She held up the tiny doll, two and a half inches long. "This is a life-sized replica of a baby at twelve weeks." Working quickly, before the clinic escort met the woman, Develyn held out a brochure. "You have alternatives. Would you like to discuss them?"

The woman's eyes opened wider. She moved her lips silently.

Develyn gave her a reassuring smile. "We can help you."

Shaking her head, the woman said, "I have no choice."

"You do. Would you like to discuss your choices?"

As the clinic escort approached, the woman said. "I have no money."

"We can help," said Develyn.

While the escort led her toward the clinic, the woman hesitated, looking back over her shoulder.

"We can help," Develyn called.

Angela watched as the escort spoke to the uncertain mother and hurried her into the clinic.

When Develyn returned to their group, Angela gave her a sympathetic grimace. "She seemed interested."

An hour later, the same woman walked out of the clinic. Her red eyes searched the crowd until she spotted Develyn. As she began walking toward her, Develyn rushed to meet her. Although Angela could not hear their words, she saw them talking. Then they bowed their heads in prayer, crossed themselves, and the woman nodded.

Develyn waved Angela over.

Angela scrutinized the young woman as she approached. *I know I've seen her somewhere.*

"Angela, can you drive my friend Maria and me to the health center?"

"Sure." Angela squinted, trying to recall. "Maria . . . now I remember. Weren't you in my Foundations—"

Wearing a startled, wounded expression, Maria's eyes suddenly peered left and right as if looking for an escape. She started nervously rubbing her hands and wrists.

"It's all right, Maria." Placing her hand lightly on the woman's wrist, Develyn spoke softly. "Angela's here to help. She's going to drive us to get a sonogram."

Angela nodded, worried she had said the wrong thing. She swallowed as she contritely glanced at Develyn. "My car's parked over here, and the health center's five minutes away."

Develyn nodded to her and then spoke gently to the woman. "You're doing the right thing, Maria. It's going to work out."

An hour later, Develyn and Maria emerged from the office, smiling, holding up a manila envelope.

"It's a boy," said Develyn.

"Congratulations." Angela shook Maria's hand. Then she looked from one to the other. "You can tell the baby's sex so soon?"

"For boys, yes," said Develyn, "as early as twelve weeks into the pregnancy."

Maria looked into space as she counted on her fingers. "May Day was twelve weeks ago yesterday." Suddenly her eyelids fluttered and she lurched as if she was going to faint.

Develyn caught her by her shoulders. "Are you all right?" She helped her sit down.

Angela got a cup of water from the cooler. "Here."

Nodding her thanks, Maria sipped it.

"Do you need to lie down?"

Maria shook her head. "I'm fine." She started to get up and then fell back into the chair.

"Maybe we can get a clinician to look at you."

Again Maria shook her head. "I'm just a little hungry. I haven't eaten today."

"That's not healthy," said Develyn, "either for you or your baby."

Angela looked at her watch. "It's almost lunch time." She turned to Maria. "Want to join us for a bite to eat?"

"That's just it. I—"

"Our treat."

Over soup and sandwich, Angela watched Maria. "What made you change your mind and leave Parentage Incorporated?"

"As I was filling out the paperwork, I read a permission slip about disposing of the 'products of conception.' Not a baby, but byproducts, waste . . ." Maria glanced at Develyn as her eyes welled up. "Since the moment you talked to me, I'd been second-guessing my decision to have the abortion." She swallowed hard. "But after reading that form, I was too uncomfortable to sign. Even in my anxious state of mind, I realized it gave Parentage Incorporated permission to do whatever it wanted with my baby . . . or its parts. The technician must have sensed a change of heart."

"Why do you say that?" Develyn's eyes caught hers.

"She asked if I was an organ donor. When I nodded, she said donating fetal tissue was the same thing. It would all be used for scientific research." Her lip curled. "Research, another name for experimentation."

"It's obvious you don't want an abortion, yet you went to the clinic." Angela asked softly, "Why?"

"I never wanted it." Maria's eyes met hers. "I just didn't . . . *don't* have any options."

"Yes, you do, more options than you may realize." Develyn shared the story of her pregnancy and how it had worked out in an open adoption.

"My birth mother, Ceren, gave me up for adoption when I was born," said Angela.

"Then, full circle, Ceren adopted my baby." Develyn smiled gently. "Those pregnancies had happy endings. Yours will, too."

"What about the father?" asked Angela. "Can he—"

Eyes focused on her chest, Maria shook her head. "When I told my fiancé I was pregnant, he simply ran out on me." She looked up. "I've texted and called, but I haven't heard from him in three weeks."

Angela grimaced. "What about your parents? Can—"

Again Maria shook her head. She took a deep breath and then spoke in a monotone. "When I told them, they said, 'You got yourself into this . . . '" Taking another deep breath, she shook her head. "They won't help."

"Where have you been living?"

"I tried crashing on my friend's couch." She raised an eyebrow. "Let's just say my friend's boyfriend was a little too friendly. I left the first night and started sleeping in my car, moving it every couple hours, whenever the police made their rounds. Thursday, when I was out looking for work, they towed it, impounded it. I didn't have money for the fines, so . . . " She shrugged.

"Where have you been sleeping the past two nights?"

"Under a bridge."

Develyn's eyes met Angela's.

Maria swallowed. "I didn't have anywhere else to go."

"That's when you decided to go to Parentage Incorporated?" Angela asked gently.

Eyes red, she took a deep breath, and nodded. "I didn't know where else to turn, what else to do."

"You said you were looking for a job." Getting an idea, Angela leaned across the table. "I work at the Alamo, and I happen to know they need an intern for the summer. Are you still a student at UTSA?"

"I was during the spring semester, but I haven't registered for the fall semester . . . "

"That qualifies you for the summer. Are you interested?"

"Yeah!"

"I can put in a good word for you, but you'll need to apply online."

Maria grimaced.

"What?"

"I don't have access to a computer."

"You still have your UTSA email address, don't you?"

"Yeah . . . "

"The library's not far. I can drive you. We'll fill out the forms online." Angela smiled at Maria as she finally recognized her. "You *were* in my 'Foundations of Communication' class at UTSA last semester, weren't you?"

When Maria gave a stilted nod, Angela studied her. "I thought so, but I wasn't sure. You look so different with short hair. Didn't you have long, curly hair last semester?"

Her shoulders drooping, the girl sighed. "I cut it yesterday."

"Because it's cooler for the summer?"

Maria grimaced. "Without a mirror and a blow dryer, let alone electricity," she took a deep breath, "let's just say this style's easier to manage."

Angela caught Develyn's eye.

At the library, all went well with filling out the form until the last page. Then Maria looked up from the keyboard.

"What's wrong?"

"It needs a mailing address . . . "

"Let me type in mine." Angela turned the keyboard toward her. "That should work."

Maria hesitated. "How will they get in touch with me for an appointment?"

Angela thought a moment. Then she glanced from Develyn to Maria. "The form needs an address, and so do you. My roommate's away for the summer, and the apartment has an extra room. Why don't you stay with me?"

Maria's eyes lit up, then faded. "I can't put you out."

"No worries, it's just till you get settled."

Maria's mouth screwed up as if fighting tears. She cleared her throat and took a deep breath as she focused on the online form. "Today's July twenty-fifth." Smiling through wet eyelashes, she said, "For me, it's Christmas in July."

The next day, Maria's smile lit up her face. "I got the job."

Angela grinned from behind the Alamo gift shop's counter. "I had a feeling you would."

"Thanks for lending me your clothes for the interview."

Angela shrugged her shoulders. "Not a problem."

"Everything I own is in the trunk of my car." A worried 'V' appeared between her eyes.

"You'll be all right. After work, we'll get your car from the impound lot." With a quick wink, Angela gave her an encouraging smile. "You're getting your life back on track one piece at a time. Don't worry. It'll all come together."

Sunday, they drove to the Mission of Divine Mercy. They chatted quietly as they climbed to the chapel. As birds chirped, a summer breeze ruffled their hair. The peppery, floral scent of sage filled the air, and Angela breathed in deeply.

As they approached, the structure began to take shape: octagonal. Native limestone veneered the exterior and interior walls of the chapel. Cedar shakes crowned its roof.

Inside, a vaulted ceiling with cedar rafters and cross-beams drew her eyes toward the crucifix hanging between knotty pine louvers. The architecture was more an open-air pavilion than a church. No glass windows or screens interrupted the birds' songs. Their chorus rang from the juniper branches only inches from the windowless walls. Ceiling fans overhead moved the cross- breeze, providing a comfortable temperature, even in late July. They took their seats at hand-fashioned pine pews topped with carpet samples.

Seeing no kneelers, Angela placed a carpet square in front of her, knelt, and began praying.

The fresh country air and birds' warbles buoyed her spirit. From the corner of her eye, she peeked at Maria. She was also on her knees, and her eyes were closed in prayer. She sat quietly beside Angela through the Mass, but when Angela stood to get in line for communion, she shook her head.

Afterwards, Angela whispered, "Do you want to go to confession?"

Hesitating, Maria mumbled.

"What?"

She sighed. "I should. I need to." She glanced at Angela and grimaced. "I just . . . "

"Go on." Angela gestured toward the confessional. "You'll feel better."

Maria waffled, making a sour face.

"What? Do you think you're the first person to make a mistake?" Smiling gently, Angela gestured with her chin. "Go on. I'll wait for you over here."

A half hour later, Maria emerged from the confessional; her eyes were red, but she was smiling.

Wordless, Angela hugged her. When they broke apart, she asked, "Hungry?"

"Starving." Maria placed her hands on her stomach. "Both of us!"

"Then you're in luck. They have a wonderful dinner after Mass each Sunday."

They walked down the hill, past the unfinished Monsignor O'Callaghan Center, and got in line beneath the canvas tent. Cafeteria-style, they picked up paper plates, napkins, and plastic utensils.

Ladies ladled out beans, rice, and okra. Then they came to a man serving pulled pork.

"Would you like some barbeque?" Rhythmically addressing each person as they moved up the line, he faltered when his eyes met Maria's.

She smiled. "Yes, thanks."

His eyes took in the girl's features. Then he swallowed, his Adam's apple bobbing.

Serving spoon suspended over her plate, he asked a beat late, "Over the rice?"

She nodded. "Please."

Angela watched his eyes follow Maria as she moved along the line. Then, seeming to catch himself, he turned toward her. "Would you like some barbeque?"

Grinning, she chuckled to herself. "Yes, please."

Their plates full, they began looking for a table in the outdoor pavilion. Angela saw Mother Mary Agnes, waved, and joined her.

She greeted the girls with hugs and smiles as Angela made introductions. "Mother Mary Agnes, this is my friend, Maria."

"Please call me Mary Agnes." Smiling, she gestured to the seats beside her and across from her. "How do you two know each other?"

Maria winced as if embarrassed. Then in halting phrases, she told Mary Agnes the story of how Angela and Develyn had met her in front of Parentage Incorporated. "Basically, they convinced me not to have an abortion." Then gesturing toward the confessional with her chin, she gave them both a shy smile. "I feel like I've been to confession twice today."

They chuckled sympathetically. Then, seeming to gather her thoughts, Mary Agnes met Maria's eyes. "Has Angela told you my story?"

She shook her head. "No."

"Years ago, I, too, found myself pregnant and unmarried."

"Were you a nun then?" Maria's eyes widened.

"No, that was before I was called. Back in college, I had a boyfriend I believed I loved."

"Did you?"

She tilted her head and gazed off in the distance. "Not really, not by my definition of love now." She turned back toward Maria. "But I found myself in a position similar to yours, pregnant and unsure what to do next. My boyfriend pressured me to get an abortion. Despite not having an answer, I knew that wasn't it."

"What did you do?"

"After a lot of soul-searching, I decided to carry the baby to term and then choose whether I wanted to give up my child for adoption or raise it as a single parent."

Angela remembered the first time Mary Agnes had told her and Develyn her story. *Was that nearly two years ago?* "You've heard Develyn's story. Mary Agnes helped her decide to give her baby up for adoption. Now she's a postulate, on her way to becoming a Sister."

Maria nodded. Then she looked at Mary Agnes. "What happened to your child?"

"My cousin and her husband adopted him." She took a deep breath.

Thinking of how her birth mother Ceren had given her up when she was born, Angela said, "All things work together for good for those who love God." Then she shared her story of how her adoptive mother had raised her. "It was an open adoption, and from my point of view, it worked well. I had two mothers. Three, if you count my aunt Pastora."

Mary Agnes smiled at her and then looked at Maria. "Do you mind if I ask you something?"

She shook her head. "No, what?"

"What are your next plans?"

Maria grimaced. "I don't know. Until a week ago, I was practically living on the street." With a dry chuckle, she added. "For two nights, I *was* living on the street, under a bridge. Then I met Angela. She helped me find a job and is letting me stay in her apartment."

Angela gave her an encouraging smile.

"My life's improved so much in this short time, I have hope now," said Maria. I feel something will work out. I don't know what. I don't know how, but I do know one thing. I'm carrying my baby to full term. I'm not aborting it."

"Do you know if God wants you to give up your baby or raise him?" She tilted her head as she watched Maria's response. "Could motherhood be the vocation God's calling you to?"

Maria blinked as if thinking it over.

Angela remembered when Mary Agnes had asked Develyn the same question.

"First seek the Lord's will. Discern what He wants you to do." Lifting an eyebrow, Mary Agnes leaned across the table. "Your first vocation is to love God. Your second vocation is to be a good prenatal mother. Take care of your baby. Take care of yourself during this pregnancy. Go to the doctor. Take vitamins. Then soul-search. Ask God, 'do I keep or give up my baby for adoption?'"

Maria nodded thoughtfully.

"At this point," said Mary Agnes, "I recommend you seek His guidance and surrender to His will."

"Mind if I join you ladies?" asked the man who had been serving barbeque.

"Please do." Mary Agnes gestured to the seat beside Maria. "Have you all met?"

"Other than sampling his delicious barbeque, no." Angela smiled. "Did you make this?"

Chuckling, he nodded.

"This is José Aceves," said Mary Agnes, "chief cook and bottle washer around here."

He grinned. "Happy to help whenever, wherever I can."

"This is Angela," said Mary Agnes, "and this is Maria." She gestured across the table.

José's eyes opened wide. "Glad to meet you."

Angela studied his dark hair and serious brown eyes. "Do you live near here?"

He nodded. "But I work in San Antonio."

"Really? Where?"

"The Menger Hotel."

Angela met Maria's eyes.

Glancing from one to the other, he narrowed his eyes. "What? Is something wrong?"

Maria turned toward him. "We work next door to you at the Alamo."

His face lit up. "Small world, isn't it?" He gazed at Maria's pixie haircut and her flashing dark eyes.

"José, you promised to help us find hearts." Two little girls came up behind him and began tugging at his arms.

Giving them a wry grin, he nodded. "I did, didn't I?"

"Hearts?" Maria cocked her head.

He turned toward her. "Fossilized shells, bivalves that look like hearts of stone."

"José, you promised." The little girls began tugging harder. "Come on."

"Okay, okay." Standing up, he reached into his wallet and pulled out two business cards. He handed one to Angela and the other to Maria. "Have you ever had a tour of the Menger Hotel?"

They shook their heads.

"Why don't you stop by, and I'll give you a behind-the-scenes tour?" Though José addressed them both, his eyes focused on Maria.

She peeked up at him as she shyly took the card.

"Maybe after work some day this week?" He held back, watching, waiting for Maria's answer as the little girls tugged at him.

Wordless, Maria bobbed her head in a curt nod.

Angela stifled a grin. "Sure, José, how about this Tuesday?"

"That'd work." He glanced at Maria, but she kept her eyes on his card.

Angela thought of Kio. "And if you don't mind, I'll ask a friend to join us at the Menger."

His smile came easily. "The more the merrier."

"José, come on!" The little girls pulled at his hands.

"My previous engagement seems pressing." He chuckled as he turned back toward the women. "Nice meeting you Angela, Maria. See you both Tuesday, and will see you next Sunday, Mary Agnes."

As the girls dragged him off, Mary Agnes smiled. "Children love him."

Maria watched him walk away with the girls, laughing as they teased him. "He seems to like them, too."

When they got off work Tuesday, Angela found Kio waiting for them outside the Menger Hotel's entrance.

Angela's heart skipped a beat as Kio leaned over to kiss her. "Hey."

"Hey." Smiling shyly, she introduced them. "This this is my roommate Maria, and this is my . . . friend Kio."

"Nice to meet you," said Kio.

Angela watched him as he held out his hand. *Why didn't I say boyfriend? But is he?*

Shaking hands, Maria said, "I've never heard the name Kio before. Is it a family name?"

"It's the Chinese name for Spica, the brightest star in Virgo."

"His great-grandmother was half Chinese," added Angela.

"The Chinese believe Spica's an auspicious star," said Kio. Since my birthday's in September, and I was born a Virgo, she said I was—"

"Born under a lucky star." Angela spoke the words along with him, and they laughed. "Which is why he's an astronomy grad student."

"Do you go to UTSA?" Maria asked.

He nodded. "Do you?"

"I did for the spring semester." Grimacing, she added, "Not sure yet about the fall."

"One day at a time." Angela smiled at her. Then, linking fingers with Kio, she glanced at him. "I'm glad you could join us."

Kio returned her smile. "The tour sounds interesting, especially with my great-great-grandfather's connection to the Menger Bar."

As they entered the hotel's lobby, Angela saw a woman look up from her knitting, as if expecting someone. When the woman did not recognize them, she pushed her wire-framed spectacles to the bridge of her nose and returned to her knitting. Then, the tassels of her beret still gently swaying from her movement, she disappeared into thin air.

Though Angela said nothing, she caught her breath. *No matter how many times I see spirits, they still startle me.*

José was standing behind the desk when he saw them walk in. "Maria, Angela, I'm so glad to see you." Eyes on Maria, he came around to the front of the desk to greet them.

"José, I'd like you to meet . . . Kio." *That avoids the issue.* Turning toward Kio, she added, "We met José Sunday at the Mission of Divine Mercy. He makes a mean barbeque."

"Glad you could join us for the tour, Kio."

"My great-great-grandfather worked in the Menger Bar before Prohibition. I've always meant to see it."

"In that case," Jose said, "why don't we start the tour there? When the bar was built, it was located in the front of the hotel. During the '20s and '30s it was dismantled and stored. Then after Prohibition ended, it was reassembled and remounted in its current location, which is just down this hall."

Acting as their personal guide, José directed their attention to an old photograph on the wall.

"See anything unusual in the photograph?"

They looked at the framed photo from several directions but shook their heads.

"Take a picture of the photo."

They looked at each other. "Why?" asked Maria.

"I'll show you." He gave her a mischievous smile.

"I don't have a phone," said Maria.

"I do." Angela took a picture of the photo and then displayed it for them.

Grinning, José asked, "See anything unusual in this picture of the photo?"

Again they shook their heads.

José zoomed in with his fingers, enlarging the right side of the photo. "See it now?"

Maria gasped. "Ohmigosh." She pointed with her finger. "See the face over here?"

Angela kept silent, but Kio's eyebrows shot up as he gave José a suspicious chuckle. "This couldn't have been PhotoShopped, could it?"

José shook his head. "This is the original, unretouched photo, and from their outfits, you can see this was taken in the early twentieth century, way before Photoshop was invented."

He led them into a dark-paneled room. "The bar's carved from solid cherry." Speaking to their reflections in the mirror, he added, "The paneled ceiling and French mirrors are said to have replicated an eighteenth-century bar in London, the House of Lords Club."

"Beautiful old wood." Angela felt the bar's smooth, polished surface. "It must have been quite the place in its day."

"They say it served mint juleps in solid silver cups, and the spittoons were gold-plated."

As Angela scanned the bar in the mirror, a mustachioed man, with big white teeth and with frameless glasses resting on his nose, nodded from the balcony overhead. He raised his drink in greeting. *He looks familiar. Where have I seen him before?* Then it dawned on her. *It just happened again.*

Angela returned the spirit's nod and glanced at José in the mirror. "Was Theodore Roosevelt ever known to frequent this place?"

"Oh, yes." His eyes twinkling, José said, "Supposedly he recruited trail drivers and Texas Rangers to be his Rough Riders by buying them a drink or two here. Then they'd wake up the next morning in basic training at Camp Wood, having signed on to fight in the Spanish American War."

"Sounds like they were shanghaied." Angela grinned. "Or in this case, would you call it sanantonioed?"

"A lot of history's happened at this hotel."

"How about hauntings?" Maria asked. "Does it have ghosts?"

"Thirty-two ghosts are said to haunt the Menger Hotel."

"Really?" Maria's eyes widened.

Grinning, José nodded. "Some say as many as forty-three. From what I'm told, there's a lot of paranormal activity here."

"How spooky." Maria's eyes danced as she looked up at him. "How exciting!"

Angela raised her eyebrow but kept still. From the corner of her eye, she saw Kio glance at her and smile to himself.

"Would you like to see Captain Richard King's suite?" asked José.

"Why? Is it 'haunted'?" Maria made quotation marks with her fingers.

"So 'they' say." Chuckling, he mimicked her. Then he took them upstairs and stopped in front of a nondescript door. "A few months before he died at the age of sixty, Captain King, founder and owner of the King Ranch, moved into this suite." José unlocked the door and gestured toward the bed. "He passed away in this very bed frame, and his wake was held in the parlor downstairs." Gesturing to the door, José turned to them. "The hotel's been remodeled several times since his death, and the door was moved to where you see it now. Before then, it had been—"

"Over here?" Angela pointed to a location several feet away.

José's eyebrows shot up. "Good guess!"

Angela smiled as she subtly nodded to the semitransparent man in denim and flannel disappearing through the wall.

"As the story goes, Captain King comes and goes from one world to the next, but through the old door that used to be here."

Then José took them to the Victorian wing. "This is the 'haunt,'" he paused as he grinned at Maria, "of Sallie White, possibly our most popular ghost."

Maria stifled a chuckle.

"Many people mistake her for housekeeping staff, since she's usually spotted carrying towels. If you see a woman dressed in a floor-length gray skirt, you might be seeing Sallie White's ghost."

Angela turned toward him. "Does she wear a bandanna?"

José nodded. "Yes, she does. Have you read about her?"

Angela shook her head as she stepped out of Sallie's way. "Just a lucky guess." She gave Kio a private wink.

With a knowing chuckle, he shook his head.

She grinned at him. *After two years, Kio finally accepts me seeing ghosts.*

José opened the door to another suite. "In this room, a guest reported a man dressed in grey pants and a buckskin jacket arguing with someone unseen. 'Are you gonna stay, or are you gonna go?' the ghost asked three times before disappearing."

"That's so sad," said Maria. "It reminds me of the lyrics to the old song, 'The One You Love.'"

"The one by Glenn Frey." José nodded as he sang the chorus. Maria joined him in an impromptu duet.

Her eyes sparkling, Maria smiled at him.

A beat late, José turned to Angela and Kio. "And now, the highlight of the tour." He grinned. "How would you like to sample the Colonial Room Restaurant's famous mango ice cream?"

"What did I read?" Trying to recall, Maria squinted. "Wasn't that served at Bill Clinton's inauguration?"

José nodded. "He liked it so much during a visit here in '92, the Menger sent him forty gallons to celebrate his inauguration."

"That's got to be good ice cream." Kio grinned.

"Judge for yourself."

The hostess seated them at an elegant window seat. A fragrant yellow rose adorned their linen covered table. Within minutes, the waiter brought out frosty parfait glasses filled with double scoops of mango ice cream set off by cookie triangles.

"It's too pretty to eat." Maria moved her ice cream next to the rose. "They're the same golden color."

"The yellow rose of Texas." José glanced at each person seated around their table. "Are you familiar with the legend of the yellow rose of Texas?"

Maria met his eyes. "Didn't it refer to Santa Anna's mistress?"

"Sort of," José grinned, "but first let me give you some historical background. During the early nineteenth century, 'yellow' was used to characterize people of mixed races, and 'rose' was a poetic term for a young woman. As the legend goes, Emily West Morgan was a mulatto servant indentured to James Morgan, a Colonel for the Texians."

"Texians . . . you mean, Texans?" asked Kio.

José nodded. "But the defenders of the Alamo preferred the name Texians. Santa Anna captured Emily and another servant named Turner. He ordered Turner to guide his Mexican troops to the Texian camp, but Emily convinced Turner to escape instead and inform the Texians. Santa Anna had other plans for Emily."

"Wasn't Santa Anna married?" Maria's eyes narrowed.

José gave a wry chuckle. "He was married to not only one, but two women."

Her eyes widened as her eyebrows shot up.

"Emily persuaded Santa Anna to camp then and there, as she entertained him with a 'champagne breakfast.' His colonels objected because of their vulnerable location, but Santa Anna was, shall we say, smitten. He listened to no one and nothing other than his . . . heart. That afternoon, Houston's army waged a surprise attack in the Battle of San Jacinto. Santa Anna was captured, and in exchange for his life, the Mexican army retreated south of the Rio Grande."

"What about Emily, the Yellow Rose?" asked Angela.

"She survived," said José, "and in reward for her heroism was given her freedom, as well as safe passage to New York."

"I remember hearing the old Mitch Miller recording," said Maria as she began to sing the chorus of "The Yellow Rose Texas."

José joined in. Then chuckling, the two broke into smiles.

Angela grinned. "You sure know your history, José."

"I come by it honestly. I have a degree in history from UTSA, but mostly it's my hobby."

"How do you mean?" Maria studied his face.

He gestured around the room. "The hotel, the ghosts, these stories come alive for me. In fact, I volunteer as a docent at the Institute of Texas Cultures, where I can dress up in period costumes." He grinned. "It's fun. History's my passion."

"So many people think it's dry, but I've always found it fascinating." Maria smiled shyly. "I'm working on my Degree in American Studies, that is, I was . . . " Faltering, she gave a silent sigh.

"What Maria means," said Angela, filling in, "is she's working this summer as a docent for the Alamo's Battlefield Tour."

Maria shot her a grateful smile.

"Really?" José's eyes lit up. "I'd like to take in your tour."

"Well, I'm still learning the outlines of the original fort as it stood in 1836, let alone memorizing the spiel." Backpedaling, she looked to Angela for support.

"This is her first week." Angela gave her an encouraging smile as she winked at José. "Maybe she'll feel more comfortable in another week or so before being critiqued."

Laughing, he turned to Maria. "Point taken. In that case, why don't you be my guest at the Institute of Texas Cultures Thursday?"

Fidgeting, Maria began wringing her hands.

At her hesitation, he turned to Angela and Kio. "All of you?"

Kio said, "That does sound interesting."

Angela shot him a dark look before responding to José. "Can we take a rain check? Maybe in another week or two? Maria's still finding her stride with her new job."

"Of course."

Pushing away his empty parfait glass, Kio grinned at their host. "You weren't kidding about the mango ice cream. It was stellar."

Angela chuckled. "Coming from an astronomer, that's high praise, indeed. It was delicious. Thank you, José."

Maria glanced up at him shyly. "And thank you for the tour and ghost stories. I really enjoyed them."

José's dark eyes met hers. "We'll have to do this again."

She blinked. Then looking down, she gave a half-smile as she hunched her shoulders.

That evening over dinner, Angela asked, "Why didn't you take José up on his offer?"

Twisting her hands, Maria opened her eyes wide. "What do you mean?"

"You know what I mean." Angela gave her a cynical grin. "Every time he came close to asking you out, even as part of a group, you'd shy away from him."

Her hands falling to her sides, Maria sighed. "Angela, I'm pregnant! I can't be dating guys when I'll be showing in another few weeks. Even . . . " Shaking her head, she tried again. "Even if I was interested, I'm not looking. I'm not in the market."

Angela grinned. "So you are interested."

"I didn't say that."

"You didn't have to."

Sunday they went to Mass at the Mission of Divine Mercy. As Angela drove along US 281, Glenn Frey's song, 'You Belong To the City' came on the radio.

"Okay if I turn that up?" Maria asked.

Angela nodded, occasionally glancing at her.

Maria stared sightlessly through the windshield as if in a trance, her eyes never blinking.

When the song ended, Angela asked, "Where were you?"

"What do you mean?"

Frowning, Angela pursed her lips. "Where were you?"

Maria took a deep breath. Then she whispered, "For those couple minutes, I was with Mal."

"Mal?" Angela peered at her.

"My boy—" She took another deep breath. "The father of my baby."

Eyes on the road, Angela nodded. "How's he fit in with this song?"

She shrugged. "We were watching reruns one night when this song came on. It was magical." Her eyes dancing, Maria gave her a wistful smile. "You might say it's our song."

"You've never talked about him."

"What's there to say?" The light in her eyes dimming, she grimaced. "He's gone."

"How do you feel about him?"

Taking a deep breath, Maria pursed her lips. "I hate him." Then swallowing, she shook her head. "I love him." She turned toward Angela's profile. "Why do you think I have such a hard time even considering dating anyone else?" Exhaling, she pushed her fingertips into her forehead. "Dumb. Dumb! DUMB! How could I let myself get into a situation like this?"

"You're not the first," said Angela gently, "and you won't be the last." She gave her a wry glance.

Maria nodded.

"You never did tell me what happened." Angela gripped the wheel. "Would it help to talk about it?"

Maria sat silently for a minute. Then she took a deep breath. "That night Mal and I heard Glenn Frey's 'You Belong To the City'?"

Angela glanced at her. "Yeah."

"That was the night I got pregnant, May first."

"Queen of Heaven," Angela murmured.

"What?"

"May Day's also the Marian feast day for the Queen of Heaven." She shook her head. "Sorry, you were saying?"

"I missed my period in May. I was concerned but not worried because I've never been that regular."

Angela nodded as she kept her eyes focused on the road.

"When I missed my period in June, I panicked." She dug her fingertips into her forehead. Then she took another deep breath. "Mal and I were at a pizzeria, celebrating the Fourth of July and his twenty-first birthday with friends." She gave another mirthless chuckle. "I had the bright idea that announcing it would be the perfect birthday present for him."

Angela lifted her eyebrow.

"I know. Dumb." Maria sighed. "Anyway, I'd bought one of those urine pregnancy tests, and I excused myself to go to the ladies' room. Within a few minutes, I got the results." She chuckled. "I was so excited. I couldn't keep it to myself. I had to tell Mal. When

25

I joined him at the table, I whispered in his ear. 'Happy birthday, you're going to be a daddy.' He scrambled to his feet and stared at me with a wild look I'll never forget."

"I gather he didn't take it well." Angela gave her a wry glance.

"That's an understatement. He ordered another pitcher of beer. Then he began drinking heavily with his buddies. I tried to get him to stop and take me home, but he ignored me, preferring his buddies' company to mine. Finally, I gave him an ultimatum. 'Take me home, or I'm walking.'"

"Did he?"

"What do you think?" Curling her lip, Maria sniffed. "I was staying with my parents for the summer. Mal didn't call the next day or the next. I tried to text him and then call his cell, but he didn't answer or return my messages. First I was worried, and then desperate. That weekend, my mother heard me in the bathroom."

"Morning sickness?"

Maria nodded. "She suspected, and I ended up telling her everything. She told my father, and they insisted I get an abortion. When I refused, they kicked me out of the house."

Angela winced.

"I figured I'd camp at my friend Linda's place. 'Sure,' she said, 'you can crash on the couch. Tony won't mind.' But her boyfriend was a little too friendly. 'Go ahead. Wear your skivvies,' he'd said. Then when I was sleeping, I felt his hands on my breasts. I screamed, turned on the light, and told him to get out."

"How did Linda take it?"

"She actually believed . . . " Maria stifled a sigh. "I told you how I slept in my car that night, then the next, and the next. I slept under a bridge. When you met me, I was broke. I had nowhere to go. Until you bought me lunch, I hadn't even eaten that day."

Angela glanced at her as they turned onto Indian Chief Trail. "No wonder you were considering abortion. Don't worry. Things are better, and they're going to keep on improving."

Maria sighed. "Hope so."

Maria sat quietly beside Angela through the Mass. Then when Angela stood to get in line for communion, Maria smiled and followed her.

Afterwards, they hurried to the outdoor pavilion to deliver a sheet cake.

José's eyes lit up when he saw Maria. "And you brought a cake. How did you know we were short on desserts this morning?"

Shrugging, Maria lifted her lip in a half smile.

"Did you make it yourself?"

Muttering, she nodded.

"We're also short on staff." His dark eyes watched her. "Would you mind helping?"

Maria glanced at Angela and then shrugged. "Okay."

After filling her plate, Angela joined Mary Agnes at one of the picnic tables. They chatted with some of the others as they ate lunch.

A few minutes later, José asked, "Mind if we join you?" Maria was at his side.

"Please." Mary Agnes gestured to the free space across the table.

"The line's slowed enough to take a break." José smiled at Maria as they took their seats.

"Did you make this?" asked Mary Agnes, sampling the cake. At Maria's nod, she said, "It's really good, moist, yet so fluffy."

"Thanks." Lowering her eyes, Maria smiled shyly.

"She made it from scratch." Angela winked at her as she spoke to the others. "She even uses a special flour."

"Just cake flour," Maria shrugged. "It makes it lighter, airier."

José nodded. "Milling makes a big difference."

Maria gave him a shy glance and then turned to the others. "Did you know José grinds his own flour?"

"Well," his cheeks reddening, he grinned. "I volunteer as a folklorist at the Mission San José grist mill. Grinding wheat is part of the historical tour."

"You keep yourself busy, don't you?" Angela studied him. *Soft-spoken, shy, yet extroverted when it comes to history.* "You work at the Menger, help here at the Mission of Divine Mercy, and volunteer at the Mission San José."

"Don't forget the Institute of Texas Cultures," added Maria.

He grinned. "Like I said, history's my passion."

Maria turned toward him. "Where do you find the time?"

"I don't have time for much else." He gave her a wry smile. "You might say I live in the past."

"What do you mean?" Maria tilted her head as she peered up at him.

"I'm so immersed in history, I don't have time for the present."

Maria gave him a puzzled glance. "I'm not following."

"I don't have time for socializing," he shrugged, "hanging out."

"All work and no play . . . " Angela looked at Maria. "I think José's saying he doesn't have time for a social life, time for himself."

"Oh." Blinking, Maria looked down at her food.

"Mother Mary Agnes," said a young woman, approaching the table, "we'd like to introduce you to the youngest member of the parish." She held up a bundled baby.

"Let me see." As the woman handed her the baby, Mary Agnes peered into its tiny face.

"His name is Gregory Allen," the woman glanced at her husband, "after both our fathers."

"Gregory Allen Smythe, that's a big name for such a little baby." Mary Agnes handed the baby back to its mother. "Congratulations, you have a fine-looking son."

Angela smiled at the beaming parents. Then she noticed José's eyes riveted on the baby.

"Could I see?" he asked.

"Sure." The couple brought the baby to the other side of the table.

José gently pulled back the blanket from the baby's face as he peered at it. Smiling at the parents, he congratulated them. Then he turned to the father. "You're a lucky man, a beautiful wife and a new baby. What more could you ask for?"

The man put his arm around his wife's waist. "We're blessed."

As a woman at the next table called them over, the couple excused themselves.

"What a cute baby." José's eyes followed them.

Maria glanced up at him. "Isn't he?"

He turned to her.

Wearing a wistful smile, Maria nodded.

As Angela watched them, she got an idea. "José, you seem so well-versed in local lore. Maybe we could visit Mission San José some time when you're volunteering. When's the next time you'll be there?"

His eyes lit up. "Actually, it's my turn Saturday." Grinning, he turned toward Maria. "I even wear a historic costume, stockings and breeches."

Saturday afternoon, Maria drove them to the San José Mission for the last docent-led tour.

"Welcome to Mission San José," said their guide. "Constructed between 1768 and 1782, this is the largest of the missions, considered by some to be the 'Queen of the Missions.' The church, outbuildings, mill, and granary were fully restored in the '30s."

He led them inside the church and its attached *convento* that had housed the early missionaries. As Angela gazed at its graceful arches, she subtly nodded to a dark-robed friar that only she could see. The spirit politely returned her nod before vanishing into thin air.

Outside, their guide pointed to an ornate window. "This is *La Ventana de Rosa*, the Rose Window. Behind it is the church sacristy. Supposedly, the padres showed the Host to the gathered worshippers during the Feast of Pentecost as they gazed through the window."

"Isn't there a story about it?" asked one of the tourists.

The guide nodded. "As the legend goes, Pedro Huízar sculpted the stone façade surrounding this window. There's circumstantial evidence to support it. He lived in this area then and received similar commissions, but there's no proof he was the sculptor. Some say he dedicated this window to a lost love named Rosa or Rosita." He grinned. "Again, there's no proof."

Next they toured the grounds and structures that had sheltered native peoples, stored food, served as workshops, and been used as a fortress.

"What are those beehive-looking things?" asked another tourist.

"Those are *hornos*, or baking ovens," said the guide. "They were also reconstructed in the thirties."

"Was this the entire mission, or did it extend past the walls?"

The guide gestured to the land beyond. "All around the compound's walls, the community cultivated six hundred acres into orchards, fields, and gardens. This mission was self-sufficient, complete with irrigation canals and even a gristmill." He smiled at the group. "Which is our next stop, where José will tell you about the San José *Acequia*."

Wearing a period shirt, buckled shoes, and blue breeches that buttoned just below the knees over black stockings, he greeted them as if he were a miller from the 1700s. Waiting for them to file into the limestone building, his eyes lit up when he spotted Maria.

"Welcome to the gristmill. Completed in the early 1730s, the *acequia* irrigated the land, supplied water for Mission San José's inhabitants and livestock, and provided the power to turn its mill's water wheel."

One of the group raised his hand. "What's an acequia?"

"Basically, it's an irrigation ditch."

Another raised her hand. "Where did it get its water? From a well?"

He shook his head. "It routed its water from the San Antonio River just below San Pedro Creek. Then it paralleled the river to the west before returning to it near the Espada Dam." He glanced at Maria before his eyes swept the rest of the group. "For those of you who like to hike, you can see parts of it along the Mission Trail. It's a great way to view the land from a historical perspective."

Then José demonstrated the gristmill, showing how the millstones ground the grain into flour. When he finished, he turned to the group with a smile. "And that, ladies and gentlemen, concludes the tour. Thank you for joining us today."

Angela and Maria waited until the others had filed out.

"I'm so glad you came." He spoke to them both but kept his eyes glued to Maria's.

This time, she met his eyes. "Me, too." She paused as she worked her mouth, as if thinking of something to say.

Angela noticed her hair had started to grow back. Dark, curly tendrils wisped around her temples, ears, and neck.

Maria's eyes fell on his buckle shoes, and she took in his appearance as she looked up into his face. "I like your costume." She smiled. "It adds to your authenticity."

"Thanks."

Angela felt unnecessary. "I . . . uh . . . I'm going to take a look around outside."

"Oh," Maria glanced at her, her eyes like a deer's in the headlights. "I'll go with you."

Angela started to object, but José acted quickly, turning toward Maria. "Maybe you can help serve food again tomorrow at the Mission of Divine Mercy?"

She bobbed her head. "Okay." With a wave, she said, "See you," and turning, walked out the door.

Startled, Angela looked from her retreating back to José's discouraged face. "Well," she said a bit too brightly, "we'll see you tomorrow. Thanks for the demonstration. I really enjoyed it."

"Glad to hear that. I'll look forward to seeing you at church." His expression was warm, courteous.

As she left, Angela raised her eyebrows. *A gentleman to the end. Impressive.* A few steps later, she caught up with Maria. "What is the matter with you?"

"What do you mean?"

Angela shook her head. "Don't play that game with me. He's been so nice to us, and you couldn't get out of there soon enough. Why? What have you got against him?"

Again she worked her mouth. "I didn't know what to say."

Frustrated, Angela stifled a sigh. "To hear you talk, you'd think you were in the seventh grade."

Maria met her eyes. "I didn't know what to say."

Angela rolled her eyes. "You said that."

"To him." She grimaced. "I didn't know what to say . . . *to him.*"

Angela blinked. "Meaning what?"

"I agree with you. José's been nothing but nice." Maria drew a deep breath. "It'd be awfully easy to," she shrugged, "you know."

Angela shook her head. "I'm not following."

"José's the kind of guy who'd stand by me, do the right thing." Her chest rose and fell in a silent sigh.

"The right thing?" Angela raised her eyebrow.

"I don't want to lead him on, use him." Maria sighed. "He's too nice a person."

Angela nodded. "Okay, now it's making sense."

"I get the feeling it would be easy to string him along. Some girls might take advantage of that, but I don't want to hurt him." She shrugged. "Rather than say too much or say the wrong thing, I'm trying not to say anything."

"So what you're telling me is you're protecting him from yourself?" Angela grinned.

Maria giggled. "When you put it that way, it sounds ridiculous." Then she grimaced. "He just seems lonely, anxious to have what that new father last week had, a wife, a family."

"What's wrong with that?"

Maria's eyes opened wide. "I'm pregnant!"

"I don't see any ring on your finger." Angela looked from her hand to her eyes. "It's not as if you're spoken for."

"But I'm carrying another man's child, and I don't want to deceive him." Maria stopped walking back to the car and turned to face her.

"Who said anything about deceiving José?" Angela stared her down. "What's wrong with telling him the truth?"

Grimacing, Maria sighed. "For one thing, I'm ashamed. For another, I'm scared. I saw how my boyfriend reacted when I told him I was pregnant. He left me, and when I told my parents, they insisted I get an abortion. When I refused, they kicked me out." She shook her head. "I don't want to be rejected a third time."

Angela pressed her lips into a thin line as she digested that. "Sounds to me like you're not as afraid of hurting him as you are of getting hurt yourself."

Her eyes bunching, Maria gave her a pained look. "Maybe. I don't know."

Angela tried another tack. "You saw how José looked at that baby last Sunday." She lifted her lip in a wry smile. "Something tells me he's the family type."

A forlorn expression came over Maria's face. "Something tells me the same thing, which is exactly why I don't want to take advantage of him." Maria sighed as she put her hands on her tummy. "I'd love my baby to have a father. Even though José seems like an answer to a prayer, he's too nice a guy to *use*."

Angela's shoulders slumped as she exhaled. "You're not listening. I'm guessing José *wants* a family. You want a father for your baby. Who knows if this . . . merger wasn't a marriage made in heaven before you even met? Who knows if this wasn't God's plan all along?"

Her eyes opening wide, Maria raised her eyebrow. "You think so?"

"Maybe." Angela gave her a half smile as she tilted her head. "Can't you just find out?" She leaned forward. "Give him a chance.

Don't be so fast to shut him out before he's knocked at your door. Who knows? You might just like what happens."

The next day after Mass, Angela and Maria hurried to the tent's food line.

"You made it." José's eyes lit up as soon as he spotted Marie. "You're a godsend." Then looking at them both, he added, "We're two people short if you'd like to help serve brunch, too."

Angela shrugged. "Sure, just tell me where to stand."

"How about the dessert section?" He gestured toward the cakes at the end of the tables. Then he smiled at Maria. "How 'bout you serve the noodles, and I'll spoon the beef tips and gravy over them?"

Smiling, she nodded. "Okay."

Catching her eye, Angela gave her a thumbs up as Maria stifled a smile.

When they started to take their places, an older woman came running up with her daughter in tow. "Sorry we're late." Pushing the young woman next to José, in front of Maria, she stepped on her toe but made no excuse. "Rosie, stand right here next to José, so he can help you."

"Your message said neither of you could make it today." He looked from the woman to Maria. "Others have volunteered to help—"

"We're here now." Then she glanced at Maria with a curt smile. "No need to stay. We've got it covered." She stepped into Maria's spot, forcing her to step aside. "Right here, Rosie."

Raising his eyebrows, José turned to the woman. "Now just a minute, Myrtle."

Maria shook her head. "It's all right." She shrugged. "I'll just sit this one out."

"And I'll take over the desserts." Myrtle rushed to the end of the line as the three of them looked on.

He glanced at Maria and Angela. "Let me straighten this out."

As he took a step toward the older woman, Maria put a light hand on his arm. "It's all right. We're plainly in what she believes is her turf."

Taking a deep breath, José shook his head. "I apologize for her behavior."

Angela shrugged. "It's not important. Maria and I'll just get a head start on dinner."

"Why don't you join us when you're through?" The corners of Maria's mouth tilted up in a gentle smile.

Watching her lips a beat too long, he caught himself with a curt nod. "Count on it."

Within twenty minutes, José joined them at a picnic table. In addition to bringing his dinner plate, he brought two dessert plates.

"This just came in," he handed each a plate, "chocolate turtle cake."

"That looks luscious, so rich and chocolatey." Angela tried a forkful. Savoring it, she rolled her eyes. "This is wonderful. It literally melts in your mouth."

"After that glowing review, what choice do I have?" Maria tasted a forkful and turned pale. Scrambling out from behind the picnic table, she excused herself.

Angela and José watched her retreat toward the restrooms. His eyes questioned hers.

I'm not letting the cat out of the bag. Angela shrugged. "Maybe she doesn't like chocolate."

When Maria came back several minutes later, her eyes were red. She took one look at the chocolate turtle cake, groaned, and pushed the plate out of her sight. Then turning toward José, she gave him a tepid smile. "Sorry, it didn't agree with me."

His concern etched in his forehead, José studied her face. "Are you feeling all—"

"I'm fine. Why wouldn't I be?" Then turning toward Angela, her eyes flashed. "Did you tell him?"

Her lips pressed tightly together, Angela slowly shook her head. "Tell me what?"

Maria glanced from his face to Angela's. "Sorry, my stomach's not the only thing that's out of sorts this morning." She ran her hand through her hair, her fingers teasing out ringlets, as she seemed to gather her thoughts.

Angela watched her. *Her hair's growing back so fast, you can almost see it grow.*

Maria moistened her lips as she looked from Angela to José. Then she took a deep breath. "I suppose honesty's the best policy."

José blinked as his spine straightened.

She caught his eye. "I don't ever want it said I hid the truth."

He raised his eyebrows but kept silent.

"There was nothing wrong with the cake. A lot of things are making me sick lately." She grimaced. "It's morning sickness."

"So you're m—"

"Pregnant, yup." Nodding, she stifled a sigh.

"So you're married." He held so still, Angela wondered if he was holding his breath.

"Oh, no." She pursed her lips. "Pregnant, but not married." She sighed. "There." Spreading her hands, palms up, she looked into his eyes. "Now you know my whole story."

Angela watched him take a deep breath. *If anything, he seems more relaxed.*

"Not married." His eyes lost their bunched, anxious appearance.

Lips pressed together, she shook her head. "Nope, I'm an unwed mother." Her eyes challenged his.

"For some reason, I thought you were married." He gave her a crooked grin.

Thursday, Angela saw José in the Alamo gift shop. "What brings you here?"

"It's been years since I've visited the Alamo. Thought I'd catch Maria's tour."

Grinning to herself, she pointed him toward the Visitor's Center. "Maria's just starting. If you hurry, you can catch up with her at the plaza."

An hour later, they met Angela in the gift shop.

"How'd you like the tour?" she asked.

José glanced at Maria and then turned back to Angela. "She's a natural. It's obvious Maria's been bitten by the history bug."

Angela grinned. "I take it your critique won't be too harsh."

"On the contrary." Teasing, he made a face. "Just a few pointers, like adding the story about Colonel Travis drawing a line in the sand with his sword. Those soldiers who chose to join him in the Alamo's fight to the death had to step across the line. Only one remained behind. That legend's become a standard in Texas, meaning to stay to the end."

"So instead of till death do us part,' Texas couples repeat that during their weddings vows, do they?" Maria's eyes twinkled.

"Only sometimes." He grinned.

As he caught Maria's eye, she laughed. "So the pro's going to give me a few pointers, huh?"

"Just one or two." His eyes flashed. "How about I tell you over nachos and cheese?" Then he glanced at Angela. "I hear you two are getting off work in a few minutes. Maybe Kio would like to join us and make it a foursome?"

"What a great idea." Maria's eyes sparkled as she turned from José to Angela. "Can you text him and see?"

What am I, a chaperone? Angela was tempted to suggest they keep it a twosome, but both pairs of eyes were focused intently on her. Stifling a sigh, she smiled to herself. *They're shy.*

"Sure."

After work, the three of them took a shortcut through the fountains and waterfalls to the River Walk. Kio met them in front of Boudro's.

They started with iced tea, nachos, and cheese, but as the conversation got more long-winded, they shared seafood samplers, and all but Maria ordered the house specialty: Prickly Pear Margaritas, drizzled with ruby-red, prickly cactus pear puree.

"Love these prickly-ritas," Kio caught Angela's eye and smiled.

Angela returned his smile as she studied his face. Thoughtful, dark eyes, sandy-brown hair, he had a sensitive mouth, quick to laugh, empathize, or console. *Have we been dating two years already?*

Then gazing inwardly, she recalled the night he had taken her for a carriage ride. As she had nestled against him, her head resting on his shoulder, listening to the clip-clop of the horse's hooves on the pavement, a concept had entered her mind for the first time. *His heart and mine?*

Watching him now, she asked herself the same question. *Maybe.* She breathed a contented sigh, still enjoying the ride.

Their eyes met in a private toast as they clinked glasses. Though nothing was official, no rings or exchanged vows, she felt they were an old married couple, comfortable, simpatico. *That's enough for now.*

"Maybe Saturday we could go to SeaWorld." José looked from Maria's face to Angela's to Kio's.

Angela and Maria caught each other's eyes. "We can't," said Angela. "We're registered for a spa for the soul."

"A what?" Lifting his eyebrow, he looked from one woman's face to the other.

Maria chuckled. "We're registered for the Catholic Women's Retreat that day."

José grinned. "That leaves Sunday. How 'bout we meet for the Mariachi Mass at San José Mission?"

Chapter 3

*"Don't shine so others can see you. Shine so that
through you, others can see Him."*
– C.S. Lewis

They went early and found seats near the front of the Henry B. Gonzalez Convention Center. A group played meditative music until Archbishop Gustavo Garcia-Siller opened the conference with a Mass and homily.

"Meaning *thanksgiving*, the Eucharist is a sign of oneness. Pray for a spirited communion of women. We don't need more pious women. We need women to be prophets of hope, like John the Baptist. Be a voice for the voiceless. Sing a new song in the desert, a message of hope, a message of repentance.

"I've given you a commission. Follow it. When are you going to announce your message? Many people are waiting to hear your voice. Don't deprive the new generation of your voice.

"Mary gave birth to Jesus. Mary wants to give birth to Jesus *in you*. Let your hearts be a reflection of His love. Mary, Undoer of Knots, wants to tease out all the tangles of your life. We've been darkened by sin. Jesus wipes away the darkness on the mirror, so we can begin to see how beautiful we are to him, so we shine."

As he exited, the emcee shouted, "*Viva Christo Rey!*"

Twenty-four hundred women shouted back, "*Viva!*"

As they broke for morning coffee, Maria turned to Angela. "Archbishop Gustavo certainly gave an impassioned homily."

"What he did was commission us all to speak up for our faith, speak up for what's right." Angela chuckled as she recalled the bossy woman at church. "I had to laugh at his line about the world not needing more pious women."

"Are you thinking what I am, Myrtle from last Sunday?"

Angela nodded.

Maria gave a wry sniff. "Do-gooders don't necessarily do good." She was quiet a moment. Then she turned toward Angela. "I liked his line about being prophets of hope. That's what you've been to me. That morning in front of Parentage Incorporated, I'd lost all hope. Then I met you and Develyn. You not only got me a job and a place to stay. You gave me hope."

"It's what anyone would've done." Angela shrugged. "It's not like you were a complete stranger. We'd been classmates."

Maria gave a mirthless chuckle. "It's more than Mal did. When I told him I was pregnant, he left. I gave him all I had, and still he took more. He stole my hope."

Pressing her lips together, Angela kept silent. She could think of nothing to say.

Maria took a deep breath. "You're the only reason my baby's alive."

Feeling the heat rise to her cheeks, Angela shook her head. "God's the only reason your baby's alive."

"You did more for us than my parents. After Mal left and I thought things couldn't get worse, I confided in them. What did they do? They left me homeless and hopeless."

Not wanting Maria's family negatively compared to her, Angela said, "We all do things we regret. We all make mistakes—"

"Mistakes? People who kick you when you're down don't just 'make mistakes.' They intentionally inflict pain. They leave scars." Maria's lip trembled.

Angela reached out for her hand. "I'm not defending them for a minute, but sometimes people give knee-jerk reactions when they're overwhelmed. A couple weeks have passed. Why don't you reach out to your family? See if time hasn't made them rethink their actions."

Red-eyed, Maria blinked back tears. As they heard the announcer call them back for the next speaker, Maria shook her head. "The wounds are too deep."

They took a lesser-used corridor back to their seats to avoid the crowd, and when they turned the corner, they ran into Archbishop Gustavo and his entourage of assistants.

Maria caught her breath. On impulse, she reached up and kissed his cheek. "Thank you for speaking to us, commissioning us to be prophets of hope."

"It's the women who'll change the world."

When they returned to their seats, Angela chuckled. "You're positively glowing."

Tears dried, Maria grinned. "I kissed the Archbishop's cheek."

As the next speaker was introduced, she gazed at the assembly. "The evangelization of America will happen through women. Stand up and say, 'I'm ready! Anoint me with the fruits of the Holy Spirit. Bring forth these gifts!'

"The Master's in each of us. Your guardian angel's whispering in your mind. The Holy Spirit's working in your heart. It's an anointing. He's saying, 'Wake up! I have so much work to do in you.'

"These gifts of the Holy Spirit are supernatural realities to guide us, so the Father's glorified. The gifts let us recognize messages to our souls. When we're inspired by the Holy Spirit, we're the daughters of God.

"Keep in mind, the Holy Spirit helps us but doesn't interfere. We have to do the work. Ask that you can enlighten others with the gifts you've been given.

"Think what we've experienced this weekend, how Jesus has led us to this moment. Uncertainty and timidity are our shortcomings, but we are blessed, anointed, sent forth by the Archbishop. We're obedient to the voice of God. Study the virtues and gifts of the Holy Spirit. Then say, 'Holy Spirit, take charge. Anoint me with the truth.'"

Maria scribbled a note in her program's margin.

41

When the conference ended, Maria drove them back to the apartment. "You know, I've been thinking about what you said."

Trying to remember, Angela blinked. "What did I say?"

"That spiel you gave me about reaching out to my family, seeing if time hasn't made them rethink their positions."

"Oh, that." Angela nodded. "What have you decided to do?"

"The memories of my parents are still too raw, but I'd like to talk to my cousin Elizabeth."

"Does she live in San Antonio?

"No, the Hill Country." Maria took her eyes off the road to glance at her. "I was thinking of calling her. If she's not busy, maybe I'll visit her next weekend."

Angela smiled. "That sounds so biblical."

"What does?"

"You going to the Hill Country to visit your cousin Elizabeth." When Maria still didn't get it, Angela added, "You know. The Visitation, when Mary visited her cousin Elizabeth."

"Oh." Maria's eyes sparkling, she chuckled. "You're right. It does."

"It also makes sense," said Angela. "A mediator might help dispel some of the family tension."

"Something else I've been thinking about. Today we heard the word *evangelization* several times." Again she glanced at Angela. "Have you ever thought about it?"

"Can't say I have." Angela grinned. "Why?"

"Evangelization." Maria spelled it out. "After the first two letters, you have the word *angel.*"

"Never thought of it that way."

"Somehow, after attending the conference, I feel surrounded by angels."

"Of course, when you're with me, you're in the company of Angela." She grinned mischievously.

Chuckling, Maria glanced at her, and she noticed something on the dashboard. "What's that?"

"What's what?"

"Is that a feather on the dash?"

Angela picked up a fluffy white plume. "How'd that get in here?" By twisting its tip, she gracefully twirled the feather between her fingers.

Maria glanced at it. "The windows were shut. The doors were locked. No bird could've gotten in."

Angela shrugged. "Maybe when we climbed in, this blew in the door."

"Could be . . . "

Sunday they met Kio and José in front of Mission San José. Taking her hand, Kio kissed Angela as Maria and José stood awkwardly, mumbling "Hi."

Then José noticed something in Maria's hair. "What's this?" Picking it out, he showed her a small feather.

Maria caught her breath as she turned to Angela. "This is the second time."

"More than a coincidence?" Angela's eyebrow lifted as their eyes connected.

Still holding the feather, José looked from one woman to the other. "What, are you raising chickens or something?"

Chuckling, Maria shook her head. "Last night after the conference we found a feather inside the car. Now this morning you find one in my hair."

"Do you sleep on down pillows?" asked Kio.

"Good question." Maria looked at Angela.

"Nope, just foam, no feathers," Angela shook her head, "but good guess." She glanced up at him through her eyelashes. "You sure are firmly grounded for someone who studies the stars."

Chuckling, Kio took her hand. "You're the one who keeps me grounded."

Angela laughed to herself. "Should we get our seats?"

As they started for the entrance, José tossed away the feather.

"Oh, no." Maria bent down to retrieve it and gasped. There on the ground, in front of the downy feather, was an owl feather. Picking up both, she blushed as she met José's eyes. "These might be lucky." Glancing at Angela, she added, "That's three. It's got to be a sign." She tucked the feathers in her purse as she reached for José's hand.

His eyes blazed and then softened into a smile as they walked hand in hand into church.

Following behind, watching them, Angela and Kio grinned at each other.

A seven-piece Mariachi group was playing as the choir accompanied them in song. The folk musicians were dressed in brightly embroidered white shirts and the traditional Spanish charro suit with silver studs on the pants. Tooled leather belts, large sombreros, and white boots completed their outfits.

"I love Mariachi Mass," Maria whispered. Then she grinned. "The sound of violins and trumpets makes me happy."

José gave her hand a friendly squeeze as Angela and Kio nodded.

Then Maria sat up straight as though listening or getting an idea. "Someday," she said slowly, seeming to think it through, "I'd like a Mariachi band to play at my wedding."

Angela raised her eyebrow as she met Kio's glance.

José's spine straightened.

After Mass, they stopped for coffee and breakfast tortillas.

"It's such a nice day." Angela smiled at them. "How would you like to walk along part of the Mission Trail?"

Nodding, shrugging, they glanced at each other.

"I hear they're making the Mission Hike and Bike Trail a pilgrimage," said José.

"Really?" Opening her eyes wide, Maria glanced at him.

He nodded. "From Mission Concepción to Mission Espada is nearly eight miles in each direction, a long walk."

"But if I recall, it's divided into sections, isn't it?" Angela glanced at him.

Again José nodded. "Many have alternate routes, so we could hike some sections roundtrip without having to backtrack."

"Sounds like a good idea." Kio winked at Angela. "We've walked the Museum Reach of the River Walk. Now let's tackle the Mission Reach."

She met his eyes as she remembered strolling the Mission Reach the night they had met.

Looking at Maria, José added, "It's roughly two or three miles between missions, so roundtrip the segments are about four to six miles. Are you up to walking that far comfortably?"

"So far, I am." She took a deep breath. "The truth is, I don't know how much longer I'll be able to hike that distance."

"In the future," Angela looked at them, "we could take two cars. Park one at the first Mission and the other at the second."

Maria smiled. "Perfect! Two-to-three-mile walks are always doable."

They drove back to San José and parked near the trail.

José pulled a map from his glove compartment.

Maria chuckled. "You're like a boy scout."

He studied her. "What? Trustworthy, loyal?"

Grinning, she shook her head. "Always prepared."

"Guilty as charged." Nodding, he chuckled. Then, opening the map, he traced his finger along the dotted line, pointing out their trail. "We'll start on Napier Avenue, walking through some of the most historical neighborhoods in San Antonio. Originally, all this land had belonged to the Mission, but centuries ago it was distributed among the parishioners. Now, many generations later, some of the original families still live on this land."

"Interesting." Then Maria started fidgeting. "Everybody ready?"

Angela studied her body language. "You seem eager to get going."

Maria shrugged. "Guess we've been sitting so much this weekend, exercise sounds good." She grinned as she took José's hand. "Come on. Let's get started."

Chuckling, he looked over his shoulder at Angela and Kio as Maria led him to Napier Avenue.

When the road dead-ended at Mission Road, Maria looked at him. "Which way?"

"If we want to walk to Mission San Juan, turn right." He glanced at them. "There's also a trail to the left that goes to San Juan Dam. Which way?"

They looked at each other and simultaneously turned right.

José laughed. "San Juan, it is." A few feet beyond the intersection, he said, "Here's where the route turns off the main road and becomes the Mission Parkway Trail."

They hiked along wide new sidewalks that followed the river.

"Did you know," said José, "Along with several agencies and non-profits, San Antonio built over fifteen miles of these hike-and-bike paths, as well as six pedestrian bridges for the Mission Reach?"

"Really?" Maria glanced at José as they walked along. "What made the city extend the River Walk so far south?"

"The Missions make up the first World Heritage Site in Texas. San Antonio considered this trail a kind of cultural connection, linking ethnic groups and neighborhoods." He gestured to the sidewalk. "It's a pathway joining the city's future to the past while it helps the current residents' quality of life."

Maria cocked her head. "What do you mean?"

"The Mission Reach also offers recreational activities."

"Besides walking and biking? Like what?" Maria watched him.

"Birding, fishing, and paddling."

Angela chuckled. "Paddling?"

José nodded. "The Mission Reach has limestone dams with chutes in the centers, so kayaks or canoes can navigate through."

Angela grinned. "Now that sounds like fun!"

Kio caught her eye and grinned. "It does."

"It's also got pavilions, overlooks, and picnic areas to connect with nature," said José.

"Let's bring a picnic lunch along for the next segment's walk," said Maria.

"And maybe try a star party at an overlook some clear night," said Kio.

Angela grinned at him. "Always the astronomer." She turned to the others. "That's why he has stars in his eyes."

"Only when I look at you." Kio's eye caught hers and held it a beat.

Feeling her cheeks warm, Angela reached up to kiss him.

Kio cleared his throat and turned to the others. "If we can find an overlook near one of the Missions, I can bring a small telescope for stargazing."

"Unfortunately, the Mission Reach is only open from dawn to dusk." José gave him a sympathetic grimace. "Maybe we can save the star party for somewhere farther away from the city?"

Angela leaned into Kio. "Great idea, though." Then she turned to Maria. "Maybe you know somewhere in the Hill Country?"

She nodded. "Blanco State Park might be a place to start."

"That's not very far," said Angela.

"It rents tubes, kayaks, and canoes during the day, and I think the gates stay open until ten at night."

Angela looked at Kio, surfing on his phone. "Would that give us enough time to view the sky?"

"It depends on the time of sunset and the cloud cover." With a surprised grunt, he glanced up from his cell. "I just found a web site with hourly forecasts of cloud cover and air transparency." He grinned. "Basically, it tells us when Blanco State Park will have the best weather for star-gazing."

"Really?" Angela caught his eye, smiling her approval.

José glanced at each of them, but his eyes rested on Maria. "Maybe we could head to Blanco next weekend."

She grimaced. "I'm going to be out of town next weekend."

José's smile melted into a somber expression.

"I'm visiting my cousin Elizabeth in the Hill Country."

His eyes softened into a smile. "Somehow, that sounds so biblical."

Maria laughed. "That's what Angela said."

"The longer we wait to go star gazing," said Kio, "the longer the nights and the earlier the sunsets. Why don't we finish hiking the Mission Reach segments before we head for points farther away?"

Agreeing, they resumed their walk. José pointed to the landscaping along the Mission Trail.

"It'll take decades for the restored native plants to cover this area, but some grasses and wildflowers have begun to take hold."

Angela gazed at the riverbanks' patchwork of textured greens. "I can't tell one from another, but I do see several different kinds of plants."

He nodded. "They planted sixty kinds of native grasses and wildflowers, but only the grasses are showing now. We'll have to come back in the spring to see the bluebonnets, scarlet sage, and prickly poppy."

"The Mission Trail has everything," Angela looked at the sun overhead, "except trees. I could really use some shade."

Kio laughed. "You're just spoiled by the century-old cypresses in the city."

"They planted over twenty thousand trees and shrubs along here," said José, "but they're still immature."

"Why, are saplings cheaper?" Deadpanning, Angela glanced at him.

"Probably," he grinned, "but mostly it's because young trees are more resistant to floods. As they mature, they'll adjust to the occasional floods and develop deeper roots. Bigger trees with shallow roots would topple in the first flood."

When they reached Mission San Juan, they saw it was closed for renovation.

"That's too bad." Angela grimaced.

Gravitating to its shade, Maria leaned against a mature red oak. "To be honest, I'm glad. It's going to take all my strength to walk back." She took a deep breath. "I wouldn't have the energy to tour this mission *and* walk back."

His forehead creased, José said, "Next time, we'll take two cars and keep these treks to two to three miles." He looked into her eyes. "Are you going to be all right?"

Maria gave him a half-hearted smile. "I'll be fine once I catch my breath."

Kio checked his phone. "According to my app, we've walked closer to two and a half miles." He looked up at Maria. "That's a hefty five-mile round trip. Tell you what. Why don't you and José wait here, while Angela and I get the car?"

"Oh, I can't put you out—"

"You're not putting us out," said Angela. "Just relax in the shade, and we'll be back for you in about forty-five minutes."

"I'll be fine once I get my second wind." Propelling herself, she gave a slight push off the tree and lurched.

José caught her before she stumbled.

Wincing, she pressed her fingertips to her forehead. "Maybe it's warmer today than I thought."

"Here." Angela took a small bottle of water from her purse. "Drink this, and sit in the shade till we get back." She looked in her eyes. "Okay?"

Pressing her lips together in a grimace, Maria nodded.

"Don't worry." José glanced from Maria to Angela. "I'll take good care of her."

Nodding, Angela and Kio hurried back toward Mission San José.

When they were out of earshot, Kio turned toward her. "I hope she's all right."

"Me, too." Angela grimaced. "I wasn't thinking. I'm just not used to being around anyone pregnant." She took a deep breath as she picked up her pace.

While they rushed along the path, ducks and cormorants flapped away noisily at their approach. Angela and Kio barely spoke while they sped back to the car, but red-winged blackbirds called in the underbrush, seeming to alert each other of their advance. Circling high overhead, near older cottonwoods above the bank's flood line, red-tailed hawks monitored their progress.

Kio checked his online map for the fastest route back to Mission San Juan. Watching the clock as they pulled into the parking lot, Angela turned to him. "We made good time. It barely took us forty minutes."

As José waved to them and Maria smiled, Kio and Angela shared a sigh of relief.

José opened the door for Maria, and they climbed into the back seat.

"Are you okay?" Angela asked.

"I'm fine." She smiled sheepishly. "I just got a little overheated."

"The last thing you need is heatstroke." Angela glanced at Kio and José. "If you don't mind, I'm going to drop you guys off at your cars and get Maria home."

Sitting in the air-conditioned kitchen, sipping iced tea, Maria wore a contented smile.

"You look like the cat that swallowed the canary." Angela chuckled as she watched her. "What are you thinking?"

She took a deep breath as she stared at nothing, gathering her thoughts. "It's finally occurred to me. I'm going to have a baby."

"Well, duh." Angela chuckled.

She shook her head. "No, I've been pregnant for nearly four months, but it's finally sinking in. I'm going to have a baby. This isn't just a 'condition' that will pass. It's the start of a new life for my baby . . . and for me."

"What brought this on?"

"It began by walking two miles—"

"You mean, two and a half miles." Angela grimaced.

Maria smiled. "And having to admit my body's changing, slowing down. Then I realized my friends are concerned about me."

"Again, duh."

"Mostly it was something José said while we were waiting for you."

Angela cocked her head. "What?"

She put her hand on her baby bump. "He said a baby is a miracle. As this life develops inside me, my life will also change." Wearing a wistful, shy smile, she glanced at Angela. "He said there was nothing more beautiful, more feminine than a pregnant woman."

Processing, Angela blinked as she took it in. "How did that make you feel?"

Maria drew a deep breath. "It didn't make me feel as much as it made me look at everything differently. From the way Mal and my parents had treated me, I'd felt pregnancy was a disease, something to be gotten over, gotten rid of. Now I'm beginning to look at pregnancy as a special time to bond with my baby."

"Wow." Angela gave Maria a sheepish grin. "What an eye-opening conversation you must've had with José. I'd never thought of pregnancy that way before. In fact, I've never thought about pregnancy before, at least not on a personal level." *Are Kio and I headed on that track?* "You make it sound magical."

She smiled. "José suggested I start a diary, record my thoughts during these days . . . these months."

"What a great idea. He seems to have his life together."

Maria nodded shyly "He's a good guy. I like him."

That Friday, José stopped by the Alamo as they were leaving. "Do you have time for a glass of iced tea?"

Angela looked at Maria. "I can wait for you if you—"

He smiled. "Both of you?"

They glanced at each other and then at José. "Sure."

After they found a shaded table along the River Walk, they discussed the weather until the waitress brought the tea.

"This Sunday's my turn to volunteer at the Institute of Texan Cultures," he said. "Would you two and Kio like to be my guests?"

Maria glanced from Angela to him. "I'm sorry, José, but I'll be out of town this weekend."

"Oh, that's right. You're visiting your cousin."

Maria nodded.

His smile faded a bit. "I'd forgotten." Then reviving his smile, he turned toward Angela. "I hope you and Kio can join me."

"Actually," Angela glanced uncomfortably from him to Maria and back. "Kio and I have other plans." Watching his expression droop, she added, "Maybe the four of us can walk another segment of the Mission Trail next Sunday?"

"But this time, let's bring two cars and hike just one way." Turning to Maria, José smiled. "Does that work for you?"

Blinking, she studied his face. Then as a slow smile lit up her eyes, she nodded. "Yes, I think that's a great idea."

"Perfect." He took a gift-wrapped package from his backpack and set it in front of her. "That subject we were discussing . . . "

Cocking her head, Maria paused. "Which one?"

He gave a nervous chuckle. "About you keeping a daily journal."

She nodded.

"I got you a little something to help." With that, his fingertips inched the small package toward her.

Grinning, her eyes sparkling, Maria lightly pressed her fingers against her chest as she looked at him. "For me?"

Leaning forward, he nodded. "Just a little something."

She unwrapped the package and found what looked like the bottom half of an antique pen. Cocking her head, she looked up at him.

He smiled. "Do you still have that owl feather?"

Nodding, she took it from her purse.

"Put the feather tip in the nub, like this." José sharpened its tip with a pocket knife and then demonstrated how it worked. "Now your owl feather can help you write wise thoughts in your daily journal."

"A quill pen, and you tied it in with the owl feather. Thank you." Maria leaned over and kissed his cheek. "You are so thoughtful." She picked up the quill, twirled it between her fingertips, and then went through the motions of using it to write. "I love this."

Flushing, he said, "It's supposedly just like the one used to sign the Declaration of Independence." His eyes lit up as he looked into hers. "I thought it might be the perfect pen to write your own 'declaration of independence.'"

Her eyes narrowed. "What do you mean my—"

"See, it's even got its own bottle of ink and some steel tips to get you started." His face became serious. "Maybe writing down your thoughts will help put things into perspective."

As Angela drove them home, she glanced at Maria. "I think José's serious about you."

Shrugging, Maria turned toward her. "He probably just felt bad about my getting a little lightheaded last Sunday."

"If anyone's lightheaded, I think he is, and I don't think the weather has anything to do with it." Angela chuckled as she glanced at Maria.

Maria smiled. Then she looked off in the distance. "What do you think he meant by the perfect pen to write my own declaration of independence?"

Shaking her head, Angela shrugged. "I don't know. Have you got any ideas?"

Taking a deep breath, Maria raised her eyebrow. "I wonder . . . "

"What?"

"I'm probably off-base here, but . . . " Palm up, she gestured feebly with her hand. "I wonder if he was talking about declaring my independence from the past, from Mal?" She turned toward Angela. "What do you think?"

Angela shook her head. "No clue, but he's certainly interested in you, and he seems concerned about your baby's welfare."

Saturday morning, Maria left for the Hill Country minutes before Kio arrived.

Angela met him at the door with a kiss. "It's good to see you alone for a change."

"Isn't it, though?" As he held her in his arms, he drew his head back and looked at her. "What's different?"

"What do you mean?" She looked up at him through her eyelashes.

"If I didn't know better, I'd say you were flirting."

Chuckling, she shrugged. "I was just glad to see you." Moving out of his grasp, she reached for her purse. "All set?"

Kio watched her for a beat and then nodded. "Still want to visit the caverns?"

"Sure." Then she turned to him. "I thought you liked astronomy and outer space."

"I do," he grinned, "but I also like inner space, the bowels and tunnels of the earth."

"I've read this whole area in central Texas is honeycombed with caves."

He nodded. "Wherever there's limestone, there are caves."

"Why is that?"

"Limestone's a base, calcium carbonate. When rainwater seeps through the ground, it becomes mildly acidic as it absorbs carbon dioxide. It's like mixing baking soda with vinegar. It bubbles. In the same way, the acidic water dissolves the limestone, creating caves."

"So it's a chemical reaction."

"Exactly." His eyes twinkling, he leaned over to kiss her. "Just like between us."

She grinned as she called to the silver-gray cat curled up on the sofa. "Good-bye, Frank. There's wet food in your bowl."

They drove through rolling hills to a cave outside Boerne.

When they arrived, Angela looked at the sign, frowned, and then looked at Kio. "What's the name of this place?"

He chuckled. "You read it right, Cave Without a Name."

Their tour guide led them along the walkway ninety feet below the surface.

As a shiver passed through her, Angela rubbed her arms.

"Cold?" Kio put his arm around her shoulders.

She huddled against him, glad for his warmth.

"It's a cool sixty-six degrees down here, year round," said the guide.

"That's why you're wearing a flannel shirt." Angela grinned.

He led them along narrow passages through six rooms filled with formations of stalagmites, stalactites, cave drapery, rimstone dams, and soda straws.

"These dripstones and flowstones are living," said the guide.

"What do you mean?"

"They're wet. Water's dripping down them, leaving behind deposits of calcium carbonate." He pointed at a fragile soda straw formation. "Slower than watching paint dry, you're seeing a stalactite in the making."

Angela caught Kio's eye, and they chuckled.

"Another few millennia, give or take ten million years, and this delicate soda straw will be a stalactite." The guide grinned.

Time. Angela thought how it affected life. *Three-month summer semesters. Nine-month gestation for Maria's baby. Two-year relationship.* She studied Kio's profile. Then she turned back toward the formation. *Millions of years to shape just one of these stalactites. Suddenly, her adoptive mother's image flashed through her mind. How old is she now? Eighty-six.* A chill swept over her.

Bringing her closer to him, Kio glanced at her. "You are cold, aren't you?"

She smiled as she huddled against him. "I should've brought a sweater." Then, her thoughts returning to her mother, Angela's smile dissolved. "Kio, do you mind if we stop by Mom's house after lunch?"

"Sure, why?"

She grimaced. "Haven't seen her in a week or two. Just want to make sure she's doing all right."

They ordered sandwiches to go and picnicked in River Road Park along Cibolo Creek. After spreading a blanket on the grassy bank, they ate lunch while they talked and watched the ducks, geese, and turtles paddle through the water.

Kio tossed them a bread crust.

"Oh, don't feed them bread. It isn't good for them."

"What should you feed them?"

"Grain." Angela dug into her purse and lifted out a bag of rice. "I figured we were stopping here, so I brought this along." She poured some rice in his hand.

His brow wrinkling, he frowned. "I thought you weren't supposed to feed birds uncooked rice, that it makes their stomachs swell up." He glanced at her. "Isn't that why you can't throw rice at weddings, anymore?"

She shook her head. "That's an urban myth Ann Landers, Martha Stewart, the Simpsons, and who knows how many others spread." Grinning, she added, "Look it up on Snopes." Then she peered up at him through her eyelashes. "But isn't that a leading question?"

He gave her a blank stare. "Isn't what a leading question?"

Raising her eyebrow, she grinned. "Rice at weddings."

Taking in her creamy complexion and dark features, he studied her. "Are you flirting with me? What's going on with you?"

What is going on with me? Watching his reaction, she felt silly, embarrassed. She covered it with a forced laugh. "Just teasing." Then she stood up, brushed herself off, and began tossing rice to the ducks as he joined her. When they had emptied the bag, she turned to him. "Ready to leave?"

"In a minute." Putting his hands on her shoulders, Kio took a deep breath and looked into her eyes. "Angela, we're both still in school. I don't think it's time to start thinking along those lines."

"Along what lines?" She gave a nervous laugh. "What are you talking about?"

He wore a wry grin. "You know what I mean. Marriage."

Hunching her shoulders, opening her lips into an O-shape, she quickly exhaled. "Who was talking about marriage? I was kidding." She rolled her eyes as she stepped back from him. "Can't you take a joke?"

He shrugged. "Maybe I heard you wrong, read you wrong."

"Well, yeah." She put up a brave front, but she shrank inside. *What is the matter with me? Maybe I've been listening to Maria and José too much.* She stifled a sigh. "Now are you ready to go?"

Again he studied her as he gave her a crooked grin. "Sure."

It was a quiet ride. They took the back roads from Boerne to Wimberley, turning onto Purgatory Road. Between feeling self-conscious with Kio and worrying about her mother, Angela kept her thoughts to herself. Then a rush of nostalgia swept over her as they turned down the familiar driveway. *Home, but for how much longer?* Again she thought about time, and she sighed.

"What's wrong?"

She turned to him. "I don't know. I just have this feeling something isn't right."

After they parked, Angela ran up to the door and pressed the bell.

Judith opened the door, wearing a robe. "Thought I heard the doorbell." She held out her arms. "What a welcome surprise." She smiled at Kio as she hugged Angela. "I'm so glad to see you both."

Angela looked at her robe, her mussed hair. "Hope we didn't wake you."

"No, I just can't seem to sleep at night, anymore. My schedule's out of whack." Smiling, she opened the door wider. "Come on in." As they walked into the kitchen, Judith asked, "Are you hungry? Can I get you something to eat?"

Shaking her head, Angela forced a smile as they sat at the kitchen island. "Thanks, we had lunch in Boerne. We just thought we'd stop by and see how you're doing."

"Other than having a little trouble sleeping, I'm fine." She smiled. "How about some iced tea?"

Angela put on a bright smile. "Sounds great."

On the drive back to San Antonio, Kio glanced at her. "Judith looks good . . . for her age. How old is she again?"

She looked up from thoughts. "Eighty-six." Then taking a deep breath, she added, "But it isn't like her to wear her bathrobe past noon." She gave a wry laugh. "Not even past six. She was always up at the crack of dawn, dressed, and on to her next project."

Keeping his eyes on the road, he shrugged. "She's getting older."

Nodding, she stifled a sigh.

He grimaced. "We all age, Angie."

Hearing him use her birth-mother's pet name for her, she gave him a wistful smile. Then it slowly faded. "True."

When Maria returned Sunday night, her eyes were sparkling, and her energy was contagious. "Elizabeth's pregnant, too."

"That's great. You and your cousin can share the experience together. Then your kids will be second cousins."

"Actually they'll be cousins twice removed, Elizabeth and I are cousins once removed."

Angela frowned. "I'm confused."

"Elizabeth is my mother's cousin."

"So she's your mother's age?"

Maria nodded. "She's forty-nine."

"This must be a miracle baby." Then Angela studied her. "I'd swear your hair's grown a half inch over the weekend. Pregnancy certainly agrees with you." Then she noticed her beaming face. "Something tells me there's more."

She chuckled. "Actually, several things." Grinning gleefully, she brought her hands together. "For one thing, I saw my guardian angel."

"Really?" Angela watched her face, half expecting a joke.

Nodding, Maria said, "It happened early Saturday morning. I was sleeping on Elizabeth's sofa, so I was out of my element, out of my comfort zone. Just as it began to get light, I woke up and saw my guardian angel standing right in front of me."

"What did he look like?"

"He was completely white, and he had humongous wings that seemed attached to his shoulders, not the puny little things on his back like the angels you see in paintings. These were immense, healthy, robust wings. I could even see the feathers."

Angela cocked her head. "Did he say anything?"

Maria scratched her head. "He didn't speak, but he gave me a peaceful feeling that all would work out, all would be well."

Angela nodded. "So you dreamt this."

"No, I was awake."

"How can you be sure?"

"When I saw him, I mentally said, 'Maria, you're dreaming. Shut your eyes, and then open them wide. If he's still here, you'll know you're not dreaming.'"

"So did you, and was he?"

Maria's eyes widened. "Yes and yes!"

"What did you do then?"

Maria gave a self-conscious chuckle. "I still wanted to be *sure*, so I shut and opened them again. He was still there. I did it again and again, and he was there until the sixth or seventh time." She hunched her shoulders. "Then he was gone."

"He never spoke to you, not a word?"

Maria shook her head. "But he had a calming effect on me." She looked off into the distance. "I just knew," she looked back at Angela. "I just *know* everything will work out for my baby and me."

Angela drew a deep breath. "Wow. That's quite an experience."

She nodded. Then Maria's eyes twinkled mischievously.

Angela grinned. "What? Is there more?"

Nodding slowly, Maria grinned back. "Oh, yeah, a lot more." She paused dramatically.

"Okay, don't keep me in suspense."

"I texted José to thank him for the pen. That led to another text and another. Long story short, we ended up talking on the phone for hours."

"Really?" Angela raised her eyebrows.

"You seem surprised."

"Well, he seems so shy." Knitting her eyebrows, she re-thought it. "Although, when he's talking about history or a topic that interests him, he seems extroverted." She sighed. "I guess what I'm trying to say is he seems like a private person. It's hard to imagine him opening up about anything personal."

"You'd be surprised." Maria gave a wry smile. "I was surprised."

Angela chose her words cautiously. "Is it anything you can share, or was your conversation confidential?"

Maria started to speak and then chewed her lip. "Some of it I'd rather not share, but there is one thing I'd like your opinion about."

Angela gave a nervous chuckle. "What do you mean, you'd like my opinion?"

"Well," she pressed her lips together as if searching for the right words. "José said something that may just put everything that's happened recently into perspective."

Angela shook her head. "Sorry, I'm not following."

"He said he had the mumps in high school." Pausing, she searched Angela's eyes. When Angela shrugged, Maria continued. "If boys get mumps after puberty . . . "

"It can cause sterility." Angela nodded. "I see where you're going with this." She thought for a moment. "He seems awfully fond of kids."

Maria took a deep breath. "I think that's the reason he's drawn to me."

Angela's eyebrows shot up but she kept silent.

"I think José sees me as an answer to his needs and sees himself as an answer to mine."

"What makes you say that?"

"As an answer to his needs, my baby and I would be a ready-made family for him, a one-stop shop."

Angela gave a rueful chuckle. "I wouldn't call you or your baby commodities."

Maria gave her a cynical half-smile. "If he's in the market for a wife, I represent a 'twofer,' two for the price of one."

Angela grimaced. "That's harsh." She took a deep breath as she watched her. "What about the second part: José seeing himself as an answer to your needs?"

She answered slowly, as if thinking it through. "I think he likes the role of protector, defender." Maria looked into Angela's face. "From everything I've seen and heard, I believe he's a sweet guy who truly wants to do the right thing."

"Which is what?"

"Make a home for my baby and me."

Angela nodded. "Then one more question. Do you see him as an answer to your needs?"

Maria sighed. "That one's harder to answer." She grimaced. "Yes, I see José as an answer to my needs . . . but not to my prayers."

Flinching, Angela exhaled. "That's cold."

"Maybe, but it's honest, practical." Maria stared into space as if gathering her thoughts. Then her eyes softened as she turned toward Angela. "Don't get me wrong. I respect him, and appreciate his thoughtfulness. We're both interested in history, hiking, and we both like classic rock music. I . . . I genuinely like him."

"But . . ."

Maria grimaced. "But dumb as this sounds, I still have feelings for Mal. No matter what he's done, I can't simply turn off my feelings for him. I'm not a faucet."

Angela tried not to roll her eyes.

"I saw that."

"Sorry, but after what you've told me about him, I can't help it. He refused to take responsibility for his actions no matter how much they've affected you or his baby. Mal's nothing but an immature, selfish kid."

Maria's expression fell. "Ever since I told him I was pregnant, that about sums him up." Then her eyes lit up. "But if you'd known him before that night, you'd see why I have such a hard time letting go of my feelings for him."

"It's moot, anyway, since he isn't in the picture, anymore." Angela gave her a sharp look.

Maria nodded.

Then Angela gave her a lopsided grin. "Who says you have to think of José, or anyone else for that matter, as potential marriage material. Maybe you prefer to be a single parent, or maybe you're still considering giving the baby up for adoption. Have you made a firm decision whether or not you want to keep him?"

As the blood drained from her face, Maria slumped into a chair. Shaking her head, she sighed. "I don't know. I can't imagine giving him up now that I think of him as a baby, not as a disease or pregnancy to terminate."

Angela grimaced. "When you came in tonight, you were so happy, you were bouncing off the walls. I'm sorry. I'm afraid I've burst your bubble."

"No, you're just being sensible."

"When you came in, you were excited about seeing your guardian angel. You said he gave you a peaceful feeling that everything would work out."

Maria nodded as the inner glow began to return to her eyes.

Angela smiled gently. "Maybe you should hold onto that."

Maria returned a half smile.

"And you seemed excited about texting José and talking to him on the phone for hours."

Shrugging, Maria mumbled, "Yeah."

"Maybe when you said José was an answer to your needs but not to your prayers, you were just being too analytical." Angela tilted her head as she watched her reaction. "Admit it. When you first came in tonight, you were all keyed up because you were beginning to connect with him."

Color returning, a smile lit up Maria's face. She nodded.

"Don't underestimate his interest. Give him time. Give yourself time. Don't be too quick to dismiss his attention as dutiful or noble. Who says marrying him would have to be a marriage of convenience? It could be a love match. Maybe this is just a budding romance that needs time to bloom."

"Maybe so." Maria stood up and hugged Angela. "Thanks for talking this through. I still don't have the answers, but I do feel it's going to work out . . . somehow."

The four of them met at Mission San Francisco de la Espada for the Sunday morning Mass.

"This is where we found Frank two years ago," Angela whispered.

Kio nodded. "At the solar illumination on October fourth, the Feast of St. Francis."

She squeezed his hand.

"You found him here?" Maria looked around the rustic stone mission.

Angela pointed to the front door. "I noticed a kitten walk through that door, jump onto that holy water font, and begin lapping up water." She smiled. "A moment later, I felt him jump on my lap. He stayed by me all during Mass, either purring in my lap or sitting on the pew, cleaning himself, when I knelt in prayer."

"Aww," said Maria, "Frank's such a cute kitty."

Angela glanced at Kio. "Hard to believe that was nearly two years ago." Shaking her head, she wondered where the time had gone.

After Mass, they left one car parked at the mission and drove the second car to the Espada Acequia.

"This irrigation system is two hundred and seventy-five years old this year," said José. "When it began supplying water to its fifteen-mile network, it served the five missions and thirty-five hundred acres of land."

Kio gave a low whistle.

Maria said, "That must have been quite an engineering project in its day."

José nodded. "It was one of the earliest recorded water projects in North America. Considering the missionaries used Roman and Moorish technology that had been brought to Spain, and inexperienced Native Americans supplied the labor, they did a great job. It's the only Spanish aqueduct left in the United States."

Maria grabbed a bottle of water from the cooler. "That water may have been potable when this was built, but I'm keeping to bottled water now." Smiling, she glanced from one to the other. "Anyone else want water?"

"Or iced tea," asked Angela, pouring a glass from the thermos jug.

As they tailgated beneath a pecan tree, Maria unpacked the food. "Hope everyone likes smoked turkey, blue cheese, and red onion on rye." Her eyes twinkled. "And pickles."

"Of course, pickles." Chuckling, Angela rolled her eyes. "We have a refrigerator filled with pickles: kosher dill spears, sliced bread-and-butter pickles, sweet pickles, gherkins, Kool-Aid pickles. You name it. We've got it."

Shrugging, Maria spread her arms, palms up. "What can I say? I like pickles."

They grinned as they unwrapped their lunch.

José bit into his sandwich and raised his eyebrows. "This is really good."

Maria laughed. "Don't look so surprised."

Angela agreed with a nod. "She knows her way around the kitchen. In fact, she does all the cooking, which works for me," she deadpanned. "Definitely not my area of expertise."

Kio caught her eye and grinned. "Duly noted."

When they finished lunch, they walked to the aqueduct to inspect its stone-arch structure.

"Even today, this carries water over Piedras Creek to irrigate the area's farms," said José.

"It's amazing it's still in use after all these years." Maria shook her head. "Some things were made to last."

José paused, studying her. "Some things still are."

Arching her eyebrow, she scrutinized him. "Like what?"

He blinked as if coming out of a trance and turned toward the aqueduct. "This is part of the nearly three-hundred-year-old Acequia Madre, or mother ditch." José's tone sounded overly bright. "Just a few years ago, archaeologists excavated another section of it in Brackenridge Park."

"And speaking of unearthing things," Angela grinned, "here's the entrance to the Mission Reach path." She pointed to the trail head as she glanced at them. "Everyone ready?"

Maria and Kio nodded. José adjusted his backpack as he glanced at Maria. "I've got extra water in here if anyone wants it."

They started along the paved trail, which crossed the creek and led them to the main path.

Angela stared up at the cloudless sky. "Another beautiful Texas-blue day." Catching Kio's eye, she smiled.

Returning her smile, he reached for her hand as they strolled along the riverbank.

Angela watched Maria and José in front of them. Their hands brushing each other's as they walked, they stole glances at each other. Then her shoulders shaking, Angela started chuckling.

Kio turned to her. "What's so funny?"

"I feel like a *dueña*, chaperoning these two."

"You don't look like one to me." His eyes twinkling in the sunlight, he gave her a mischievous smile as he bent to kiss her.

When they broke apart, she stifled a grin as she pretended to think about it. "For some reason, I don't feel as much like a dueña, anymore." She winked at him.

As they approached Mission Espada, Angela noticed a gray, longhaired cat hiding in the underbrush. While she watched, it seemed to connect with her, cautiously creeping out of hiding, one paw at a time.

"Look at that cat." She glanced at Kio and then back to the cat. "Did you ever see markings like that?"

Following her eyes, he looked in the same direction. "Like what?"

"Its paws look lacy with the white scalloped trim on its toes."

His eyes darted as he searched the area. "Where are you looking?"

She pointed. "Right there."

"Where?"

Angela did a double-take. "Don't you see it? A longhaired, silver-gray cat that looks just like Frank except for its white-tipped paws."

Pressing his lips together, he shook his head while the cat slowly pussy-footed toward her, purring.

She grinned. "Well, this is a first."

He raised his eyebrow. "What is?"

"A ghost cat's walking between my feet, rubbing against the calves of my legs." She chuckled. "And it tickles."

His eyebrows shot up. "What?" Then he sighed. "This could only happen to you."

She reached down and began petting it.

Kio shook his head. "I see your hand moving, but it's touching thin air."

"Says you." She grinned.

Several yards in the lead, Maria called to them. "The mission's just ahead. We're almost there."

"Okay." As Angela called back, the cat jumped away and started to slink toward the underbrush. "Kitty, where are you going?" She bent down, and it cautiously returned.

"What are you doing?" His lip curled, Kio raised his eyebrow.

"Just petting the cat. I didn't mean to scare it." She scratched the cat under the chin and behind the ears. Then she stood up. "Goodbye, kitty." Taking Kio's hand, she turned and started walking away. When she glanced over her shoulder, the cat was shadowing them. "Uh, oh."

He rolled his eyes. "What now?"

"It's following us." She stopped and bent down again. "Whatever the reason you're here, kitty, I think this is where you're supposed to resolve it. Sorry, but you have to stay."

Kio took her hand, and they started walking again. Glancing at her, he tugged at her wrist. "Don't look back."

"Are you kidding?" Pursing her lips, trying to take a firm stand, Angela instead burst out laughing when she saw the cat scurrying after them.

"What are you going to do?"

She shrugged. "If it wants to follow me, there isn't much I can do." She grinned. "Besides, it won't eat much."

Kio tilted his head back as he looked at her. "Not funny."

"Then look at it this way: Frank will have a playmate."

"I wonder how he'll react." He caught her eye. "Maybe he won't see him, won't even notice him."

"Or maybe this kitty spirit will frighten him." Angela grimaced. "Only one way to find out." Then she remembered the cave. "No Name."

"What?" Kio turned toward her.

"Remember the Cave Without a Name? That's what I'll call the kitty, No Name."

Rolling his eyes, he grinned. "It makes perfect sense to name a cat no one else can see, No Name."

They met up with Maria and José and climbed into the car.

Just as No Name scampered in after them, Maria slammed the door. Gasping, Angela flinched.

"What?" Maria's eyes opened wide. "What's wrong?"

Then Angela saw the cat curling up on her lap. Chuckling with relief, she said, "You're not going to believe this . . . "

As the fall semester started, Angela's roommate Tulah returned from her summer job. To make room for Maria, they converted a storage room into a third bedroom.

Over breakfast coffee the first morning, Angela turned toward Tulah, noting her blue eyes, tanned rosy cheeks, and shoulder-length blond hair swept back in a ponytail and tucked through a baseball cap. "How was your summer, working at your family's winery?"

"I loved being in the Hill Country, plus I got to see a lot of my boyfriend Clay and the horses."

"Horses?" Maria looked up.

Tulah's eyes lit up. "Clay's family and mine have Texas Mustangs, a non-profit group that rescues wild horses."

"Sounds wonderful." Maria smiled.

"It is." Giving a wistful smile, Tulah nodded. "But I miss 'em all: my family, Clay, and the mustangs." Then she looked at Maria. "Are you taking any classes?"

Eyes cast down, Maria shook her head. "Not this semester."

Angela pressed her lips together. "Maybe you could apply for a student loan at UTSA."

Maria patted her growing belly. "Think I'll sit this one out."

Chapter 4

"All God's angels come to us disguised."
— James Russell Lowell

The next few weeks flew by as the fall semester got in full swing.

Angela studied Maria over breakfast coffee. "I can't get over how fast your hair's growing. It's past chin length already."

Wearing a lighthearted smile, Maria shrugged. "Just healthy, I guess."

"I've been too busy to notice, but have you seen José lately?"

"Yes, in fact, we've met for lunch a few times."

Alone? Angela lifted her eyebrow. "So you've gone out with him?"

Maria's cheeks flushed. "Not on dates, just lunch."

Ducking her chin, Angela hid a smile. "How's he doing?"

"Between working and volunteering, he keeps busy." Maria sat up straight. "That reminds me. I promised I'd bring a side dish to the Mission of Divine Mercy Sunday."

Frank padded into the kitchen and began rubbing against Angela's legs. She bent down to pet him, saw No Name, and began petting him, too.

"I promised Kio we'd watch the eclipse." Angela grinned. "He loves celestial events."

"That's not till after dark," said Maria. "Why don't the four of us go to Mass at the Mission, spend the afternoon in Blanco State Park, and watch the eclipse together?"

"According to Saint Thomas Aquinas, there are nine choirs or ranks of angels," said the priest during the homily. "It's a celestial hierarchy, with the highest order of angels being the Seraphim, Cherubim, and Thrones. The next order are the Dominions, Virtues, and Powers, and the lowest order are the Principalities, Archangels, and Angels. Our guardian angels usually come from the angelic rank.

"Tuesday's the Archangels Gabriel, Raphael, and Michael's Feast day. Michael protects and defends. Gabriel announces and clarifies, and Raphael guides and heals.

"Friday's the Feast day of the Guardian Angel. We each have our own guardian angel to serve and protect us. Guardian angels encourage us to be virtuous, just as fallen angels or demons try to discourage us and turn us away from God.

"This is nothing new. We're each tempted every day. A temptation could be called a demon or even a spirit. For instance, if someone's tempted to doubt their faith, you could refer to it as a spirit of doubt. In the same way, there's a spirit of jealousy, a spirit of defeatism, fear, pride, lust, and so forth. We could call them spirits, as well as demons.

"So don't listen to the voices of the fallen angels. Ask Jesus to drive out the demons, so you're not distracted. Listen to your guardian angel, and then be 'guardian angels' to each other, giving hope to a wounded world.

"Our faith includes traditions, such as the Prayer to Saint Michael to defend us, and the Chaplet of Saint Michael, asking for the intercession of all the angels. These prayers can help prevent evil from taking root in our hearts. Listen to your guardian angels, spread their encouraging messages, and have an angelic week."

After Mass, they shared dinner at the Mission of Divine Mercy. Then they changed clothes and headed for Blanco State Park.

As they left the grounds, Angela pointed out the statue of the Archangel Michael. She smiled to herself. "Odd we never noticed it before."

Forty-five minutes later, they pulled into Blanco State Park.

"They rent canoes and tubes here," Maria looked to them for approval, "but only until four. Why don't we do that first, and then swim or hike until it gets dark?"

Nodding, they agreed.

"And I have a surprise." Maria grinned. "I rented a screened shelter, so we have a retreat in case of sunburn or mosquitoes and a place to relax after dark, at least until the eclipse begins."

"Good thinking." José fist-bumped her.

"Okay," again Maria glanced at them. "Tubing or canoeing?"

They looked at each other and said in unison, "Canoeing."

After renting two canoes, they paddled the calm waters of the Blanco River, side by side.

"Do you know how the Blanco River got its name?" Maria called.

Angela and Kio shook their heads.

"White River?" Leaning into her space, José looked to her for the answer.

She nodded. "When the Spanish first came to this part of Texas, they noticed how the riverbed's pale limestone reflected the moonlight, so they named it the Blanco."

"We'll have to be sure to see this river in the moonlight," said José.

Maria swiveled in her seat to grin at him.

After they returned the canoes, they hiked one of the nature trails. Then they swam and splashed in the river to cool off. After showering, they reconvened in the screened shelter.

"Renting this place really was a good idea." Nodding, Angela winked at Maria.

She shrugged. "Like I said, it gives us a place to retreat between events." Then she brought her hands together. "Who's ready for dinner?"

"I am." José grinned at her.

"If you guys can build a campfire, we can unpack the cooler and have dinner *en brochette*." Maria smiled at José.

Within fifteen minutes, they were sitting in a ring, roasting brats over a crackling fire.

"Buns, potato salad, coleslaw, and pickles are on the table," said Maria.

"Of course, pickles," added Angela, "and water or iced tea if you're thirsty."

They sat quietly, either lost in thought or listening to the sounds of the Hill Country as the moon began to rise. Angela heard the brats hissing and sizzling in the flames. Birds called to each other while the dusk faded into night. As a breeze rustled through the cottonwoods, the leaves trembled and shook, sounding like rain.

Kio got up, fixed his plate and Angela's, and rejoined them. Looking at their faces around the campfire, he smiled. "This was a good idea."

Angela took her plate from him. "Thanks." Then returning his smile, she took a deep breath of fresh air. "It's good to get away to the Hill Country, even for a few hours."

"Now if the clouds can just hold off long enough to see the eclipse," said José, "it'll be a perfect night." Bringing back his and Maria's plates, he sat close to her, their shoulders touching.

"The moon enters the earth's umbral shadow just after eight o'clock," said Kio. "Sixty-four minutes after that, the moon is completely within the shadow, lasting another seventy-two minutes."

Angela turned to the others with a grin. "What my scientific friend is trying to say is the eclipse runs from roughly nine-fifteen to ten-thirty."

"Don't forget," said Maria, "the gates close at ten."

As they ate dinner, they watched the moon gradually enter the earth's shadow. Afterwards, they packed their gear in the cars and put out the campfire. Then Kio attached his portable telescope to a tripod, and they took turns watching the eclipse through the lens or with their naked eyes.

Angela groaned. "The clouds are rolling in. I can barely see the moon, let alone the eclipse."

"Got an idea." Kio brought his iPad from the car, found a link to the eclipse's live coverage, and set up the screen, so they could watch remotely.

As the four huddled together around the small screen, Kio smiled. "This is streaming live from Germany. No cloud cover there."

Angela chuckled as she curled up against him. "My astronomer, the genius."

Chatting quietly, they alternated between watching the screen and glancing up at the sky.

"Another name for this full moon is Comanche Moon." José's voice had a confidential tone to it. The three turned toward him. "In the 1800s, the Comanche raiding parties rode across the Texas plains at night. The early settlers dreaded full moons for good reason."

Angela met Maria's eyes in a smile. "I think I hear a story coming on."

José nodded. "You're familiar with the Devil's Backbone, all 4700 acres of mountains, ridges, ravines, and hardscrabble?"

Everyone nodded.

"Ranch Road 32 follows the crest of the backbone's spine. For miles, there's nothing but undeveloped land on either side of that lonely stretch, except for a 1930s bar." José glanced at them. "People say it's haunted. They tell of pictures falling off walls, doors opening, and televisions changing channels mid-program. They talk of hearing galloping hooves as bands of wild horses once again stampede across the land. They whisper about seeing confederate soldiers, war parties of Comanches, and a friendly, little girl with a bullet hole in her head." He paused, glancing left and right.

"And they tell of seeing two red eyes peering at them from the darkness. Watching them. Following them." He shrugged. "Who knows how many of these stories are true, if any, but my college roommate Jay once experienced something he couldn't explain."

Angela raised her eyebrows as she sat back to listen.

"He was working nights, tending bar at that honky-tonk tavern. On his way home one night, his 'check engine' light came on. Moments later, his car rolled to a stop along the shoulder of Ranch Road 32. He tried to use his cell phone but couldn't get a signal. Miles from home, he debated whether to wait it out in the car or start walking.

"He was bone tired. He'd been on his feet the whole day. The idea of walking along a deserted road at night didn't appeal to him, but he figured it was better than doing nothing. He grabbed his cigarettes, put on his car's blinkers, and began the six-mile hike home. Within minutes, the blinkers' pale light became a hazy glow, fading in the distance. Only the moonlight lit his way. At three in the morning, no cars passed him.

"He said it became deathly still. Not even crickets chirped. He could hear the sound of his own breathing. Then he began hearing footsteps following him, hollow, echoing like the wooden heels of cowboy boots. At first, he thought it was his imagination. Then, as he listened, the steps became louder, closer. He walked faster, but the footsteps matched his, even seeming to gain on him.

"Though it was January, he began sweating. 'This is ridiculous,' he told himself. 'It's just my imagination.' He debated whether looking behind him would put his mind at ease or confirm his suspicions. Then he remembered something his grandmother had once said: Never look directly at an evil spirit. 'But how do I know if it's evil?'

"He stole a glance over his shoulder and saw what looked like a man in a reddish sports jacket and loose-fitting, dark pants following him. The man's eyes seemed to glow an eerie red in the dark. Nearly tripping over his feet, Jay began power-walking. Still the figure was closing in on him. The footsteps got closer and closer, until they were right behind him. Then he felt the man's breath on the back of his neck.

"He remembered something else his Native American grand-mother had once told him: Tobacco is a peace offering. He pulled his cigarettes and lighter from his pocket, lit a cigarette, and tossed it in the air. From the corner of his eye, he saw a half-human, half-goat-like figure covered with a mat of curly, black hair pause as its black hooves glimmered in the moonlight. He watched its broad hand with long, gangling fingers catch the cigarette mid-air.

"Then throwing the pack of cigarettes behind him, Jay ran until he was out of breath. After that, he power-walked until the foot-steps behind him faded into the dawn. It was seven before he got home that morning, and he never could explain how it took him four hours to walk six miles."

Angela looked at him and chuckled. "Good story! Dang, José, you're a natural-born story-teller."

He shrugged. "My roommate swore it happened."

"No lonely walks for me along the Devil's Backbone." Maria's eyes sparkled in the moonlight.

Kio glanced at the sky, his eyes on the moon. "And look! The clouds are parting."

They followed his gaze. "Ohmigosh, it is turning a bloody hue." Angela stared up at the deep red orb.

They took turns peering at the eclipse through the telescope, but when the clouds began rolling in again, Angela stifled a yawn.

"Getting sleepy?" Kio whispered.

She nodded. "A little. I was up early finishing a class project that's due tomorrow."

"Maybe we should start back. It's nearly ten, anyway." Kio turned to José. "Want to drive back—"

Angela glanced at him. "Anything wrong?"

Grinning, Kio gestured toward José and Maria, entwined in a kiss.

When the two drew apart, Kio and Angela tried not to grin.

"So," Kio said loudly, "ready to start back?"

The two spun toward him. When Maria realized Kio and Angela had caught them, she flinched and then hid her face against José's chest.

Wearing a sheepish grin, José nodded as he put his arms around her protectively. "Sure."

Halfway home, Cornelius Brothers and Sister Rose's 'Too Late to Turn Back Now' came on the oldies radio station.

From the backseat, Angela could hear José and Maria singing along.

A few minutes later, The Spinners' "Could It Be I'm Falling In Love" came on.

Again from the backseat, José and Maria sang along with the refrain.

They said goodnight in front of Angela's apartment.

"See you in the morning." Maria's fingers were still entangled with José's as she slowly drew away from his touch.

When they got inside, Angela scratched Frank and No Name behind the ears. Then she glanced at Maria. "What's going on with you two?"

Maria wore a mischievous grin as she shrugged her shoulders. "What do you mean?"

"You and José seem to have stepped things up a notch."

Wearing a wistful smile, Maria stared at nothing as she gathered her thoughts. "I don't know. The more time I spend with him, the more I find myself . . . "

"What?" Angela lifted her eyebrow. "Falling in love?"

Maria sighed. "José's always seemed an answer to my needs, but as I get to know him . . . "

Angela smiled. "Is he beginning to be an answer to your prayers?"

Maria's eyes twinkled as she turned toward her. "Maybe . . . " Hugging herself, she nodded. "Maybe!"

Two nights later, after José dropped Maria off at their apartment, she burst in the door, eyes twinkling. "Guess what?"

Angela looked up from her book as Frank and No Name sat beside her on the sofa. "What?"

"José made dinner for me, and you'll never guess what he prepared in honor of today's Feast of the Archangels."

"Probably not." Angela chuckled as she closed her book. "What did he make?"

"Archangels on Horseback."

"Okay," Angela shrugged, "what is that?"

Maria grinned. "Sea scallops broiled in bacon and served on buttered toast points." She groaned. "And that was just the appetizers. For the main course, he made roast goose stuffed with minced apples that was absolutely mouthwatering."

"He sounds like quite the chef."

"He's sure got me convinced."

Angela thought for a minute. "I get the Archangels on Horseback for today's Feast of the Archangels, but what's the significance of the roast goose?"

"I was hoping you'd ask me that." Maria grinned mischievously. "José said the Feast of the Archangels is also called Michaelmas, and is considered a day of thanksgiving in gratitude for a good harvest."

Chuckling, Angela shook her head. "Where does he learn this stuff?"

"I don't know, but I like it." Her face lit up. "He's also got something planned for us for Friday, the Feast Day of the Guardian Angels."

Angela gave her a wry chuckle. "What's he going to cook up for that?"

"Actually," Maria gave a mischievous grin, "he's made reservations to go out for dinner with his parents and then attend an event at Our Lady of the Angels church."

"His parents?" Angela's eyebrow shot up. "This is getting seri—"

"I know!" Maria squealed. "Isn't it exciting?"

Nodding, Angela studied her. *Her hair's growing back so fast . . . and she looks so happy, she's beaming.* "I've never seen you like this. You're positively glowing."

"Am I?" Maria grinned. "Does it show?"

"Does what show?"

"I think I am falling in love with him."

Friday night, Maria bounded in the door. "Guess what?"

"This is getting to be a habit." Angela chuckled. "What?"

Smiling proudly, Maria held out her left hand.

Angela gasped when she saw the ring. "Ohmigosh! He popped the question?"

Grinning ear to ear, Maria nodded.

"It's gorgeous!"

"And did you see the setting?"

Angela took a closer look. "It almost looks like two angels holding the stone in place."

"That's exactly what it is." Maria grinned gleefully. "José had the mounting especially made for tonight, the Feast Day of the Guardian Angels. He wanted us to always remember this night."

Chuckling, Angela shook her head. "He thinks of everything." Then she stood up and hugged Maria. "Congratulations! You couldn't have found a nicer guy, and José couldn't have found a better choice. It's a match made in heaven. I'm so happy for you both." She hugged her again. "So when's the wedding?"

Maria paused. "Not sure."

"What do you mean?" Angela puckered her brow.

Maria sighed. "José thinks the excitement of a wedding might be hard on the baby."

Angela's eyebrows rose as she thought it through. "Maybe he has a point." Then she saw Maria's smile fade. "How do you feel about it?"

She grimaced. "It's not like I'd wear white or anything, but . . . " She pressed her lips together into a thin line.

"But what?"

"Even though José wants to wait, I'd like to be married when the baby comes."

Angela nodded. "Understandably."

"November." Blinking, Maria's eyes shone when she smiled. "I'd really like to be married in early November, before Thanksgiving. I've always wanted to be married around the holidays."

"The weather would be perfect then." Angela grinned. "But it wouldn't leave you much time to plan a wedding, only about seven weeks."

"It wouldn't have to be anything fancy," she shrugged, "just a few friends and José's family at a nuptial Mass."

"So tell me. What prompted this proposal tonight?"

"Would you believe he had a dream on the Feast of the Archangels?"

"Really?"

Smiling gently, Maria nodded. "He dreamt an angel spoke to him." Whispering, she added, "He took it as a sign."

"As I recall, you dreamt of an angel, too, but yours never spoke."

"True," Maria nodded, "but mine had such a calming effect, I knew everything would work out." She sighed and then turned to

Angela with a smile. "And now it has, and so much of it's because of you."

Angela shook her head. "Because of God, I just happened to be in the right place at the right time."

"Would you be willing to do it again?"

"Do what again?" Angela drew her eyebrows together.

"Be in the right place at the right time?"

Angela cocked her head. "Huh?"

"Once I know when," Maria grinned, "would you be my maid of honor?"

"Of course, I would!" Angela hugged her and then grinned. "Just let me know where to show up for the wedding."

"More than that, I'm hoping you help me plan it."

"It'd be my honor," she chuckled, "as maid of honor."

Arms still around each other, they were laughing as the doorbell rang.

"That's Dev." Angela opened the door and hugged her. "Wait till you hear the good news."

Develyn's eyes opened wide at the size of Maria. "Look at you." She grinned. "You've grown. How many months pregnant are you now?"

Hunching her shoulders, Maria's smile was shy. "Five, nearly to the day."

"You're positively glowing."

"And for more reasons than you think." Angela winked at her. "Tell Dev your good news."

Maria held out her left hand. "I'm getting married."

"Congratulations!" Develyn hugged her. "God's always got a plan, no matter how bleak things might seem at times. From the looks of you and your baby, His plan's definitely working." Then she turned to Angela. "That reminds me, are we still on for tomorrow?"

"Yup!" Angela nodded and then glanced at Maria. "We're going to the abortion clinic to do some sidewalk counseling in the morning. How would you like to join us?"

Slowly shaking her head, Maria hunched her shoulders. "Oh, I wouldn't know what to do."

"Just pray." Angela turned toward Develyn. "Pray and watch how Develyn approaches the mothers." She smiled. "You know the difference it can make."

"First hand." Maria took a deep breath. Then she nodded. "I've been on the receiving end of this ministry for over two months. Maybe it's time to start paying back."

The doorbell rang again. Angela went to answer it, glancing at Develyn.

"Ceren," they hugged, "come on in." Then Angela bent down to the little girl carrying the stuffed lamb. "Ginny, how big you're getting." The girl hugged her with one arm and presented her lamb with the other. "Who's this?"

"Amkins."

"Lambkins," whispered Ceren.

Standing up, Angela turned Ginny toward Develyn. "Look who's here to see you."

Develyn's eyes looked glassy. Blinking back tears, she put on a big smile, got down on her knees, and held out her arms. "Ginny, are you ever a sight for sore eyes." She hugged the girl tightly to her chest.

With a sympathetic grimace, Ceren glanced at Angela.

Lips pursed, she nodded. Then Angela turned toward Maria. "I'd like you to meet my birth mother, Ceren."

Maria smiled and held out her hand.

"And this is Ginny," said Develyn, still on her knees hugging the child, "Ceren's adopted daughter."

Maria's jaw dropped as she made the connection. Catching herself, she smiled at the girl. "I like your little friend. What a cute Lambkins." Then Maria's eyes went from woman to woman as if piecing the parts together.

Angela smiled as she stood with them. "We're family."

The next morning, as Develyn drove them to the clinic, Maria asked, "How did you get involved with sidewalk counseling?"

Looking in the rearview mirror, Develyn smiled at Angela in the backseat. Then she glanced at Maria beside her. "When it comes to abortions, I know how just controlling, how influential partners, parents, even Parentage Incorporated can be."

Her lips pressed into a tight line, Maria nodded.

"Women are more sensitive during pregnancy." Develyn said. "Rising hormone levels are changing their bodies, making them emotionally more vulnerable, more volatile. They need someone to give them a lifeline, someone to stand with them."

"What prompted you to begin this ministry?"

Again glancing in the rearview mirror, Develyn exchanged a look with Angela in the backseat. Then taking a deep breath, she turned toward Maria. "Ginny."

Maria nodded. "I wondered."

Her eyes on the road, Develyn nodded. "My pregnancy ended in adoption, not abortion, despite pressure at the time from my boyfriend. Then I attended a conference." Develyn glanced at Maria. "The topic was the Christmas story, but with a twist. The focus was Herod's slaughter of the innocents, and Mary and Joseph's flight to Egypt with their newborn baby."

"That story's hardly mentioned, anymore," said Maria.

"It's not the uplifting message people want to hear at Christmas," said Angela from the back.

"Exactly." Nodding, occasionally glancing into the rearview, Develyn kept her eyes on the road. "People love to hear about the nativity, the angels on high, the shepherds in the fields, and the three wise men following the Christmas star—"

"In other words, they like to hear about the season's joy," said Angela.

"But they forget about the dark side of Christmas."

In the rearview mirror, Angela saw Develyn arch her eyebrow. Angela shivered and then rubbed her arms. "You gave me a chill."

"It's a chilling tale. Herod's slaughter of the innocents is about the cold-blooded murder of babies. Some people haven't heard the story. Others confuse it with the Exodus story of the plague on the firstborn. Basically, it's about King Herod. Egocentric, set in his ways, fearful of anything that threatened his kingdom, he was the keeper of the status quo."

Maria wrinkled her brow. "What do you mean, 'keeper of the status quo'?"

"Herod had become so entrenched, so established in his empire, he lashed out when he felt threatened. History tells us Herod killed three of his own sons because he was afraid they would take his throne."

"Nice guy." Angela grimaced.

"To maintain his monarchy, to stay in power, he killed everyone he perceived as a threat, even his wives. Then just before his death, Herod ordered his men to kill a member of every family."

Maria's face contorted. "Why?"

"To ensure his subjects would genuinely grieve his death."

"That was so senseless." Lifting her eyebrows, Maria shook her head.

"Senseless?" Develyn sniffed. "What about Herod's decree to kill all the male infants after Christ's birth? He was so afraid of losing his monarchy to the new King, he murdered all the baby boys."

"The slaughter of the innocents," said Angela.

"This conference stressed the conflict, the life-and-death struggle between the old and the new. 'What is' confronts 'what wants to be.' What's strong and entrenched, confronts what's easily crushed. Power is heavily weighted towards the status quo. The new has only its desire to be born. For every concept, every vision, every new step forward, every 'child,' there are hundreds killed and slaughtered, never to have the chance to grow and mature."

"Wait a minute." Squinting, Maria said, "I thought we were talking about Herod."

"We are."

"But it sounds like you're talking about Parentage Incorporated."

Develyn arched her eyebrow as she glanced at her. "We are."

"So you're telling us, this conference was comparing Herod to Parentage Incorporated."

Develyn nodded.

Blinking, seeming to process her thoughts, Maria said, "Christmas is about the birth of Christ. Are you saying the joy of Christmas is like the joy of a baby's conception?"

Develyn nodded.

"And the abortion mills' slaughter of the innocents," said Maria, "is like Herod's historic butchery."

"That's part of it."

Maria studied her. "What else?"

"Herod's fear wasn't unlike that of Parentage Incorporated." Develyn's mouth was grim. "Whether kingdom or corporation, the real reason they kill babies is to protect their bottom line—greed."

Chapter 5

"You Belong To the City"
– GLENN FREY

José, Maria, Kio, and Angela attended Mass at the Mission San Juan Capistrano chapel Sunday. Afterwards, they hiked the Yanaguana Nature Trail between the chapel and the San Antonio River.

"It's a short hike," said José, "about a quarter mile west of here, along a part of the San Antonio River's original channel. This section's returned to its natural ecosystem."

Maria looked at the underbrush and lush canopy. "What do you call this kind of environment?"

"South Texas riparian brush country."

"And Yanaguana, what does that mean?" She looked up into his face.

"To the *Coahuiltecan* peoples, it meant 'refreshing waters.'" He smiled. "This river was life. It was the only constant water supply, providing water not only for the native people, but for fish and wildlife, too. I came across a letter written nearly two centuries ago that mentioned the abundant fish, turkey, and buffalo in this area."

"Buffalo *here?* Really?" Maria caught his eye and smiled.

José grinned. Then he stopped in front of a tree and rubbed one of its leaves between his fingers. "This is called a sandpaper tree."

Maria chuckled. "Why?"

"Feel this leaf. The tree's scientific name is *Anaqua*, and its leaves were once used to polish wood."

"I can see why." Recoiling, she dropped the leaf. "What are you, a Texas Master Naturalist or something?"

He winked. "Actually, yes."

She grinned. "Show-off." Then she proudly pointed to a nearby bush. "I know this one, Mountain Laurel."

"Did you know Native Americans would trade a six-foot strand of its beans for a horse?"

"That's ridiculous. These beans are everywhere. Why would they put such a high price on them?"

"The shells of its beans are so dense, they're hard to drill through. It was the labor that added value."

They looked at the river as they walked along the trail. Then José stopped in front of a tree and ran his fingers lightly over its rough, warty bark. "Not the most attractive tree, this is a Hackberry, but it's considered *the* most valuable tree for wildlife in North America. Over two hundred species of birds eat its fruit."

Running her fingers over its spongy bark, Maria studied it. "It looks like bumpy layers of cork."

Nodding, José reached for her hand. As they led the way, the foursome strolled along the well-maintained trail. Stopping at each boardwalk observation point, gazing out at the views, they were still back to the car within a half hour.

When Kio turned the car's ignition, Glenn Frey's 'You Belong To the City' began playing on the oldies station.

Ears perked, Maria paused as she climbed into the back seat. Then amid the song's base beat, her phone chimed. She glanced at the text and blanched.

Watching her, José's forehead creased. "Anything wrong?"

Shaking her head, she shrugged. "No, just a doctor's reminder for tomorrow's appointment." She gave a forced smile. "Good thing they texted, or I might've forgotten it."

Scrutinizing her, Angela narrowed her eyes.

Behind the wheel, Kio turned toward them. "Anyone hungry?"

Angela grinned. "Starved."

"I know a new Brazilian restaurant that just opened," said José. "They've got a mean *Feijoada*."

"A what?" Angela raised her eyebrows.

"It's a hearty, traditional chili made with black beans, meat, and sausage."

"Mmm, sounds delicious." Angela grinned.

Maria turned pale. She put her hand to her forehead as beads of sweat broke out above her upper lip. "All of a sudden, I don't feel well."

Hand on the doorknob, ready to spring into action, José watched her. "Do you need to visit the restroom?"

Maria shook her head. "No, please just take me home. I need to lie down."

Kio pulled up to the apartment in under ten minutes.

José jumped out, opened Maria's door, and held out his hand to her. "Do you need me to help you in?"

Her eyes cast down, avoiding his gaze, she shook her head. "No, thanks, I just need to lie down."

Angela turned toward Kio. "I'd better go in with her." Grimacing, she whispered, "Sorry." Then she kissed him, got out, and opened the front door. Once inside the apartment, Angela turned to Maria. "Okay, what's really going on?"

Taking a deep breath, Maria handed Angela her phone. "Read the text."

"Where are you?"

Angela scowled as she shook her head.

"Look who sent it."

Angela gasped. "Mal."

Maria dragged her hand through her thick hair. "What should I do?"

Angela shook her head. "This is your call entirely."

Maria's face screwed up as if she was going to cry. "Why did he have to contact me now?" She glanced at Angela. "I haven't heard from him since July Fourth. If he's stayed away this long, why is he showing up now?"

Again Angela shook her head. "I don't have the answers."

"Neither do I." Maria frowned. "I guess only Mal does." She reached for her phone.

Angela momentarily clasped it tightly, sighed, and then handed it back to her. "What about José?"

Her face pinched, Maria mumbled "I have to lie down."

Angela watched as she closed the door to her room.

When José called a half hour later, Angela crossed her fingers as she fibbed. "She's resting." *At least, I hope so.*

"I figured she was. That's why I didn't call her cell. Please let her know I called."

"Sure."

He gave a wry chuckle. "I worry about her."

So do I. After she hung up, she paused at Maria's door, debating whether to check on her or leave her alone. Hand poised to knock, she heard Maria's voice talking on the phone. Then, shoulders slumping, Angela stifled a groan as she walked away.

Three hours later, Maria emerged from her room. Though her eyes were red and her lashes were wet, she wore a tranquil smile.

Angela studied her, trying to read her body language. Finally, she asked. "What's changed?"

Wearing a Mona Lisa smile, she sighed. "Everything." Seeming to float, she crossed to the refrigerator and took out a carton of yogurt.

Her forehead creasing, Angela watched her. "A little more detail, please."

Maria stirred her yogurt as she gathered her thoughts. "I texted Mal, and we texted back and forth a few minutes. But so much has happened to us, we decided it would be easier to talk." She gave another peaceful smile. "We ended up talking for almost three hours."

Angela had a sinking feeling. She pressed her lips together to keep from voicing her concerns.

"Don't look so happy for me." Maria's tone was sarcastic, but her smile was friendly.

Angela sighed. "I'm waiting for the other shoe to fall."

"What?" Maria cocked her head.

"The text from Mal, you hiding it from José, your three-hour phone call with Mal," Angela met her eyes. "That's the first shoe falling. Now, I'm waiting for the second."

Again Maria's face took on a wistful calmness. "Just before Mal texted me, when we got into the car, did you hear Glenn Frey's 'You Belong To the City' come on the oldies station?"

"Vaguely. Why?"

"That was our song. The moment I heard it, I sensed an energy, an electricity in the air. The next moment Mal texted me."

Angela could not keep the words from spilling out. "Did he happen to mention why he deserted you or hasn't contacted you in over three months?"

Maria lifted a warning eyebrow. Then she returned to her calm disposition. "As a matter of fact, he did." She paused.

Angela spread her hands impatiently. "And . . . "

"He was in jail."

Angela's eyelids flew open. "Jail!"

"I knew you'd take it this way—"

"What way should I take it? The guy dumped you, left you to fend for yourself, then when he finally does text you after three months, he tells you he's been in jail." Shaking her head, Angela sighed. "How would you suggest I take it? Give him a good conduct medal, a good citizenship award?"

"No." Maria shrugged. "It just wasn't the way it happened." Frowning, she sighed. "I mean, it just sounded that way. It wasn't the way it was."

"That's exactly how it 'sounded' to me." Angela narrowed her eyes as she scrutinized her. "How did he sugar-coat it to make it sound any different?"

Maria looked down at the floor, swallowed, and then met Angela's eyes. "His birthday, the night I told him I was pregnant, the last time I saw him," she sighed. "The police picked him up for drunk driving. They gave him one call. He called his father to get him an attorney. Then they took away his cell phone and—"

"Drunk driving! Really?" Angela rolled her eyes.

"No, it isn't the way it sounds. It was his first—his *only* DWI. Even so, they still fined him and kept him in jail ninety days with no outside contact other than his lawyer."

"I don't buy it." Angela sighed and tried again. "If Mal really had wanted to get in touch with you, don't you think he'd have found a way?"

Maria held out her hands, palms up. "I got a new phone. My number changed. No one knew where I was."

"Couldn't he have gotten word to you somehow? Email? Facebook?"

Maria slowly shook her head. "I don't know." She looked into Angela's eyes. "He said he couldn't."

"And you believe him?"

Finishing her yogurt, she nodded. "I do."

"Then how did he find you now?"

"He ran into my cousin Elizabeth. She gave him my new number."

Curling her lip, Angela lifted her eyebrow. "By the way, José called while you were listening to Mal's alibi. He's worried about you." She scowled. "Have you given José any thought during this?"

"What's that supposed to mean?" Her face tightening, Maria's tone challenged her.

"I guess I'm still waiting for the other shoe to fall." Sighing, Angela grimaced. "Before I jump to any more conclusions, let me ask you something. Are you planning to stay in contact with Mal?"

Maria glanced at the clock, and a tranquil smile lit up her face. "He's picking me up for coffee in twenty minutes."

"I'll get it!"

When the doorbell rang, Maria raced across the living room to answer it.

Angela did not want to meet Mal. From what she had heard, he was the devil himself. She felt nothing but disgust for him, yet she had to see who could hold Maria in such a grip. Not wanting to be a part of it, yet intrigued, she stood on the sidelines, watching as the scene unfolded.

When Maria opened the door, Angela caught her breath. *He's drop-dead gorgeous, easily the most stunning man I've ever seen.* Suddenly, the reason for Maria's fascination became clear.

The man standing in their doorway was tall, blond, and blue-eyed. Perfectly proportioned, he exuded an easy air of command. His cheekbones flawlessly symmetrical, his angular jaw and chin seemed to give his full lips a perpetual pout, but it was his crystal blue eyes that mesmerized, captivated. Angela could not take her eyes off him.

When he saw Maria, he took a step forward as if to hug her, but stepping back, she deftly avoided him.

"Mal, I'd like you to meet my roommate, Angela."

His smile was like the clouds parting and the sun shining. From across the room Angela could feel his magnetism. "Hello, Angela. I've heard so much about you."

Not moving from her spot, she nodded coolly. "Hi."

If he noticed her hostility, he did not let on. He turned his charismatic smile toward Maria, and she visibly basked in his glow. Never taking her eyes off him, her face took on its earlier tranquil, Mona Lisa smile.

The look of love. Inwardly, Angela groaned.

Mal's eyes ran up and down Maria's body, seeming to take in the transformation since the last time he had seen her. "I've never seen you lovelier. You're beautiful."

As she stared back, Maria's smile turned into a gaze of mute adoration.

Angela stifled a sigh. Watching Maria, she thought of José, and her heart sank. Then she did a double take as she saw a spirit lurking beside Mal. Except for the tattoos, piercings, shaved head, and sneer, he looked exactly like José. Amazed by the resemblance, she openly stared.

As if sensing her, the spirit turned his gaze from Mal to Angela. "You can see me?"

She gave a subtle nod.

"And hear me?"

Again she bobbed her chin.

His dark eyes narrowed as he strode toward her.

Angela swallowed hard. She had never sensed a spirit harboring such anger. As it approached, she began feeling nauseous. A heaviness gripped her chest. Breathing became labored.

"Look at that pretty-boy face." The spirit pointed at Mal and then focused his steely eyes on Angela. "That face laughed as he emptied his semi-automatic's magazine into me."

Gulping, Angela's eyebrows shot up.

"See ya," called Maria from the door.

Blinking, Angela tuned in to the other conversation. "Sorry, I didn't catch that. What did you say?"

"I said, we're going for coffee. See ya."

"Follow them," said the spirit in her other ear. "Wait till they leave, and then tail 'em. Don't trust him for a minute."

Glancing from the spirit to Maria, Angela lifted her hand in a feeble wave and mumbled, "'Kay."

"Get your keys." The spirit looked out the window. "Okay, they're taking off. Go!"

Angela dashed out the door, jumped in her car, and tried to follow Mal's fire-engine-red Corvette without being seen.

She gave a frustrated sigh. "This is ridiculous. The speed limit's thirty-five in this zone. He's gotta be doing sixty. I can't keep up."

"Don't worry," said the spirit. "I'll guide you."

Lifting her eyebrow, Angela gave him a disbelieving sidelong glance. *He looks like the devil incarnate, and he's my guiding angel?*

The spirit began chuckling and ended by throwing back his head, howling with laughter.

Angela kept her eyes on the traffic as she spoke. "Great, so you can read my mind?"

"Every nuance." He gave a final chuckle, and then said, "Turn left at the next intersection."

She followed his directions and ended up parking down the street from Mal and Maria.

"Now what?"

"Keep your eye on them." He raised his pierced eyebrow. "I'll fill you in on what you don't see."

Slouching down in her seat, Angela peeked over the steering wheel. As Mal and Maria crossed the street, she saw Maria hold out her left hand and show him her engagement ring. Relieved, Angela took a deep breath.

They sat down at one of the coffee shop's sidewalk tables. Although Angela couldn't hear their conversation, she could watch their body language.

Then she saw the spirit begin hovering over Mal. First it knocked his silverware off the table. Ten minutes into their conversation, it tipped over his water glass, soaking the tablecloth and spilling on Maria's dress. When the waiter brought the two coffees, it moved the table's third chair, so the chair leg tripped the waiter. Hot coffee splashed on Mal's leg. Though she could not hear, she could see him jump up and swipe at his trousers with his napkin. Chuckling to herself, she could only imagine the expletives.

An hour later, Mal paid the tab, and they crossed to his Corvette. As Angela followed them home, the spirit sat beside her. Suddenly, the Corvette's left blinker went on. Then his right. Then his windshield wipers began going full speed. Angela glanced at the spirit, chuckling evilly next to her.

"Grow up."

"Why?" He turned toward her. "I'm dead. I'm done growing."

"No, you're not." She glanced at him.

He met her eyes and sneered. "It's over for me."

Angela shook her head as she kept her eye on traffic. "You've still got another round to go." She glanced at him. "It's not too late for you."

Sniffing, he grimaced. "Game's over, and I lost."

Shaking her head, Angela pursed her lips. "It ain't over till it's over, and it ain't over." She glanced at him, "If you like, I can help you through this final round."

"Why?" He sneered.

Angela shrugged. "Why not?" Again she glanced at him. "What's your name?"

"Gabe. What's yours?"

"Angela."

When they neared her apartment, she slowed and kept at a distance. After Mal parked, Angela pulled into a slot down the street. Again she watched them as Mal walked Maria to the door. When he tried to kiss her, Maria ducked her chin.

Angela gave a sigh of relief as she pulled into traffic and then turned into their driveway. "Oh, you beat me home." Glancing at Gabe before she spoke to them, Angela asked innocently, "Have fun?"

As the four walked into the apartment, the phone rang.

Gabe gave Angela a puzzled look. Then, his eyes narrowing, he crinkled his forehead as he glanced from the phone to Maria and back to Angela.

She shrugged. *What?*

Gabe blinked, seeming to process his thoughts, while Maria held back as if frozen.

Scowling at her, Angela answered the phone. "Hi José," she said loudly.

Maria shook her head and subtly held up her hands as if saying she was not there.

"Why, yes, she just got . . . up." Despite Maria's dark glance, Angela handed her the phone.

Mal gestured with his thumb and pinkie he would call as he slunk away, closing the door behind him.

Angela rolled her eyes and heaved a silent sigh.

His ears perking, Gabe cocked his head.

"Yes, I'm definitely feeling better." Maria glanced at her. Although she spoke into the phone, she raised her voice for Angela's sake. A worried look came over her face, and she added, "I'm still a little tired. I think it'd be better if I just take a bath and turn in early tonight. Maybe we can meet tomorrow?"

Angela and Gabe shared a look.

As Maria hung up, Angela started in. "What kind of game are you playing?"

"What do you mean?"

Angela gave an exasperated growl deep in her throat. "Mal's playing you. You seem to be playing him against José. José's the only one not playing, and now you're playing games with him."

Her forehead furrowing, her eyes snapping, Maria turned toward her. "What is your problem?"

"Although I didn't go along with it, I could understand your interest in hearing Mal's story," Angela grimaced, "but now you've crossed a line."

"What are you talking about?"

"You lied to José, making it sound like you were home resting instead of being out with another man. I fibbed for you, saying you just got up, not just got in with Mal. That changes the game." Angela paused as she drew a deep breath. "You're hiding something from José."

"José who?" asked Gabe as Maria talked over him.

"It was a white lie, and to tell the truth, I am a little tired. Good night." Raising her eyebrow, Maria started toward her room and closed the door.

"José who?" asked Gabe.

"Aceves." Angela looked at him. "Why?"

"Does he work at the Menger?"

She nodded. "Why?"

The streetwise sneer left his face as he looked at her. "Just curious." Then he spotted the cat. "Who's this?"

"No Name. He followed me home."

Gabe picked up the cat and then turned to her. "How is it that you can see me, hear me?"

"It's a gift." Angela shrugged. "I was born with it." She met his eyes. "Tell me what you know about Mal."

Instantly, the spirit seethed with anger and revenge. Again she began to feel nauseous, and her breathing became labored. No Name jumped down from Gabe's arms and hid behind the sofa.

"Last July, I met a business associate outside Alpine. The deal went sour." He sneered as he gestured toward the door. "Pretty Boy emptied his semi-automatic's magazine into my stomach and chest."

That explains the nausea and difficulty breathing. She filled her lungs and then let it out with a sigh. "Why? Was it a fight over something, robbery, self-defense? Why did he do it?"

Gabe grimaced. "It was a drug deal gone wrong."

She raised her eyebrow. "He's a murderer and involved with drugs?"

He nodded. "He's part of a group that I," he shrugged, "did business with."

Angela took in that information with another deep breath. *How did Maria ever get involved with Mal?* Then her attention focused on Gabe. "Why haven't you moved on? Why are you still here?"

His lips turned down in disgust as he recalled the memory. "I want to see him pay for what he did. He got away with murder, while I . . ."

"You what?"

"My bones are bleaching on the Chihuahuan Desert outside Alpine. I want a Christian burial on consecrated land!" his voice bellowed, "and I want payback."

She nodded solemnly. "Okay, how can I help?"

He sneered, said, "Stand by," and disappeared.

Two weeks later, Mal showed up at the Alamo with a single rose for Maria. Angela watched her eyes sparkle as she smiled up at him. Angela heard her talking on the phone with him that night and the next. At lunch Friday, Angela saw her leave with Mal. She took a deep breath but said nothing. Saturday, he showed up in his red Corvette, wanting to take her out for dinner.

"Maria, can I see you a minute?" Angela stepped into the kitchen, and Maria followed. "I don't want to butt into your business, but I'm worried about you. Have you thought this through?"

"Thought what through?"

Arching her eyebrow, Angela glared as she gave her a warning look.

"You mean Mal." Maria nodded. "Yes, I've . . . I'm working through it."

"This path you're walking is narrow." Angela grimaced. "Be careful, or you're going to get hurt."

"I can take care of myself."

"What about José?"

"What about him?" Maria shrugged. "I'm not hurting him."

"I thought the four of us were going to a late dinner tonight."

Maria's jaw dropped. "I forgot."

"I thought so." Angela grimaced.

Maria's face fell. "Now what am I going to do?" She sighed. "I can't just tell Mal to leave."

"Why not?" Angela gave an exasperated sigh. "He showed up unannounced. Tell him you've got other plans."

She shook her head. "I can't do that."

"You've got to start making some hard decisions." *And about more than just dinner.*

"I don't know what to do." Maria pointed to the living room. "Mal's here now. Our dinner date's not for hours." Then her eyes lit up as she grinned. "Since I can't choose between them, why not do both? Double the pleasure, double the fun. A quick bite with Mal, and I'll be home in time for dinner with José."

"You're walking a fine line." She gave her a wry smile. "What about our plans to meet Dev at the abortion clinic this afternoon?"

Maria thumped her forehead with her hand. "Oh, Angela, I'm so sorry. I forgot. Next time, I promise."

Angela grimaced as they stepped back into the living room. Apparently catching Mal unawares, he stopped pacing mid-stride. Gabe was hovering behind him like a dark shadow, yet Mal seemed oblivious to him. Instead, he homed in on Maria. "Ready?"

For what? Angela shared a dark look with Gabe.

"Let me get my—"

"Purse," Mal interjected.

Gabe raised an eyebrow.

Not understanding, Angela frowned slightly as she shrugged her shoulder.

Chuckling, Maria said, "I'll be—"

"Right back." Edgy, Mal rushed to finish her sentence.

Gabe shot her a 'See that?' expression.

Angela subtly shook her head.

While Maria got her purse, Mal fidgeted, checking his watch, cracking his neck, scratching his head, never holding still.

Angela finally gestured to a chair. "Would you like to—"

"No, I'm good." He walked to the window. Then as an after-thought, he glanced back at her. "Thanks." He continued pacing to the bookcase to study a knickknack, to the coffee table to glance at a magazine, and back to the window until Maria appeared. Then he scrambled to open the door. "Let's go."

Angela took a step forward. "What time will you be back?"

Maria shrugged as she looked at Mal. "Two, two and a half—"

"We'll be back by three," called Mal, his arm around Maria's waist as he quickly ushered her out the door.

Angela turned to Gabe. "What was that all about?"

His lip curling, he sneered. "Ice."

Angela gave him a blank stare.

"You know, Glass, Crystal, Methlies Quik."

"What?"

His eyes opened wide. "Speed, Meth, Methamphetamine."

"Drugs?"

Rolling his eyes, he threw his hands in the air. "Yeah, *drugs.*" He grimaced. "Didn't you pick up on his interruptions?"

"I wondered about that. He couldn't seem to wait for Maria or me to finish a sentence. He had to finish it faster."

He nodded. "He's feeling the high right now. His system's so sped up, you're all speaking, moving in slow motion for him."

"And he's driving?"

Arching an eyebrow, Gabe nodded.

Angela took a deep breath as she said a silent prayer. "What was all that fidgeting about?"

"He may be entering the tweaking phase. You saw him scratch-ing his head?"

She nodded.

"Intense itching is one of the first signs. I've seen people scratch and pick so much, they look like they have chicken pox."

"That's called tweaking?"

"Yeah, it happens when a user's coming to the end of a binge, when ice doesn't give them a rush or a high anymore."

Angela shook her head. "I shouldn't have let her go."

"Like you could've stopped her?"

"Maybe we should follow them again?"

"Not a bad idea."

Angela glanced out the window and then back at him. "Problem is, he's got a few minutes' lead on us. I don't know where they're headed."

"Just drive. Leave the navigating to me." Gabe grinned. "I'll meet you in the car."

Angela started to answer but realized she was speaking to thin air. She found her keys and got in the car. Before she could turn the ignition, Gabe was sitting beside her again.

"Go to the second light and make a right," he said.

"Where'd you go?"

"I 'popped in' on Pretty Boy." His grimace almost passed for a smile. "Make a left at the next corner. Then another left at the first light."

"Is Maria safe, at least for now?" Angela thought of Develyn and her boyfriend Travis. The memory of him killing himself made her shudder.

He glanced at her. "What's wrong?"

"Something similar happened to a friend of mine. Her boyfriend combined too much alcohol with a death wish." She took a deep breath. "I don't want to repeat that experience . . . ever."

He nodded and pointed to a parking space. "Pull in here. It's got a clear view of the patio. If I know Pretty Boy, he'll want to sit outside, so he can smoke and keep his eye out for customers."

Raising her eyebrow, she glanced at him.

"He's picked up a few habits in jail." Gabe gestured toward the seating area. "There's Pretty Boy and your friend now."

Angela watched the hostess seat them in the patio. Still fidgeting, Mal pulled out a pack of cigarettes and lit up. She saw them order, and then Mal seemed to recognize someone at another table. He excused himself, got up, and joined the other man.

"Keep your eyes on his hands," said Gabe.

As she watched them talking, she noticed an exchange under the table. "Was that what I thought it was?"

Gabe nodded. "Pretty Boy's dealing."

"If you hadn't told me to watch his hands, I never would've noticed. His hands seemed to work independently of him." Angela cocked her head. "How'd you know he was going to do that?"

"Let's just say I've had a lot of experience."

She appraised his tattoos, pierced ears, and gruff appearance. "You seem to know a lot about surveillance for a drug dealer."

He sniffed. "Glad to see my cover's still working."

Drawing her eyebrows together, she studied him. "Cover?"

He nodded. "I was an undercover agent for the DEA."

Her eyes opened wide as her jaw dropped. "The Drug Enforcement Administration?" Then she nodded slowly as the situation became clear. "You were acting in the line of duty when he shot you."

He let out another wry chuckle. "I was trying to keep him from making a big mistake."

"What happened?"

"My partner and I'd been lining up the deal for weeks. Posing as buyers, we spent months infiltrating the *Diamante Verde* gang. Then the night of the bust, the *Lobos Grises* cartel brought in Pretty Boy to drive the heat vehicle."

She wrinkled her brow. "The heat vehicle, what's that?"

"It's a decoy, someone they hire to speed down the road, so highway patrol pulls them over and lets the cars behind him carrying the drugs get through."

"So that was Mal's role in all this, a driver."

"Initially, but Pretty Boy was a rookie, drunk, high, and itching for a fight, *literally itching*." He shook his head. "I'd never seen him before. I figured it was his first time, so I tried to let him off."

She hunched her shoulders. "How could you do anything without blowing your cover?"

He raised his eyebrows. "Good question. I pointed out he was in no condition to drive, that he was a liability, not an asset to the job. If he'd been smart, he would have left then."

"But he didn't . . . "

Gabe snickered. "I think he'd seen too many movies. Instead of leaving, he got confrontational. He pulled out his semi-automatic and started waving it around, making threats. Everyone there tried to talk sense into him, but he was so high on drugs and alcohol, he wasn't listening."

"When all you were doing was trying to protect him." Shaking her head, she sighed.

He gave her wry smile. "No good deed goes unpunished."

So this is what Maria's dealing with. "What happened then?"

"One thing led to another, and he emptied his magazine in me."

"Wow." The hair stood up on the back of Angela's neck. Shuddering, she glanced at the table. Mal had returned and was again sitting with Maria. "How could someone so evil be so incredibly good-looking?"

"He won't be for long. Meth's hard on the body. It ages users quickly. The fact that its effects aren't showing proves he hasn't been using it that long."

"He was behind bars for three months. Maybe he got it out of his system and is just redeveloping the habit."

He sniffed. "If he's been cold turkey for three months, as you think, he's probably been using it for only a few weeks. On the other hand, we don't know how long he'd used it prior to his incarceration. He's already showing signs of addiction."

Angela watched Maria. "What does she see in him?"

"Before he became a meth user, he might've been a nice guy, someone completely different from what he is now." He shrugged. "Who knows? She may still see who he was, not who he's become." Shaking his head, he glanced at Maria and Mal. "Pretty Boy's playing with matches, while she's sitting on a powder keg."

Her lips pressed together, Angela sighed. "I'm worried about her."

"You should be."

As they sat in the car watching, Angela called Develyn. "Sorry, but Maria and I can't join you today." She told her the story.

"Mal sounds a lot like Travis, only worse—alcoholic *and* drug-addicted." Develyn sighed. "I'll add him to my prayers."

"Do me a favor," asked Angela, "add Maria, too?"

Develyn's smile came through the phone. "I've been praying for her and her baby since we met her."

Gabe gestured toward them. "They're leaving."

"Gotta go. Thanks, Dev. Talk to you later." Angela hung up and started the ignition. "That was fast. Seems like they hardly sat down, and they're leaving."

"Pretty Boy's losing his appetite." He glanced at her. "Another sign of a meth abuser."

She eased into traffic, trying to follow Mal without being seen. "The hard part's trying to keep up with him."

"Uh-oh."

She glanced at Gabe. "What's wrong?"

"Be right back." With that, he disappeared.

Angela kept Mal's car in view as, block after block, she passed street signs. A few minutes later, Gabe appeared beside her.

"This isn't the way back to our apartment. Where's he taking her?"

"He had something else planned, but luckily . . . "

Angela watched as Mal slowed down and then abruptly pulled into a parking lot. "What just happened?"

"His fuel pump died." Gabe grinned. "Pull over. Let's give them a few minutes and then just happen to drive by."

Ten minutes later, Angela pulled alongside Mal's Corvette and rolled down the window. "Anything wrong?"

Maria sighed with relief. "Angela, am I ever glad to see you." Then a puzzled look came over her face. "What are you doing in this part of town?"

"Just running a few errands." Angela smiled innocently. "What's up?"

"Mal's car broke down. It just suddenly stopped working, and he's having a heck of a time finding a tow truck. He's going to be here a while. Can you give me a ride home?"

"Sure, hop in." As she spoke, Gabe vanished from the passenger seat.

Maria climbed in, and Mal leaned over to kiss her goodbye. Just then the car lurched forward, slamming the open door against him.

"Oops . . . sorry!" As surprised as everyone else, Angela had to think fast. "My foot must have slipped off the brake."

From the back, she heard Gabe gasping in between fits of laughter.

Mal gave her a dark look as he straightened his back and winced. Then he slammed the door.

"Bye, Mal," called Maria, wearing a worried frown.

"Hope your wait's not too long," called Gabe, bursting out in a new round of laughter.

Angela tried but couldn't suppress a grin as she glanced at Gabe in the rearview mirror.

"What are you smirking about?" Maria gave her a suspicious look. "Did you do that on purpose?"

Angela momentarily took her right hand from the wheel and raised it as if taking an oath. "I didn't do it." Then forcing a smile, she glanced at Maria. "So how was your date?"

She shrugged. "It wasn't a date. It was a quick sandwich."

"It was quick all right. Weren't you . . . getting along?"

Maria took a deep breath. Staring into space, she seemed to mull it over. "Mal seems different."

Angela glanced at her. "Really? How so?"

"For one thing, he's nervous, antsy, always fidgeting."

Angela nodded. "I noticed that. He was pacing, practically climbing walls while you went to get your purse."

Maria made a face. "And he smokes now."

"Now? You mean he'd never smoked before?"

Maria shook her head. "He said it was a habit he picked up in jail."

What other habits? "Anything else?"

She took a deep breath. "Nothing, everything, it's hard to put my finger on. It seems like he's always in motion . . . and he talks so fast. I feel constantly rushed when I'm around him to the point I can't calm down." She clenched her hands. "I just feel so anxious around him, so agitated."

"So he makes you . . . uneasy."

Maria nodded slowly as she thought it over. "That's exactly how I feel with him, and it never used to be that way." She turned toward Angela. "I'd loved him so much. I was crushed when I told him I was pregnant, and he ignored me. In the weeks after, when he didn't contact me, I was stunned, in a daze. Then I got numb, just stopped feeling . . . and gradually stopped thinking about him." Her eyes lit up. "But after he texted me, and then when we talked on the phone, after he explained how he'd tried but couldn't get in touch with me, my old feelings for him began resurfacing."

Angela's shoulders slumped as Maria gave her a dark look

"I know what you're thinking." Maria swallowed. "I've steadily fallen in love with José over these past months. How couldn't I? He's a gift from God." She turned to Angela as she sighed. "But Mal's the father of my child. Part of him is *in* me, will always remain *physically embedded in me.* If you had any idea how much I'd loved him," looking down at her belly, she slumped, "how much I love Mal, you'd begin to understand."

When they got home, Maria went into her room and closed the door. A few minutes later, Angela heard strains of Glenn Frey's 'You Belong To the City' wafting from her room. Then she heard the muffled sounds of Maria crying into her pillow.

What can I do? Angela lifted her eyes in prayer. *José is goodness personified, but he lacks Mal's magnetism. Mal is evil incarnate, yet Maria loves him. What is his hold on her?*

At six o'clock sharp, Kio and José rang the doorbell. Maria wore a smile as she met them, but her eyes were red and swollen.

When José kissed her hello, his eyes lingered on hers. "Are you feeling all right?"

"Yeah, I'm fine," she smiled, "just a little tired."

Then Angela saw Gabe standing beside José, and she did a double take.

Although José lacked the tattoos, piercings, shaved head, and generally rough appearance, the similarities were uncanny. The eyes, cheekbones, and rise of their foreheads were the same. Sans Gabe's sneer, their mouths and chins bore more than a family resemblance.

"José," asked Angela as they walked out to the car, "do you have any brothers or sisters?"

Shoulders abruptly sagging, his eyes turning down at the corners, he blinked. His smile drooped. "Why do you ask?"

"I thought I saw someone who looked like you." She lifted a shoulder. "Just wondered."

Gabe wore a pensive smile as he watched José help Maria into the back seat.

José seemed lost in thought. Then a few minutes after they were underway, he said, "Yes, I have a twin brother."

Angela glanced at him in the back seat. "Really?" Wondering how to broach the subject, she asked, "Have you seen him recently?"

"No, we haven't heard from him in nearly three months." José frowned. "I haven't . . . hadn't sensed him, either."

"What do you mean?"

"Twins share a connection." José's mouth lifted in a half-smile. "Even if he was undercover and couldn't call, I'd know on an intuitive level. I'd sense he was all right, but . . . " He winced.

"What?" Ears perked, Angela studied him.

Subtly shaking his head, he grimaced. "I've lost that sensation, that connection. I don't know what's happened to him, although recently . . . "

Gabe appeared between Kio and Angela in the front seat. "Tell him."

I can't just blurt it out. She chose her words carefully. "You mentioned undercover. Was he in the FBI or CIA or something?"

The question brought a smile to José. "Ever since we were kids, he loved playing cops and robbers."

Angela chuckled. "I take it he was always the cop?"

José nodded. "That was my brother, always the good guy."

Her smile faded as José continued.

"He earned his undergraduate degree in the NROTC. Then he served in the Navy. After attending law school, he served several years with JAG."

"What's JAG?" Maria looked at him.

"The Judge Advocates General's Corps, where he was a trial attorney. He liked it, but it was a desk job. His only commute was from his office to the courtroom, and he wanted more."

"More what?" Maria studied him.

"More action, more excitement. He wanted to work in the field, yet use his legal training. Finally, he joined the Drug Enforcement Administration, where he could do both."

Angela did another double-take. Guessing was one thing, but learning Gabe was José's twin brother was another. "Why? What compelled him to risk his life?" Angela glanced from one brother to the other.

"He said working on the streets gave him an adrenaline rush." He smiled to himself. "He never stopped playing cops and robbers."

"Then he likes being an agent?" asked Kio, glancing into the rearview mirror, oblivious to Gabe sitting between them.

José chuckled. "Every nuance."

Again Angela's ears perked as she recalled Gabe using the same phrase.

Gabe turned toward her with a sad smile. "Tell him."

She nodded. *I will. I'm just waiting for the right time.*

Kio parked in front of a brightly painted blue and yellow building. They passed through a courtyard of delicate wrought-iron work with a gurgling fountain. Then as they walked inside, they saw millions of twinkling white lights suspended from the ceiling. *Papel picado* or colorful, lacy flags made of cut paper hung from the rafters. Cheery red tablecloths covered the tables.

The hostess seated them beneath a busy, hand-painted mural splashed across the back wall. As they made themselves comfortable, Angela gazed at the mural's painted figures, some holding photos. *I wonder if those photos are of deceased friends and family.*

Angela glanced from José to Gabe. *As with the mural's 'photos,' our loved ones stay with us in spirit.* Then she scrutinized Maria. Suddenly she realized Maria must be the connection between Mal and Gabe. *Right?* Mentally speaking to Gabe, she glanced at him.

He nodded. "Until Pretty Boy led me to her, I was fused to him. I despised him so much for what he'd done, I was blind to everyone else. I could see only him."

Now?

"Now it's more complicated." He looked at José. "My brother's in love with the woman who's in love with my murderer." He gave a wry chuckle. "Ironic, isn't it? The one who separated me from my family has accidentally led me back to my family."

Everything happens for a reason. Maybe now you can make peace.

"Not yet." His sneer returned. "I want my body found in the desert outside Alpine. I want a Christian burial on consecrated land, where my family can find closure." His voice became gruff. "And I want Pretty Boy to pay."

"What's wrong?" Kio tugged at her hand. "You seem a million miles away."

Angela flinched. Then she gave him a wry smile. "Actually, about four hundred miles."

"What?" He cocked his head.

"Alpine's about four hundred miles from here."

He gave her a blank stare.

Leaning toward him, she whispered. "I'll tell you later."

Everyone except Maria ordered margaritas.

"To tonight," she said, toasting with her glass of water.

"To the future." José gave her a warm smile.

"To the past." Lifting her eyebrow as she raised her glass, Angela included Gabe in the toast.

Joking, Kio mispronounced tequila. "To kill ya!"

Everyone laughed but Gabe and Angela. She gave him a sympathetic smile.

Maria ordered *Flautas De Pollo*, dainty chicken tacos as thin as flutes.

Angela ordered *Gallina En Mole*, chicken topped with chocolate mole sauce. "My birth mother loves this dish. I think I developed a taste for it in her womb." She chuckled.

José ordered *Agujas Asadas*, charbroiled rib steak, and Kio ordered Steak Ranchero.

The food was good, the atmosphere festive. They chatted and laughed among themselves until, from Maria's purse, Mal's ring tones cut through their conversation.

Angela gave her a dark look. Then she noticed the scowl on Gabe's face.

José stopped speaking mid-sentence as the phone continued to ring. "Aren't you going to get that?"

Lips pressed together tightly, Maria looked uncertain whether or not to answer it. She blinked. "Sure." Then she reached for her purse and muted her phone. "Sorry."

Five minutes later, Maria excused herself.

José rose to his feet to get her chair. "Aren't you feel—"

"I'm fine," she snapped. Then she forced an awkward smile. "Be right back."

Angela glanced from José's uncomfortable expression to the grim set of Gabe's features.

"Angela, can you follow her?" José's eyes pleaded.

She exchanged a look with Kio and then nodded. "Sure." Catching up with Maria in the ladies' room, she saw her cell phone pressed to her ear.

Maria held her index finger to her lips as she listened to a message.

Angela waited quietly until she put down the phone. "Let me guess, Mal wants to meet you."

She nodded.

"You're walking a narrow path." Angela pointed toward the dining area. "There's a man out there worried sick about you, and you're in here pining after some jerk who broke your heart." She held up her hands. "What is wrong with you?"

"It isn't that simple." She took a deep breath. "I love José . . . "

"But?"

"There's no electricity. I miss the zing, the high."

She echoed Gabe's words about Mal. "Maria, you sound like a drug addict looking for a fix."

She flinched. "I never thought of it that way."

"You've got a lifetime commitment from José. What's Mal ever given you but heartache?"

Maria stared at the floor. She grimaced. She sighed. "I know you're right . . . "

"But?" Angela rolled her eyes. "Is that all you're looking for? Kicks? Fireworks?"

Without answering, Maria lifted one shoulder.

"You'd better open your eyes before it's too late." With that, Angela turned and walked back to their table.

"Is she all right?" Worry lines etched José's forehead.

Angela crossed her fingers as she put on a bright smile. "She's fine."

Maria returned to the table a few minutes later, her eyes red. Conversation slowly resumed, but not the festivity. Gabe vanished. They finished early and walked back to the car in silence.

Kio turned toward them as he started the engine. "Want to take a walk on the River Walk?"

They silently looked at each other. Finally, Maria shook her head. "Actually, I'd . . . I'm a little tired."

Kio caught Angela's eye as he shrugged. Then looking in the rearview mirror, he tried again. "Any other suggestions, or should we call it a night?" When no one answered, he shrugged again. "Okay." Then he turned on the radio.

The opening strains of 'The One You Love' began. They listened to the plaintive cry of the saxophone. When Glenn Frey sang the chorus, José began softly singing along.

Angela saw he was singing to Maria. The expression in his eyes tugged at her. She had seen that same look on Maria's face when she had gazed at Mal.

José's words hung in the air as the song ended.

Swallowing, Angela turned from them toward Kio and reached for his hand. When he glanced at her, she gave him a wistful smile.

Again they heard the yearning sounds of a saxophone as Glenn Frey's 'You Belong to the City' came over the air. Then the opening notes gave way to the driving beat of the drums.

Angela's grip on Kio's hand tightened. Lifting his eyebrow, he glanced at her.

As the song finished, Mal's ring tones chimed from Maria's purse. She fumbled through her purse, trying to mute it. Instead, her finger pressed the speaker.

"Maria, is that you?" Mal's voice came over the speaker.

At the sound of Mal's voice, Angela watched Gabe reappear between Kio and her. She let go of Kio's hand and glanced at the back seat.

"I thought you muted it." José's dark eyes glittered in the dim light.

Maria turned off her phone. "Sorry."

After a beat, José said, "When we get back, we need to talk about drawing a line in the sand." He spoke up for Kio's benefit. "No need to wait for me. I can take a cab home."

Angela glanced at Kio. "Or why don't you come in for a cup of coffee? That is, if you'd like to wait."

Nodding, Kio said, "Sure." Then he spoke to José in the rear-view mirror. "Take your time."

José nodded. "Thanks, Maria and I have something to discuss."

When Kio parked in front of the apartment, José did not help Maria out of the back seat. Instead, unblinking, his face stony, he watched her struggle.

Angela sighed. Then Kio reached for her hand, and they walked into the apartment, leaving the other couple to work out their differences.

"Do you really feel like coffee, or would wine work?" She grinned.

"You talked me into it."

She brought a bottle and two glasses onto the small balcony. Then they pulled up lawn chairs around a tiny table.

"It's finally cool enough to sit outside."

She poured and handed him a glass. "October nights are the best in Texas."

He glanced at his watch. Then he turned toward her. "You know, the Draconids meteor shower reaches its peak tonight." He glanced up at their small piece of sky. "There's light scatter, but there isn't much moonlight to interfere." His eyes shining, he turned toward her. "This isn't a bad spot. Want to watch the shooting stars tonight?"

She grinned at her best friend. "Heck, yeah!" She clinked her glass against his. "These chairs recline, so we wouldn't have to crane our necks. We can just lean back, look up, and star gaze." She smiled. "What a great idea."

Then Kio's face took on a serious expression as he sipped his wine. "What's going on with José and Maria?"

Angela took a deep breath and told him the story.

"You mean this guy Mal impregnated her, deserted her—"

She sighed. "He does seem to be telling the truth about not being able to contact her." She shrugged. "Gabe verified his jail alibi."

"Mal's a meth addict, involved with a drug cartel, and has killed José's twin brother." He shook his head. "What does she see in him?

"That's what we're wondering."

"Does José know about Gabe?"

"Not yet," she grimaced, "and I don't know how to tell him."

"Yeah, tonight might not be the best time." Raising his eyebrows, he sighed. Then he gave her a wry grin. "It was a good idea to talk out here."

"Comfortable, cozy," she smiled, "plus I'm with my best friend."

He touched glasses with her. "Is that what we are, best friends?"

"We're more than casual dates, but we're not serious." She watched him through her lashes. "Yet there's no one I'd rather be with." She sipped her wine. "If not best friends, how would you characterize us?"

"Boyfriend and girlfriend?" He leaned over to kiss her.

"Mmmmaybe." She took a deep breath as if making up her mind, then playfully kissed him back.

Grinning, he nodded. "I think we've officially graduated." Again they tapped their glasses together. "To our new roles."

They heard the front door. Then they heard Maria and José's voices, followed by another door slamming.

Moments later, José called to them.

"Back here," called Kio, "on the balcony."

"Let me get another glass." Angela stood up and found José in the kitchen. She grabbed a glass. "We're having some wine. Join us."

"No, I'd—"

Seeing Maria's closed bedroom door and his woebegone expression, she gave him a sympathetic smile. "Come on. Join us."

Kio drew up a third lawn chair while Angela poured José a glass of wine.

"To starry October nights," said Kio, raising his glass.

The three touched glasses together and then sat sipping in silence. Angela looked at Kio. When he shrugged his shoulders, she decided to break the ice. "So did you go for a walk?"

José grimaced. "Not exactly." Digging in his pocket, he pulled out the engagement ring and set it on the table. "I drew a line in the sand."

"I'm sorry." Sighing, she rubbed his shoulder. "Do you want to talk about it?"

He sighed uneasily. "You saw and heard most of it." Then he took a deep breath. "Those two calls from her old boyfriend . . ." He shook his head. "No matter how much I love her, she wants to go with the one she loves."

"She said that?" Angela looked at him and saw double. Gabe was standing behind him.

"Not in so many words, but her actions clinched it."

"Give Maria time to think it over—"

Setting down his glass, José studied her. "When did this all begin?"

She pressed her lips together.

"Be honest. Tell me."

"The day we hiked the Yanaguana Trail at Mission San Juan Capistrano was the first time he texted her."

"I had a feeling." José nodded slowly as it sank in. Then he turned to them. "Tonight I mentioned my twin brother and that I'd lost that connection with him." He grimaced. "That's only partly true."

"Tell him," said Gabe. "Tell him."

Ignoring him, she tried to focus on José. "What do you mean?"

"It's hard to describe, but ever since that afternoon, I've had the sensation my brother's been trying to communicate with me." He sniffed. "Maybe this is what it's about."

"Tell him," said Gabe, "or I will . . . "

She glanced at him and mentally dismissed him. *Not now!*

Gabe swept the ring off the table with his hand, but to Kio and José it looked like the ring flew from its own volition.

"What just happened?" José turned toward her.

She took a deep breath. "I don't think this is the right time to tell you, but I don't seem to have a choice." She winced "I see spirits."

Even in the dark, she saw his eyes widen. "Are you telling me—"

She nodded. "He's passed—"

"No!" José put his hands to his head.

"Tell him the truth!" thundered Gabe. "I was murdered."

"He wants me to tell you—"

"You really speak to spirits?" As she nodded, he cautiously lowered his hands. "What does he want?"

She struggled for the words to break it gently. "There's a reason you began to feel Gabe's presence that afternoon."

A look of wonder came over his face. "I've never mentioned his name to you. This is proof." Lifting his eyebrows, he nodded. "What does he want to tell me?"

She glanced at Kio, grimaced, and then looked José in the eye. "Your brother was killed in the line of duty."

José's mouth turned down. His bottom lip quivered. Then he cleared this throat. "Go on . . . please."

"He and his partner were trying to bust a drug cartel." She sighed. "And one of the gang shot Gabe."

"One of them . . ." His eyes glittered. "It wouldn't have been Maria's old boyfriend, would it?"

"Mal." Angela stared at him. "How did you guess?"

"I felt a loathing toward him that goes beyond jealousy. Gabe and I've had a connection since birth. I think I subconsciously felt his repulsion toward Mal."

Grimacing, she nodded. So Gabe's anger has somehow entered José's psyche.

His expression was so sharp, it seemed to pierce her. "Did she know anything about it?"

Angela shook her head. "None of it. Maria has no idea what Mal's done. She only knows what he's told her, that his one brush with the law was drunk driving." She filled him in on the details.

José reached over and picked up the ring. Turning it slowly between his fingers, he studied it as he seemed to collect his thoughts. Then he spoke softly, as if thinking aloud.

"I had this made especially for her since I didn't . . . " He took a deep breath. "Gabe and I'd made a pact. Whoever got engaged first would give their fiancée our grandmother's engagement ring."

His eyes focusing inwardly, Gabe thought a moment. "It was filigreed gold surrounding a blue sapphire."

Angela looked from him to José. "Whatever happened to it?"

"Until one or the other of us needed it, Gabe wore it around his neck as a kind of good luck charm."

Her chest caving in, Angela felt her heart sink. As she pressed her lips together, she shook her head.

José drew a deep breath. "Where's Gabe buried?"

She shook her head. "He isn't, and that's a point of contention with him."

"Then where's his body?"

She lifted a shoulder. "All he's told me is it's somewhere in the Chihuahuan Desert outside Alpine," she lowered her voice, "and he wants a Christian burial on consecrated land."

"Chihuahuan Desert outside Alpine." José knitted his brow as he thought aloud. "Could it be . . . ?"

"What?" Angela searched his face for clues.

"Ask Gabe if his body's on our grandfather's land."

Angela glanced from José to his brother.

Gabe grinned. "I knew he'd figure it out." Beaming, he slapped José on the back as he gave Angela the details.

José straightened his spine. "What was that? Did my brother touch me?"

Smiling, Angela nodded. "He wants to know if you remember the old gate by the cattle guard."

José smiled as if reliving a memory, and then his eyes teared. "Yeah," he sniffed, "it's where we used to play cops and robbers." His lip trembling, he cleared his throat. "I know exactly where it is."

"Gabe wants you to call Detective Hadd at the DEA. Tell him 'Christmas Mountain.'" She gave him a wry smile. "Apparently it was the code name for the bust. He'll know what to do."

Head bowed, José nodded.

"He suggests you and I meet Detective Hadd there, so you can find the land," she grimaced, "and identify his body." She stiffened. "He wants me there, so he can speak through me."

Putting the ring in his pocket, José set down his glass and stood. Sighing, he glanced at Angela. "Thank you for telling me the truth."

"I'm just sorry the news was so bad." She grimaced.

He shook his head. "My family and I suspected as much. Though this confirms our worst fears, it'll give us closure."

Nodding, Gabe's mouth lifted in a half-smile.

Angela looked from him to José. "It'll also help your brother find peace."

Kio tossed him his car keys. "Take the car."

"No, I can call a cab."

Kio was adamant. "Take the car."

"I can drive Kio to your place to pick up his car." Angela gave him a wry smile. "Let me know when Detective Hadd wants us to meet him in Alpine."

"Thanks, both of you." He half-hugged Angela's shoulders. "I'll call you tomorrow." Then he held up the keys. "Thanks, Kio. I'll leave them in the car under the driver's seat."

Kio shook his head. "Lock it. I've got a spare in my wallet."

"Speaking of locking up," Angela stood up, "I'll walk you out and lock the front door." Back five minutes later, she looked up at Kio. "Poor José. Not one, but two losses tonight."

Kio raised his eyebrows. "A double whammy, but at least you can help him and his brother."

She nodded absently, thinking of José. Then feeling Kio's eyes watching her, she turned toward him with a smile. "Okay, which way should we turn our chairs?"

Kio grinned as he looked from her to the sky. "The shower's radiant point should be right over there." Standing up, he pointed. "See the Big Dipper?"

Nodding, she followed his finger with her eyes.

"On a straight line above the pointer stars, you'll see Polaris, the tail end of the Little Dipper. Just above that is the constellation Draco, the Dragon." He glanced at her and smiled.

Returning his smile, she moved closer.

He put his arm around her shoulders and pointed with his other arm. "Do you see the head of the Dragon?"

"Yeah."

He traced the sky with his finger. "There are the Dragon's eyes, the stars Rastaban and Eltanin. That's the radiant point, the center of activity. The shooting stars make the Dragon's eyes sparkle and snap." Turning toward her, he studied her face. "Do you know your eyes twinkle in the starlight?"

She smothered a grin. "No."

He bent his head toward her. "If I look closely enough, I see the stars in your eyes."

Lifting the corner of her lip in a smile, Angela murmured, "Really?" Standing on tiptoe, she reached around his neck with her arms and gently pulled him closer until they were eye to eye. "What do you see now?"

As he brought her to him in a kiss, he murmured, "My guiding star."

Chapter 6

"Runnin' with the Devil"
— VAN HALEN

When Angela dropped Kio off in front of José's place, he met them outside. "Glad I caught you. I called Detective Hadd, and he wants us to meet him Monday. Can you get off work? Do you have classes that day?"

She smiled. "It just happens, I don't have classes Monday, and I'm not scheduled to work. What time do you want to leave?"

"Early." José grimaced. "It's going to take at least five hours each way. Are you up for this?"

She knew he was talking about more than just the ten hours of driving. Taking a deep breath, she nodded. "Glad to help any way I can."

"Really appreciate it." Then holding up the keys, he turned to Kio. "And thanks for lending me your car. You're both good friends."

Monday morning, José picked her up at seven. They took I-10 West to US-67 South. With José deep in thought, conversation was minimal, and Angela had time to daydream, reminisce. As they approached Alpine, she recalled her birth mother telling her about her whirlwind courtship to her father.

"We'd attended a Southwest Art seminar at Sul Ross University in Alpine," said Ceren. "On the way back, we stopped for dinner at a steakhouse. We'd been argu—" She had looked at her daughter, and her expression softened. "We'd had a disagreement. Very long story short, your father proposed."

"And you accepted just like that?"

"Not just like that, but almost." She gave a bemused grin. "It was a two-hour drive to Carlsbad, so I had two hours to mull it over and back out. Even with a frantic, last-minute search for the county clerk's office, we had our marriage license in hand, had said, 'I do' in front of the county judge, and were out the door before the courthouse closed at five for the weekend."

"How did you feel about marrying so suddenly?"

Ceren's eyes flashed momentarily. "It all happened so fast, none of it seemed real. When I say it was a fairytale, I'm not exaggerating. I kept waiting to wake up from the dream."

Angela couldn't resist asking. "Was it his kiss that woke you?"

Nodding, Ceren smiled at the memory. "It was our first kiss as husband and wife. We were standing beneath an ancient live oak on the courthouse grounds that hot August afternoon while we planned our next step." She laughed to herself. "As he put his arms around me, I got a bad case of the giggles."

"What was so funny?" Ceren's mirth was contagious—Angela could not help smiling.

"That's pretty much what he wanted to know. As soon as he pressed his lips against mine, I got the silliest notion. An image of Snow White popped into my head. All I could think about was the Prince waking her with a kiss."

"Why?"

Ceren shrugged. "The proposal, our wedding had all happened so fast, none of it seemed real until he kissed me." She took a deep breath, collecting her thoughts. "It's as if his kiss grounded me, making the whole idea take root, have substance." She looked at her daughter. "As I held him, as I felt his arms around me, it occurred to me he was the only thing tangible in what otherwise seemed a fairytale."

Angela and José pulled into Alpine a little after noon. Driving south on TX-118, they turned off the highway onto a dusty, caliche road and followed it until the road branched in two. A dark, unmarked car was parked alongside the road.

As José pulled up behind it and they stepped out, Gabe abruptly appeared beside her. Rubbing his hand over his head, his fingers brushed against the peach fuzz that recently sprouted. His movements were jerky, brusque.

You seem agitated. Angela spoke mentally.

"Wouldn't you be if you visited the scene of your murder?"

Guess I would, at that. She grimaced.

As the car door opened, and a man stepped out, Gabe stiffened. "Charlie?"

"José Aceves?" asked the man in a tan polo shirt and dark Dockers.

José nodded. "Detective Hadd?"

Holding out his hand, the man said, "Charles Hadd, Charlie."

As they shook hands, José introduced Angela. "It's because of her gift we're here today."

Angela saw the skeptical twist to his mouth and silently sighed. *Cynicism's nothing new.*

"Ask him how Dorothy and Little Gabe are doing." Eyes twinkling mischievously, Gabe winked.

She glanced from him to Charlie. "Gabe wants to know how Dorothy and Little Gabe are doing."

His jaw dropped. "How . . . ?" Then his eyes narrowed. "Who are they?"

Gabe grinned. "How could I forget his wife or my godson?"

"They're your wife and Gabe's godson."

Charlie's eyebrows shot up. "You've either got some outstanding intel, or you really are communicating with him."

She smiled wryly. "Pleased to meet you, too."

He gave her a wary grin. Then he turned to José. "You lead, and I'll follow."

They climbed back into their cars, and José took the road to the left, turning onto a caliche driveway. A half mile in, they came to an old cabin. The windows were boarded up, yet roses bloomed on the overgrown brambles surrounding the timeworn building.

"That's where our great-grandfather homesteaded," said José. "Our father was born here, but his parents moved when he was small. Later, this became our summer getaway and then the hunting cabin." He smiled. "Our father used to bring us here a lot, but now," he shrugged, "it's just an old shack."

"Yet the roses continue to bloom."

"Wood's roses. My grandmother planted them." He gave her a wistful smile.

She returned it with a sympathetic grimace. "Bet this place holds a lot of memories."

"Bittersweet." Nodding, he put the car in park. "We'll have to walk from here." Then turning toward her, his eyes took on a somber expression. "You don't have to do this, you know. It's still not too—"

"It's okay." Her smile was shy, embarrassed. "It's something I need to do, want to do for Gabe."

As they got out, Charlie joined them.

"This way." José led them behind the cabin along an overgrown trail. Hidden by scrub mesquite, green brier brambles, cactus, and overgrown rose bushes, they came to a gate with a cattle guard behind it.

Straightening his shoulders, José took a deep breath. Then he turned to Angela.

"Do you want to take it from here?"

She nodded.

Gabe was walking along the barbed-wire fence line. "Over here," he called.

Calling to the others, Angela followed him. "This way," she said.

About a hundred feet away, Gabe stopped as he stared at the ground.

"Over here," she called, joining him.

There on the dusty caliche lay scattered human remains. Blooming rose bushes stood silent sentry.

"Picked clean." Gabe sneered. "The coyotes and vultures did a thorough job."

Sorry. She grimaced as she spoke mentally. *At least, now you can move on.*

He shook his head. "Finding my bones is just step one."

I know. Next you want a Christian burial on consecrated ground.

"I do, but while we're here, you need to find the evidence to put Pretty Boy away."

What do you mean?

"Tell Charlie to sweep this area for prints."

José joined her and followed her glance. "No!" Sharply inhaling, he hung his head.

"Why don't you take a minute," said Charlie, "while I get pictures of the crime scene."

José nodded. Blinking back tears, he turned away.

Angela met Charlie's eyes. "Gabe wants you to sweep this area for prints."

He raised his eyebrow. "He thinks there's something here?" Charlie pulled on a pair of rubber gloves. "Don't touch anything."

"I know better than that." Her lips pursed, she scowled at him.

Shrugging, he handed her a pair of gloves. "Still don't touch anything, but this way at least you can help me search."

Gabe chuckled. "Don't mind Charlie. He only believes in the tangible." Then his eyes narrowed. "Now that I'm at the scene, I remember something else."

What? She looked at him.

"Follow me."

"Got a hunch," she called to Charlie. "Be right back."

"Don't touch anything."

She rolled her eyes.

"Pretty Boy tossed a beer can over here somewhere." He sneered. "I doubt he wiped off prints."

Wouldn't the heat and sun have degraded fingerprints?

"Possibly," Gabe nodded, "but I've read forensic reports where they've been able to lift them from aluminum cans three months after the fact." He glanced at her. "Let's find that can. It's the only evidence."

Where were you standing when you met with the cartel?

"Over here."

Angela walked cautiously through the Chihuahuan desert. Though searching for the can, she kept an eye out for cactus and rattlers. Then she spotted something glimmering in the sunlight. On closer inspection, she called to Charlie. "Think I found something."

"Don't touch it."

She stifled a frustrated groan. "Gabe said the murderer had tossed a beer can. This may be it."

Using a stick, he picked up the can by slipping the stick through its opening, inverting it, and carefully depositing it in a plastic bag.

"Good work," he mumbled without meeting her eyes.

Gabe grinned at her.

"I'll finish taking photos," said Charlie, "and then gather the bones and belongings in a body bag."

Suddenly, the finality of the situation sank in. Sighing, she nodded. "I'd better check on José."

She found him standing over his brother's remains, praying, talking. Gabe stood beside him, his arm around his shoulders. Not wanting to intrude, Angela hesitated, but Gabe saw her and waved her over.

"Can you tell him something for me?"

Of course. She looked at Gabe, wondering how he felt at the site of his murder, at the sight of his bones.

"How do you think I feel?"

Crap! I keep forgetting you can hear my thoughts. Well, how do you feel?

He exhaled. "Sad for José and our parents. Angry at Pretty Boy for ending my life and stealing our grandmother's engagement ring."

He stole your grandmother's engagement ring?

His hand going to his throat, he nodded. "After he shot me."

Talk about adding insult to injury. How—

"It was on a chain. He ripped it off my neck."

She narrowed her eyes. *Why?*

His eyes narrowed. "Like a big game hunter cuts off a rhinoceros's horn or a bear's paw, he wanted a trophy, bragging rights."

Her eyes opening wide, she shook her head. *That's so cold.*

"Cold-blooded murder." Then taking a deep breath, he focused on her. "You'd asked how I feel." A peaceful smile slowly came over his face, replacing the hostility. "Mostly I feel lighter, relieved."

How's that possible?

"You were right. This is the first step in moving on."

I'm glad you're beginning to feel that way. She nodded. *Then she cocked her head. What was it you want me to tell José?*

He hesitated as if easing into the message he wanted her to give. "Our father's name is David."

Okay . . . She gave him a quizzical look.

Gabe's smile seemed bashful. "Are you familiar with the Christmas story according to Matthew?"

She shrugged. *Somewhat.*

His eyes became somber. "Please give him this message."

Turning around, José flinched. "Oh, I didn't see you standing there."

"Didn't mean to startle you." She gave him a grim smile. "Actually, Gabe has something he wants me to say to you."

José lifted his eyebrows expectantly. "What is it?"

Gabe gave her another shy smile. "Paraphrasing the Book of Matthew, tell him, 'José, son of David, don't be afraid to take Maria as your wife. She'll bear a son, and you're to name him Jesus.'"

Her eyes widening, Angela looked at him. *Are you sure this is what you want me to say?*

He nodded solemnly.

She took a deep breath. Then she met José's eyes. "These are Gabe's words, not mine. José, son of David, don't be afraid to take Maria as your wife . . . "

Avoiding José's sharp eyes, she looked to Gabe for the remaining words.

"She'll bear a son, and you're to name him Jesus."

She repeated his words as she watched José's eyebrow arch skeptically.

"Now tell him, Olly, olly oxen free."

Reciting Gabe's words, she watched a chuckle replace José's skepticism and then quickly turn into a sob.

She felt like crying along with him. "What?"

José faced her with a melancholy smile. "Olly, olly oxen free was our catch phrase to return to base."

"Where was base?"

His eyes glassy, José gestured to the area around them. "Here." He took a deep breath. "What's Gabe really saying?"

She turned to Gabe for the answer.

Gabe held up his hands. "I'm just the messenger delivering the message."

Whose message?

"Whose do you think? Heaven's."

Her brow puckering, she struggled to hold back the tears. Stifling a sob, she covered her mouth with her hand.

Now it was José's turn to ask. "What?"

Swallowing her tears, she was overcome with the enormity of his words. "I'm . . . " She took a deep breath. "Gabe says he's simply a heavenly messenger," she cleared her throat, "delivering God's word to you."

Delivering God's word . . . and if I'm relaying the message, translating . . . She turned away, feeling so small, so insubstantial in the magnitude of that revelation. Then, it occurred to her. *All the training, career counseling, or aptitude tests in the world couldn't have prepared me for this.*

Angela remembered the stories her mother and Ceren had told her when she was a child. Her 'heritage,' they had called it, had prepared her for something. She looked inwardly. *Until this moment, I hadn't known for what. Gabe said he's a messenger . . . so am I.*

They heard Charlie's call and doubled back to meet him.

He was struggling to carry the body bag, a smaller bag, and the camera.

As José froze at the sight, Angela rushed toward Charlie. "Let me help."

On the drive back to San Antonio, Angela glanced at José in the driver's seat.

He gave her a depressed smile.

"You've been so quiet," she said. "How're you doing?"

"All things considered, not bad." He took a deep breath. "Just have a lot on my mind, a lot to digest."

She nodded. "So much has happened in the past forty-eight hours, I can imagine."

"Did Maria tell you I'd dreamt about her?"

"She mentioned you'd dreamt it on the Feast of the Archangels."

His smile was grim. "It's what prompted me to propose."

"Why are you mentioning this now?" She peered at him.

"That Christmas story from the Book of Matthew that you . . . that Gabe paraphrased was about an angel speaking to Joseph in a dream."

She nodded. "I recognized it."

"The dream I have is recurring." He took his eyes from the road momentarily to glance at her. "No angels have spoken to me . . . unless you count Gabe today. The details are always a little different in the dreams, but the theme's the same."

She watched his profile. "What is it?"

"Marry Maria." He shook his head. "Yet . . . "

"What?"

"After what I've learned in the past two days, I have a hard time even looking at her."

She inhaled sharply. "All you can do is pray about it."

"And not just her. When I think about her baby being the son of Gabe's murderer . . . " Shaking his head, he sighed. "I can't see myself raising him as my own."

"That's something only you and God can decide." Then a thought came to her. "You have to admit, though, you're in a unique situation."

He chuckled wryly. "That's an understatement."

"You have the opportunity to give this baby the father he'd never have had otherwise."

He took a deep breath. "That's what I'd thought before . . . before I learned the circumstances of Gabe's death." Sniffing, he shook his head. "Now . . . "

"What I mean is, not just for him but also for yourself."

His eyebrow arched, he glanced at her.

"You have the opportunity to forgive your brother's murderer by raising his son as your own." A smile flickered at her lips. "What a beautiful testament to Gabe."

When José dropped Angela off at her apartment, she paused before opening the car door. "Would you like to come in for minute, have a bite to eat?"

"Thanks," he shook his head, "but no, not really."

"I understand," Angela took a deep breath, "but don't be a stranger. Let me know how I can help."

Maria was waiting for her when she walked in the door. "Wasn't that Jenny?"

Angela studied her. "Jenny?"

"Wasn't that José's car?"

Angela nodded and then cocked her head. "Why did you ask if it was Jenny?"

Maria twisted her mouth into an annoyed grimace. "That's what he calls her."

"Why?"

"He says cold weather makes her engine balk, and she has a mule-like stubbornness." Her eyes narrowed. "Why were you with him?"

Angela took a deep breath, debating how much, if anything, to tell her before police reports corroborated Gabe's story. *Honesty's always the best policy.* "Let's sit down."

As she told Maria the story of Mal's role in Gabe's death, Maria's eyes first widened and then became stony. Before she finished, Maria stood up.

"Are you serious?" Rolling her eyes, she scoffed. "You accuse Mal of drug running and murder and then expect me to believe some ghost story?" Shaking her head, she scoffed. "I thought you were my friend."

"I am. That's why I'm sharing this with you." Angela grimaced. "I'm worried about you."

"Well, don't be." She took a deep breath. "Angela, I can't tell you how much I appreciate what you've done for me, taking me in and getting me an internship." She shook her head. "I just don't understand why you're telling me these lies now."

"They're not . . . " Not wanting to argue, Angela took a deep breath and counted to five. "What I'm trying—"

"Hi." Letting herself in, their roommate Tulah dropped her books on the coffee table. "Can't believe we're all here at the same time. This must be a first." She chuckled. "Well, maybe a second." When neither responded, her smile drooped as she looked from one to the other. "I'm not interrupting anything, am I?"

After a strained silence, Maria said, "No." She gave Angela a sharp look, adding, "I'm going out in a few minutes, anyway, just as soon as Mal—"

The doorbell rang.

"There he is now." She arched her eyebrow at Angela. "Right on time." Maria opened the door. "Hey."

Angela did a double-take at the changes in Mal.

Instead of the drop-dead gorgeous hunk she had met a few weeks earlier, the person standing in their doorway looked pale, pasty. His crystal blue eyes that had mesmerized her, seemed unfocused. Even in the two days since she had last seen him, Mal's looks had declined. Scratches covered his face and arms. When he opened his mouth, she saw a front tooth had chipped.

She could not help but stare. Had meth done this? She calculated the time frame.

If he started it before his jail sentence, he's been taking it four months, at least. Could all this have happened in that short span? Or has it been much longer?

"Ready?" His expression sullen as he scratched, picked at his arms, he ignored the others.

Is she blind? Angela wanted to say something, stop her from going with him, but she felt stymied. *If Maria can't see the changes herself, what can I say to convince her?*

"Don't wait up," Maria called over her shoulder.

When they left, Tulah raised her eyebrows. "Who is that guy?"

"The father of Maria's child."

Tulah slowly shook her head. "Did you see his face, his mouth? That guy's got 'meth mouth.'"

"What?"

"'Meth mouth.'" She grimaced. "You saw the chipped tooth. Users get a dry mouth. When they can't neutralize the digestive acids, their teeth decay, loosen, fall out, or break off."

"And his complexion." Angela slowly shook her head. "He's covered in scratches."

"What does she see in him?" Tulah scowled.

"When I met him nearly a month ago, Mal was gorgeous," she rolled her eyes, "at least externally. It almost made sense that she was attracted to him then, but now I don't have a clue . . . unless she still sees him as he once was." Angela took a deep breath. "I don't get it."

"Me, either." Tulah grimaced.

"Could this have happened in just a few months?"

Tulah nodded. "I've read it depends on whether the meth's smoked or injected, how often it's taken, and the level of oral hygiene. But, yes, some people show these symptoms in as short a span as four months. I've heard of people going blind after just one use."

"Wow." Angela stared into space, trying to grasp the ruthlessness of the drug.

"There's just something so dark about him." Tulah's eyes narrowed to suspicious slits.

Dark? Angela recalled the homily from the Archangels Feast Day. *We're all tempted every day. A temptation could be called a demon or even a spirit.*

Angela nodded. "You're right about a darkness. There's definitely something shadowy, murky about him." She shivered. "Just thinking of him gives me the willies."

Later that night, with Frank and No Name beside her, Angela sat on the sofa, reading, when she heard Maria and Mal come in the front door.

"Look what Mal gave me!" Gone was her former cool reserve. Hands splayed across her chest, she gushed as she showed off her new jewelry.

Angela peered at her ornate, heavy necklace. "Is that—"

"Yeah, solid gold and diamonds," said Mal, pride gleaming in his eyes.

"I was going to ask if that's the Grim Reaper." She turned from Mal to Maria. "Is it?"

Mal shook his head. "*Santa Muerte.*"

Angela turned back to him, a frown creasing her forehead. "Saint Death?"

"Yeah, 'the sinner's saint.'"

The opposite of joyful, his laugh was a fiendish yowl. It drove off the cats and sent vile chills down her spine. No longer scratching his arms or acting anxious, now he seemed exhilarated, confident, a completely different personality from several hours earlier.

Angela took a closer look at him. His pupils were dilated. Remembering Tulah's description of 'meth mouth,' she watched as he licked his chapped lips, then clenched and twisted his jaw.

Then she saw something disturbing. Her eyes opening wide, she watched as he seemed to separate. It was as if his shadow momentarily lost sync with his body and then just as quickly rejoined it.

"Did you catch that?" Gabe appeared, and No Name shyly began rubbing against his legs.

What was it?

"You just witnessed a dark spirit."

She cocked her head. *A what?*

"Demon, dark angel, evil spirit, they're called many things, but that's what you just saw." He bent down to pet No Name.

133

She glanced from Gabe to Mal. *He's possessed?*

"Not possessed. Very few are ever possessed. He's what you'd call demonized."

She cocked her head. *What's the difference?*

"When a person's possessed, the demon or demons have complete control of the body. When a person's obsessed or oppressed, the demon can temporarily seize control, but the person maintains free will most of the time." Gabe grimaced. "In Pretty Boy's case, even when the demon doesn't take control, meth does."

So if he isn't a prisoner of one, he is of the other?

"Exactly."

She inhaled. *Wow!*

"Scary stuff."

"So, you wanna see it?"

From the lull in conversation, Angela realized she had been asked a question, and she forced a quick smile. "Sorry, could you repeat that?"

Mal stifled a sigh. "*I said*, you wanna see it?"

As she gave him a blank stare, Maria filled in. "Mal just bought a new car. Would you like to see it?"

"Sure." She glanced at Gabe as they stepped outside. *Where did he get the money for all this stuff?*

Gabe's arched eyebrow and sneer said it all.

Gone was Mal's fire-engine-red Corvette. In its place was a black car, custom-painted with ghost flames.

Looking at its virtual blaze, she gave him a sarcastic smile. "Hot stuff."

"Hot stuff." As he ran his shaky fingers over the paint job, he gave the same bone-chilling laugh he had before. "It's a Dodge Challenger SRT Hellcat." He turned toward her, wearing a proud smile. "It's the sixth most powerful production car in the world, after a Bugatti, McLaren, Porsche, and a couple Ferraris."

While she walked around the car, she noticed the skull-decorated license plate holder. "What an . . . " she searched for a better word than *odd*, "unusual license plate holder. Is that—"

"The Bony Lady." He grinned, the chip in his yellowed teeth visible.

"Bony Lady? Santa Muerte?"

He nodded. "She protects me."

"From what?"

"Enemies." Mal shrugged.

Enemies? Angela looked from him to Gabe.

"Gangs, law enforcement." Gabe smirked. "She's known as the 'narco-saint.' Drug bosses exploit their soldiers' susceptibility. Santa Muerte establishes a kind of religious discipline, keeping their foot soldiers in line, while raising their cause to a quasi-holy level."

You're kidding, right?

"It's a Robin Hood mentality."

She subtly shook her head. *Not following.*

"Robbing the rich gringo addicts to give to the—"

Poor? Disbelieving, she gave him a skeptical glance.

He shook his head. "To give to the foot soldiers." Then he gestured toward Mal. "Where do you think he got the money for the jewelry and car?"

He's into robbery, too?

"In a manner of speaking. He drives for the Lobos Grises drug cartel. That's aiding and abetting, part and parcel." His lips pursed, Gabe gave her an emphatic nod.

Angela sighed. *How did he even get involved with Santa Muerte and the Lobos Grises?*

Gabe shrugged. "Probably the way a lot of them do. Underage kids cross into border towns, drink cheap Tequila, and then end up getting introduced to the wrong people. Recruiters have gone beyond looking for experienced soldiers with Special Forces training. They want *norteamericana* kids as foot soldiers for their ability to blend in and do the grunt work."

Kids?

He nodded. "Young adults, but even as young as third graders, eight years old." He grimaced. "Once in, they're in for life . . . which usually isn't long."

Do you know how Mal got involved?

"I've got a pretty good idea. He crossed into Mexico with his buddies, started drinking Tequila, got introduced to meth, and then, while feeling good, was recruited to earn thousands of dollars for an hour or two's easy work."

What about this demon? She grimaced. *How did he—it—get inside Mal?*

Gabe pressed his lips into a thin line. "This is all new to me, something I've only begun to understand since I passed onto this plane. My guess," he sneered, "is that while he was drunk, high, he wasn't in control. Senseless, without his *senses*, his common sense, he was *unaware*. With nothing to prevent it, the demon found an open door."

Common sense isn't that common.

Then Angela watched as Gabe focused on something suspended from the rearview mirror. Stiffening, his spine straightened.

What?

"You'd asked if he was into robbery." He sniffed. "Ask him what's hanging from his rearview mirror."

Her eyes narrowed. *Why?*

"Just ask him."

Angela turned toward Mal and, pointing at the suspended ring, repeated the question.

"That?" His lip curling in a smug sneer, Mal's eyes glittered. "That's a souvenir."

Angela blinked. "From what?"

"My first job."

Taking a deep breath, Angela looked at Gabe. *Is that your grandmother's engagement ring?*

A grim set to his mouth, he nodded.

Angela's shoulders drooped as her heart sank. *I'm so sorry.*

"It's Maria I'm worried about," said Gabe. "Possession of stolen goods criminalizes the receiver. It's a crime if you *should have known*—that is, suspected—the item you received was stolen."

After Mal left, Angela turned to Maria. "We've got to talk."

"Okay." She took a seat in the living room.

Angela sat on the sofa as the cats snuggled around her. Then she pointedly looked at Maria's necklace. "Where's Mal getting the money for gold jewelry and sports cars?"

Maria shrugged. "I don't know."

"Doesn't it seem odd that he's just out of jail and has all this disposable income?" Angela watched her. "Has he ever talked about his job?"

"Sure, he works as a consultant."

"For what?"

Some import/export company." Her eyes narrowed. "Why?"

Angela hesitated, again wondering how much to say. "I have reason to believe he stole that ring hanging from his rearview mirror."

"What?" Maria sneered. "You just won't let up on him, will you? You just can't give the guy a break. He's paid his dues to society, but you just won't forget he spent time in jail."

Angela sighed. "That's not—"

"You accuse Mal of drug dealing, drug running, murder, and now theft, but what proof have you got? Some dreamt-up ghost story?" Scoffing, she stood up. "I'm not going to sit here and listen to you insult him." Taking out her phone, she began texting. Then without another word, she walked out on the front stoop.

A few minutes later, Angela heard a car screech to a stop in front of the apartment house. She glanced out the window in time to see Maria get into Mal's black Hellcat. As he pulled out, his tires squealing, all she saw was the fiery glow of its paint job.

The phone woke her. Groggy, Angela glanced at the clock. *Eleven forty? Who's calling at this hour?* Yawning, she answered her cell.

"Angela, can you pick me up?"

Her eyelids opening wide, she recognized Maria's panicked voice. "Are you all right?"

"For now, but please hurry!" The tone was urgent.

Already out of bed, Angela had the phone on speaker as she pulled on a pair of jeans. "Where are you?"

"Off I-35, at Buc-ee's near the outlet mall."

"Be there as soon as I can."

Angela called Maria's cell as she pulled into the immense parking lot. "Where are you?"

"I'll find you. Where are you parked?"

"Near the Creekside Crossing entrance."

Five minutes later, Maria tapped on the passenger window, and Angela unlocked the car.

"Thanks for picking me up," said Maria. Then, locking the doors, she hunched over to keep out of sight.

Angela did a double-take. "What are you doing?"

"Please just get out of here." When she did not immediately respond, Maria's eyes widened. "Hurry! Please!"

"Not until you tell me what's going on."

"I'll tell you the whole story. I promise, just please *drive!*"

Against her better judgment, Angela started back to their apartment. "What happened?"

Lifting her head, Maria peeked behind them. "No headlights are following us." She sighed.

"Last time I'm asking, or I'm pulling over and stopping." Angela glanced at her. "What's going on?"

Maria swallowed. "After Mal picked me up, we stopped at a drive-in. I thought he was hungry, but when we got there, first one person, and then another came up to the car, asking 'to score.'"

Angela's head snapped as she turned to see Maria's expression.

Pressing her lips together, Maria nodded. "You were right. He's dealing drugs."

"What did you say to him?"

Maria sniffed. "I told him to take me home. I'd seen enough, too much."

"Did he?"

"Mal started to drive me back, but then he got a call on his cell." She took a deep breath. "He seemed to argue with the person on the phone, trying to stall him. Finally, he hung up, saying there was something he had to do before he could take me home."

Angela glanced at her. "What was it?"

"He met some people in a parking lot. They told him to take I-35 north. They'd follow, and he'd know what to do." She swallowed. "He waited until his phone rang. That seemed to be their cue because he stepped on the gas and began speeding."

Angela looked at the narrow temporary lanes, then turned toward Maria. "Not through these detour lanes?"

Her lips pressed tightly together, Maria nodded. "He kept picking up speed. The more I told him to slow down, the faster he went. I told him to let me out, if he cared at all for his baby or me, to let me out of the car. It didn't matter what I said. He just kept picking up speed. Finally, I screamed at him. 'What are you doing?'"

Trying to keep within the detour's winding, interim lanes, Angela glanced at her briefly. "What did he say?"

"That he had a job to do."

"Which was?"

"Apparently to act as some kind of decoy. Then when he saw flashing lights in his rearview mirror, he floored it. The speedometer needle was off the chart." Shaking her head, Maria exhaled. "I was petrified. He was taking potholes and curves so fast, I was bounced and tossed all over the front seat."

"What about the baby?"

Maria nodded. "That's what I was worried about. When he wouldn't stop, I said whatever kind of crazy job he had wasn't worth endangering his baby. Just quit the stupid job, get off the road, and stop playing this game with death."

"What did he say?"

Staring straight ahead, Maria recalled the scene.

"I can't quit." Mal glanced at her.

"Why not? Just get off the road."

He shook his head. "I work for the Lobos Grises cartel. I *have* to do this."

"A cartel? You mean a drug cartel?"

He nodded, keeping his eyes on the road as the necklace swung from the rearview mirror.

"Where did you get this?"

"I told you. It's a souvenir."

"From what?"

He shrugged. "From my first . . . job."

"Did you steal it?"

He shrugged. "It's a war trophy, victory souvenir." He snickered.

"Then you took it from somewhere . . . someone."

"What difference does it make?" His face contorting, he shouted, "Shut up. Just shut up!"

The car hit a large pothole, and something fell from the driver's sun visor. It fell onto the dash and then, as Mal swerved around a car, it flew across the dash to the passenger's side.

"A gun! What are you doing with a gun?"

He reached for it, but as he did, he saw the red sea of brake lights ahead. Changing his focus at the last moment, he slammed on the brakes, and the gun went flying.

Maria lifted her eyes to meet Angela's as she continued her grim tale. "When the gun dropped into my lap, I screamed. I don't know if it was a road block, an accident, or just a traffic snarl, but Mal screeched to a stop just inches behind the car in front of him. We were in the middle lane on the interstate at a dead standstill. I didn't stop to think. I tossed the gun in my purse, yanked the ring hanging from the rearview mirror, and jumped out."

Angela turned toward her. "You jumped out into moving traffic?"

Maria shook her head. "The cars were at a dead stop, but I didn't know for how long. I saw my chance, and I just reacted."

"How did you get to the gas station?"

"Though Mal was screaming at me, I figured he wouldn't follow on foot since the police were only a few cars behind him. I slid down the incline, crossed the green area and service road, and then ran toward the outlet center. Even if he followed me, I knew he couldn't find me there."

"What happened to him?"

She shrugged. "I lost sight of him. The traffic jam let up before I made it across the grass, and he took off with the squad car in close pursuit."

"And you have his gun?" Angela glanced at her.

"Yeah." Her body hunching, she sighed. "Angela, I'm sorry I didn't believe you. I . . . I don't know what to say. I just didn't . . . couldn't see Mal for what he was. I kept seeing the person I'd known, the man I remembered."

"Now you believe me?"

Maria's voice was barely above a whisper. "Yeah."

"All of it?" When she did not hear an answer, Angela glanced at her. "All of it, even the possibility Mal shot José's brother?"

Her shoulders drooping, Maria sighed. "From what I've seen and heard tonight, I believe anything you say about him's possible. Before that, I wouldn't . . . I couldn't recognize the truth."

That's definite progress. "The first thing we have to do is call José—"

"Why?" Her plaintive tone made Angela look.

"He's got Detective Hadd's contact information." Angela grimaced. "You've got to go to the police with this gun, but the local police won't know the background. Detective Hadd's the only one who'll understand the connection between this handgun and Gabe. I'll call José and see if he can meet us at the apartment."

When he answered, Angela briefly described what had happened. "Maria may have evidence involving Gabe's death."

Silence.

"José, are you still there? You seemed to cut out for a minute."

"Yeah." He took a deep breath. "What kind of evidence?"

"The gun."

"And she got this . . . how?"

Angela gritted her teeth. "Better let Maria explain it."

His voice monotone, he said, "I'll try to get hold of Charlie. I'll call you when I know something."

The phone clicked in her ear. What a double loss for José. Mal murdered his brother and destroyed his happiness with Maria. Now, whether he wants to be or not, he's thrown back into the mix.

Moments later, José called her cell phone.

"Charlie's in San Antonio on a case. I'll meet him at your apartment in a half hour."

"Can you meet us there sooner?"

"Yeah, sure." The line went dead.

Chapter 7

"Ain't Talkin' 'Bout Love"
— Van Halen

When they got home, José was waiting outside.

Angela gave him a sympathetic smile. "Thanks for coming on such short notice."

He kept his eyes on Angela, never once glancing in Maria's direction. "Charlie will be here in a few minutes."

As he spoke, an unmarked car pulled in front of the apartment, and Charlie stepped out, wearing plain clothes.

Angela made the introductions and invited everyone into the living room. She sensed the chill as her eyes swept the room. Charlie stood near the bookcase. José sat across the room, his eyes dark as he glanced at Maria. Maria sat beside Angela on the sofa, her eyes focused on her pregnant belly.

Charlie turned on a tape recorder. "The date is October 23, 2015." Turning to Maria, he said, "Would you state your name for the record?"

"Maria Ramirez."

"What is your relationship with Malachi Straub?" he asked.

Maria glanced at José, paled, and spoke in a whisper. "He's the father of my child."

"Would you speak up, please," said Charlie.

She repeated her statement loudly.

"And have you seen him recently?" asked Charlie.

She swallowed and again glanced at José. "Yes, I saw him tonight."

"Would you describe the circumstances surrounding the meeting?"

Maria repeated what she had told Angela, describing how the gun had fallen from its holster above the visor, and she had grabbed it before making her escape.

"Would you produce the weapon you allegedly took from Mal?"

Blanching at the word *allegedly,* Maria reached into her purse.

Detective Hadd raised his eyebrows. "To keep the fingerprints intact, please don't handle the weapon any more than you have already. Instead, hand me your bag."

Using gloves, he carefully lifted out the gun and handed back her purse. Holding it gingerly, he noticed the gun's caliber and stated it for the tape recorder. "A .32 ACP Walther PPK." Then he took out a plastic bag and placed the gun in it.

José looked at the detective. "Do you think that's the murder weapon?"

"We'll need to run a ballistics test, but the bullet casings we found near the body were from a .32 ACP Walther PPK."

Closing his eyes, balling his hands into fists, José shuddered.

Then Angela saw Gabe standing beside him. "Tell him not to grieve for me. The system will catch Pretty Boy, and justice will be served, but first Maria needs to lure him."

What? She gave him a blank look.

"She needs to be wired, meet Pretty Boy, and entrap him."

Before Gabe finished speaking, Detective Hadd said, "Maria, if you'll work with us, I'll put in a good word for you."

She frowned. "Why would I need any reference from you?"

"Your prints are on an alleged murder weapon. You could be charged with being an accessory after the fact."

"What?"

"If you helped a felon avoid capture or arrest, you can be charged with being an accessory after the fact—"

"I never even knew about any crime—"

"If it ever comes to light you've helped a felon, you'd be charged with a similar offense."

"What?" Her eyebrows knit into a tight V.

Detective Hadd shrugged. "Of course, if you'll work with us . . . " His implications hanging like a noose at the gallows, he studied her.

Gabe shook his head. "Tell him she had nothing to do with it."

Angela said, "Maria knew nothing about the murder—"

"Then how did she know about a murder weapon?"

". . . until I told her earlier tonight." Angela glanced at her. "She didn't even believe me. In fact, that's why she called Mal. He hadn't planned to see her, which may be why he dealt in front of her and unintentionally dragged her along on the police chase."

Gabe's smile was ironic. "Tell him not to be so hardnosed."

Lifting her eyebrow, tilting her head at a skeptical angle, Angela glanced at him.

"Go on. Tell him not to be so hardnosed."

Angela repeated Gabe's words, expecting an angry reaction. Instead, a hint of a smile crossed Charlie's face. "A message?"

Giving him a wry grin, she nodded.

"Point taken." He turned toward Maria. "You're still going to have to answer questions about your fingerprints on the alleged murder weapon, but I'll get what immunity for you I can. All I ask is that you agree to meet with the suspect."

As she sighed, her shoulders slumped, her face drooped. She shook her head. "After the way he endangered my baby's life, I never want to see him again."

Charlie met her eyes. "It's the only way we can lure and entrap him."

She shrugged. "What can I say to him? I took his gun and," she caught her breath, "escaped. I'm not sure he'd even want to see me again."

"I am," José said softly. Maria turned toward him, and their eyes met. After a beat, he looked at the detective. "But in her condition, she'd need protection."

"Sure, we can have a few plainclothesmen in unmarked cars, but we'll need to wire her."

She gave a nervous laugh. "I don't even know what I'd say to him."

"Tell him you ran because you were afraid for yourself and your baby," said the detective. "Tell him you're uncomfortable with a gun in your possession and that you want to give it back."

"Okay, but since you're going to wire me, you obviously want a confession or something from him, right?" She shrugged. "What?"

"Ask him why he had a gun in the first place." His tone changed. "By the way, it won't be this weapon. It'll be the same model, but this one won't fire."

"Thanks." Grimacing, she pressed her lips together.

"And if you can work it into the conversation, ask him what happened July Fourth after you left. That's when he was picked up for drunk driving. That's the night he . . . allegedly shot Detective Aceves. Once we have it on record, our men will move in."

She nodded. "You want me to be the decoy."

"You're our 'in.'"

Mal's ring tones chimed from Maria's purse. Maria's eyes met José's. Swallowing, she turned toward the detective. "That's him. What should I do?"

"Answer it. Say you want to meet him."

"Hello." She clicked the speaker button.

"What the hell were you thinking, jumping out of the car?"

Maria again looked to the detective. "You were driving so fast, I was worried about the baby. When you stopped, I ran."

His tone challenged. "Why did you take the gun?"

"Why did you have one?" Lifting her eyebrow, she glanced at the detective for confirmation.

He nodded.

"I need it for protection."

"Who from?"

"Never mind who. I need it back. Where are you?"

She paused a moment. "On my way home, Angela picked me up."

"I'll be there in a few minutes."

"Give me a half—"

Charlie shook his head. Holding up his index finger, he mouthed *one hour*.

"Make that an hour. I'll be home in an hour." She looked at Angela as if corroborating her story. "We have to stop for groceries."

They had just moved the cars and finished wiring Maria when Mal drove up.

"He's here," Angela called from the window.

"Meet him outside," said the detective.

José mumbled through pinched, white lips. "Be safe."

Nodding, she gave him a quick hug. Then she pressed something into his hand as she whispered in his ear. "You probably despise me, but take this ring. I want you to know I'm only doing this for Gabe, for you." With that, she hurried out to meet Mal.

"Hey," they heard her say through her microphone.

"Hey." Mal sounded sullen. "Got the gun?"

"Yeah, here." They heard her close the car door as she got in.

"Where's the ring?"

"I . . . I must've left it in the apartment."

"Get it."

"Can't I get it when we go back? I'm just really exhausted. I've been up all night."

"'Kay."

"Mal, we've got to talk."

"About what?" He started the engine.

"Where are we going?"

"My favorite drive-in. I've been up all night, too, and I need breakfast."

Angela, José, and the detectives heard highway sounds and chitchat. Then they heard a muffled intercom. "What'll you have?"

Mal called in the order. Then his voice got louder as he apparently turned toward Maria. "Want anything besides coffee?"

"No thanks."

After they picked up their breakfast, Mal parked and turned off the motor.

She took a deep breath. "Look, that gun raised a lot of flags. Why did you have it?"

"I told you," he snapped, "for protection. What do you want, my life story?"

"No, just what happened after I had to walk home July Fourth."

"I was—"

They heard tapping at the window.

"Mal, I'm looking to score. What ya got?"

"The usual. What ya need?"

"A coke dime bag and a gram of meth."

"Can do, Pal. Show me the green."

As Charlie nodded grimly, Angela, José, and the detectives heard papers rustling.

After the drug deal closed, they heard Maria. "So getting back to our discussion. What happened after I walked home July Fourth?"

"Got buzzed with my buds. Geez, you're getting nosy."

"Hey, man," said another voice. "What you got?"

"Whatever you want," said Mal. "What you need?"

As they listened to the conversation, Angela gave José an empathetic smile.

When that drug deal ended, they heard Maria's voice. "How can we talk with these . . . interruptions?"

"What, the drugs? This is how I make my living." His tone was quarrelsome, belligerent. "If you want nice stuff, this is how I earn it."

She sighed. "Then why bother trying?" She took off her necklace and handed it to him. "I don't want 'nice things' if this is how you get them. There's nothing to talk about. Take me home, or do I have to walk . . . again?"

They heard another tap at the window.

"All right, this is my last deal," said Mal. "Then we'll talk."

When that deal ended, they heard the engine start up. A few minutes later, Mal cut the motor.

"So," said Maria, "what happened after I walked home on your birthday?"

"Look, I can BS you, but I'm not going to."

"The truth?"

"The truth. That was the night I made my first run."

"Run?" she asked.

"Yeah, like I did on I-35 last night. It's easy money."

"But you got caught for speeding and drunk driving, and now you've got a police record. Plus, I've seen you deal drugs. This is bad stuff, Mal, bad. And what was that you'd said about the ring you had hanging from the rearview mirror?"

"Oh, that." He laughed his fiendish howl.

"You told Angela it was a souvenir."

"Yeah, a war trophy." Hs snickered. "That was what you might call icing on the cake."

"I'm not following."

"It was my library card for paying my dues."

She paused. "What?"

"It's how I got accepted into the Lobos Grises cartel, all right?"

"You got that ring for speeding?"

"No, geez, *icing*. I iced a man."

"I don't—"

Frustration in his voice, he shouted. "I shot someone, all right?"

"What? No, it's not all right. Ohmigosh. Take me home." They heard the door open. "Take me home, or I'm walking."

"Shut the damned door." He heaved a sigh. "I'll drive you. Just give me back my ring."

"Oh, you'll get it . . . once I get home." She slammed the door.

A few minutes later, Angela called from the window. "His car's parking now."

"Back in a sec," they heard Maria say as she opened her door, then slammed it shut.

"I'm coming with you."

"No . . . after Angela had to pick me up, she doesn't want to see you."

When Maria was safely inside, Detective Hadd radioed the order. Within seconds, squad cars surrounded Mal's Dodge Challenger, blocking his escape.

Angela watched from the window as the officers hauled him from his car, screaming expletives she could hear inside. Spread-eagled against the car door, still shrieking, he struggled as the plainclothesmen cuffed him and read him his rights.

For a second time, she watched as his shadow seemed to briefly lose sync with his body. Only this time, it locked eyes with her. Angela recoiled, momentarily pulling her head back from the window. Then as quickly as the silhouette had detached itself, it rejoined Mal's body.

That was weird. Angela blinked, wondering if she had seen right. Then she watched the officers help Mal into the back seat of a squad car.

"Saw it again, didn't you?"

Angela flinched. Gabe was standing beside her.

Yeah, that thing gives me the willies.

Maria took off the microphone and handed it to Detective Hadd.

"Appreciate your cooperation." Then his eyes hardened. "Don't leave town. You're still a suspect."

Grimacing, she nodded as she held the door open for him.

"I'd better be going, too," said José.

"Oh, please don't go yet." Maria's eyes pleaded. "Can't you stay for a cup of coffee?"

He hesitated, then glanced at Angela.

"I think we could all use a cup." She gave him a crooked smile. "It's been a long night."

His smile was shy. "Okay."

A few minutes later, they were sitting around the kitchen table.

José took the gold-filigreed, blue sapphire ring from his pocket. Turning it slowly between his fingers, he studied it as he seemed to collect his thoughts. Then he spoke softly, as if he was thinking aloud.

"This was our grandmother's engagement ring . . . " He took a deep breath. "Gabe and I'd had a pact. Whoever got engaged first would give this to their fiancée."

Maria looked at José. "Why did your brother have it?"

"Until one or the other of us needed it, he wore it as a kind of good luck charm."

"Why Gabe? Why didn't you wear it?"

Angela saw Gabe sitting beside his brother.

"He was the oldest . . . by three minutes." A smile stole across José's face as he set the ring on his saucer. "He never let me forget it."

Gabe chuckled. "I loved to lord it over him."

Maria looked at her bare left hand, stifled a sigh, and added sugar to her coffee.

José glanced at her. "You never said why you took this ring."

"Angela tried to tell me Mal had stolen it. I couldn't believe her, but after some of the things I saw, I began wondering. Then when he admitted . . . " Shaking her head, on the verge of tears, she gulped. "I am so sorry, José, so sorry for . . . everything."

Angela watched José's internal struggle through his stilted body language. He would start to get up or move toward Maria and then press his back against his chair, restraining himself, his mind apparently in conflict with his body.

Rather than watch her friends agonize, Angela broke the tension. "Was Mal always a troublemaker?"

Maria shook her head. "He was a happy, outgoing kid until his mother died. Then his father began drinking. After that, he started beating him and taking him to some weird church. Mal began to get withdrawn. At times, he'd be his old sunny self, but then other times he'd be so angry, nasty." She took a deep breath.

"So you've known him since grade school?" Angela sipped her coffee.

"Middle school. We lost touch when I started at UTSA, but then last Christmas we met at a party and," she glanced at José, "renewed our friendship."

Expressionless, eyes cast down, he stirred his coffee.

Angela caught her eye. "Was he his old self?"

"Sometimes," Maria stared at nothing, seeming to remember. "It was like he was two different people. Sometimes he'd be the good-natured kid I remembered. Other times," she shook her head, "he'd seem so dark, I couldn't recognize him. He was like someone I didn't know, someone I'd never met."

Angela glanced at Gabe.

"It sounds like DID."

Did what?

Gabe shook his head. "D.I.D., Dissociative Identity Disorder, basically what psychiatrists used to call multiple personality disorder. There's a close relationship between DID and satanic ritual abuse. Ask her more about the 'church' he attended."

"You'd mentioned his father took him to 'some weird church.'"

Maria shook her head. "I don't know much about it. After the first few times he attended, Mal said they danced, handled snakes, and lit black candles. Then he shut up. He never talked about it again."

Gabe raised his eyebrows. "From what I've read, nearly all DID sufferers experienced childhood abuse. It's a coping device, a defense mechanism."

So another personality or a demon?

Gabe shrugged. "Either, both."

Angela turned toward Maria. "It sounds almost evil. And you said he was abused?"

Maria nodded. "I saw bruises on his arms, and I saw him limping more than once."

"Did he do drugs?"

"Not that I know of. Mostly, he was a nice guy. He just developed a dark side that gradually seemed to take over." She sighed. "Looking back on the last few weeks, he's become someone I don't recognize." Her forehead wrinkled. "I just hadn't realized it, couldn't see it. Why? Why was I so blind?"

"*Ciega de amor.*" His eyes dull, José gave her a sad but sympathetic smile. "Love's blind."

Nodding, grimacing, Maria caught his eye.

José's phone rang. After listening to the caller, he thanked him and hung up. "That was Detective Hadd. He expedited the ballistics test, and the results just came in." Pressing his lips together, he looked from Angela to Maria. "That's the gun that killed my brother."

Her shoulders slumping, Maria closed her eyes and sighed.

"And they've made a positive ID on the fingerprints, both on the aluminum can and the gun." José glanced at Angela. "They belong to Malachi Straub."

As she watched Gabe relax, Angela recalled the first time she had seen him. He had been so filled with anger, his presence had made her nauseous. Oppressive, his presence had gripped her chest and hampered her breathing.

Now you look almost peaceful.

Gabe turned toward her with a tranquil smile and then chuckled. "I almost am. When you met me, you asked why I was still here."

She dipped her chin in a nod. *You'd said you wanted Mal to pay for what he'd done.*

"Now he's in custody, and they've got enough evidence to put him away." He smiled at her. "Thanks to you, they've found my bones. All that's missing before I can move on—"

Is a Christian burial on consecrated land. Angela nodded.

Maria reached across the table for José's arm. "I'm so sorry for your loss, but at least now you can lay your brother to rest." When he flinched, she drew back her arm.

"His remains are being cremated." Struggling to keep his composure, José spoke to Angela. "We'll hold a memorial service and bury his ashes in the family plot."

Gabe's smile was bright as he looked from José to Maria to Angela. "Just one more thing."

Angela glanced at him. *What?*

"Remind him to take Maria as his wife. She'll bear a son, and he's to name him Jesus.'"

Now? This isn't the time. She shook her head.

José studied her. "Why are you shaking your head?"

Angela took a deep breath. *What do I say?*

"Tell him the truth." Gabe's nod confirmed his words.

As both twins stared at her, Angela glanced from brother to brother. *How much alike you two look.* Sighing, she turned toward José. "Gabe's here."

"Now?" He looked around the room. "Where?"

"He's sitting beside you."

José turned to his right.

"The other side." She rubbed her chin. "He wants me to give you a message."

José's eyebrow rose skeptically. "This isn't like the message you gave me the last time, is it?"

Angela gave a nervous laugh, then nodded. "Actually, it is."

"Save your breath." José glanced at Maria, scowled, and turned back to Angela. "Consider your message delivered." Then he turned to his left. "You're asking too much of me."

"Tell him," Gabe chose his words, "what I'm asking is for his own good."

Pressing her lips together, Angela shook her head at Gabe. *I can't.*

"I can." Standing up, he lifted his grandmother's ring from José's saucer and placed it on the table in front of Maria.

Maria gasped as she sat back in her chair. Her eyes widening, she stared at the ring.

José paled as he glanced from her to the ring. Pointing, he asked Angela, "Is he standing here?"

She nodded. "Between you and Maria."

He spoke to the air. "Gabe, I need time to think about your message."

"Tell him, time's precious. You never know when it'll run out. Seize every moment. *Live* every moment, and take love when and where you find it."

Swallowing, Angela repeated Gabe's words.

Hands cupping her face, Maria sat at the table, vainly trying to hide the tears running down her face.

His eyes red, José whispered, "I need time to think." With that, he stood up and rushed toward the door.

"José," called Maria, "you left your ring."

Sunday, Angela drove Maria to the Mission of Divine Mercy.

"Angela, I've been . . . blind." Maria sighed.

"We all have blind spots, whether driving," she checked her side-view mirror as she changed lanes, "or trekking through life. 'There are none so blind as those who will not see.'"

"Ain't that the truth?" Maria grimaced.

"'The most deluded people are those who choose to ignore what they already know.'" When Maria did not answer Angela glanced at her. "John Heywood, remember?"

"No . . . should I?"

She grinned. "Our 'Foundations of Communication' class last semester. Don't you remember?"

Maria shook her head. "I don't know. It seems I've been walking around with my mind shut down, my eyes closed the past six months. It's like I've been wearing blinders. I didn't even sleep last night, thinking about . . ." Maria sighed. "Just thinking."

Angela gave her a sympathetic smile as she parked the car.

The Gospel reading was from Mark: "Then Jesus spoke, 'What do you want me to do for you?' The blind man said to him, 'Rabbi, let me see again.' Jesus said to him, 'Go; your faith has saved you.' And at once his sight returned."

As the reader sat down, the priest began his homily. "How many of you wear glasses or contacts? Let me see a show of hands."

Angela turned in her seat to see how many of the congregation raised their hands. Then she spotted José and gave him a surprised smile.

"Roughly two-thirds of us wear lenses to improve our eyesight," continued the priest. "If we're in a room where the lights suddenly go out, we're lost. We don't move until the lights come back on. Eyesight's such an important sense. We treasure clear vision and clarity, yet in some ways we may be living 'in the dark.' We may not even be aware of blind spots in our lives. Do we cherish our faith, the gift of being able to see beyond this moment, this problem?

"Today's Gospel describes Jesus meeting the blind man, who cries out for pity. What should we learn from this? It's a call to raise our voices and cry out to Jesus. Maybe there are times when we need to be the strong, silent type." He grinned. "More often, we need to raise our voices in prayer, but we can only do this if we believe God hears and answers our prayers.

"The crowd told Bartimaeus to shut up. What did he do? He shouted louder. 'Son of David have pity on me.' Instead of bowing to the bullies or being discouraged, he tried harder. He summoned all his strength and shouted at the top of his lungs.

"In a way, we're all Bartimaeus: frail, wounded, begging for God's mercy. And in one way or another, we're all blind. Blinded by sin, pride, greed, the drive to succeed, to excel. Or maybe we're not seeing or thinking clearly because of some personal injury, perhaps a broken heart or broken spirit. Or maybe we're struggling to find our way through a haze of addiction and have given up or given in to darkness. What can we do?

"First, we have to believe Jesus will help. Next, we have to be persistent. Keep crying out for God's mercy. No matter if your heart's sinking, cry out louder, 'Son of David, have pity on me.'

"Then, after Jesus calls you to Him, what will you do? Will you follow Bartimaeus's example? He threw off his cloak, possibly his most treasured possession. Blind, he groped his way to Jesus. He left behind everything familiar, all he knew, all he owned. Though most likely his life wasn't comfortable, he left his comfort zone and found his way to God. Risking all he had, he began his journey of faith." He looked out over the congregation. "What would you do?

"Finally, don't be afraid to respond when Jesus asks, 'What do you want me to do for you?' Do you want your eyes opened to something or someone? Do you want clarity of thought? Do you want insight? Are you living in darkness? Look to Jesus, the light of this world. Then once you see the light, decide. Will you follow Bartimaeus's example? Will you give up your old ways and follow Jesus?

"These are the questions to ask yourself today." The priest gave them a benevolent smile. "Have an insightful Sunday of reflection!"

After Mass ended, they were walking past the confession cabins, when Maria slowed her pace and paused. "Would you mind starting lunch alone?"

Angela glanced from her somber face to the cabins and back. "Not at all." She clasped her hand. "Take your time."

Fifteen minutes later, Angela raised her eyebrow when she saw Maria approaching the table with José.

Apparently noticing Angela's surprise, Maria quickly explained. "He was just coming out of confession as I went in."

"And I finished my penance just as she came out," José promptly added.

Angela swallowed a grin. "Small world." She gestured toward the bench seats across from her. "Have a seat."

As they joined her, José blinked as if thinking. "I enjoyed the homily today about clarity, blindness. It's amazing how short-sighted we can be."

A smile tugged at the corner of Angela's mouth. "It's universal. Think of all the idioms about it. Can't see past their nose. Can't see their hand in front of their face. Can't see the forest for the trees."

Maria joined in. "Begin to see daylight. See the light. See the light at the end of the tunnel."

"See it from my perspective. As I see it," said José.

"Don't see you much, anymore," said Angela. "Long time no see."

"Come back and see us," added Maria.

"Good to see you," said José, turning toward Maria at his side. "See you later. Could I see you again?"

As they gazed into each other's eyes, the phrases' meanings clicked. Stiffening, they blinked and looked away. As the playful banter lagged, the game ended.

They ate in thoughtful silence until Angela glanced at José. "I didn't know we'd see you here."

"Hadn't planned on it. I had to see if the Institute needed me today."

Maria began chuckling.

His eyes twinkling, a smile played at his lips. "What?"

"See you here, see if—" She chuckled.

José's eyes crinkled in a smile. "I see."

"Mother Mary Agnes." Angela waved the woman over as she approached the table. "Please join us." Scooting over, Angela made room beside her.

"Thank you." Mary Agnes gave her a quick hug, then looked at José. "I read your email, just hadn't responded yet." As Mother Mary Agnes sat down, she reached out for his hand. "I'm so sorry to hear of your loss." Pressing her lips together, she shook her head.

"Thank you." He nodded. "When we hadn't heard from Gabe, we'd suspected foul play, but now it's been confirmed."

"The good news is you'll have closure. He'll have a proper burial, and his spirit will be put to rest."

Gabe's words almost verbatim. Does she sense his presence? Angela turned quickly to see Mother Mary Agnes's expression. From her sad smile, all she felt were concern and sympathy, but Gabe stood beside her.

"When is the funeral?"

"Next Monday," José swallowed, "*Dia de los Muertos.*"

"All Souls Day." Mother Mary Agnes nodded. "What better day to commend your brother's soul to God?"

Maria had remained expressionless throughout the conversation, but on hearing those words, she turned toward him. "Where? In San Antonio?"

José turned bloodshot eyes toward her. "No, Alpine."

She repeated the word in a whisper, then sighed. Pressing her lips together, she grimaced. "Could I—would you mind if I," she glanced at Angela, "if Angela and I attend his funeral?"

His dark eyes brooding, José studied her. Finally, he took a jagged breath. "If you want to show your respects," he nodded slowly, "you're welcome to join my family in saying goodbye."

Angela watched Gabe's face relax into a smile, comparing his appearance to the first time she had seen him. Gone was the sneer. His initial anger now dispelled, it no longer coarsened his features. The tattoos had faded, and his shaved head sported hair. She compared him to his brother. Though there had always been a strong resemblance, they were beginning to look like twins.

Then she glanced at Maria. Her hair had nearly grown back, and her face had a rosy glow. *Maybe now that she's free of Mal's hold on her, she can move forward. Is it time that heals all wounds? Or is it God?*

Chapter 8

"The One You Love"
– GLENN FREY

Angela and Maria attended Gabe's memorial Mass, followed by his interment in consecrated ground. Afterwards, Angela spotted Maria speaking to the priest. Then they joined the family and friends at José's parents' house, where on the Day of the Dead, they celebrated Gabe's life.

They admired the family altar containing Gabe's photos and memorabilia, along with painted sugar skulls, marigolds, crucifixes, statues of Our Lady of Guadalupe, and lit candles. Then they joined the family in remembering Gabe's life through anecdotes and stories.

They ate the anise-flavored *pan de muerto*, bread of the dead, candied pumpkin, marigold-pressed tortillas, and gingerbread cookies shaped like pigs. They drank *champurrado*, a thick hot chocolate, and sipped marigold-infused tequila to 'raise spirits.'

Said one of the guests, "*Viva la Vida!*"

As the day wore on, José progressed from being a perfunctory host toward Maria to being courteous, and then to being attentive. When she leaned over, reaching for a marigold, the chain around her neck swung out from her blouse, revealing Gabe's ring. José's eyes widened.

Maria swallowed as she met his gaze. "This morning, I asked the priest to bless this ring, remove all negativity from it." Undoing the chain, she slid off the ring and handed it to him. "I was waiting for the right moment to return this."

He looked at the ring, at her hand. "The right moment," he repeated softly. Then he looked into her eyes. "Is this the right moment, the appropriate time?"

Angela saw Gabe standing behind him, smiling his consent.

"If you're asking what I think you are," Maria nodded, "yes."

As José slipped the ring on her left hand and kissed her, Gabe looked on wearing a lopsided grin.

"Remember what they told us at the Women's Conference?" asked Maria.

Angela glanced at her as they drove back to San Antonio. "What part?"

"When they told us about being the daughters of God. When they called the Holy Spirit to anoint us with the fruit of the Spirit: love, joy, peace, patience, kindness, generosity, faithfulness, gentleness, and self-control."

Angela's eyes on the road, she nodded.

"I finally feel the Holy Spirit's working in me." Maria splayed her fingers, admiring her ring. "For the first time in six months, I feel peace." She smiled gently. "Joy and peace."

"That's two," Angela grinned, "only seven to go."

"Last month, I struggled between the flesh and the spirit, between Mal and José."

"That's the first time you've mentioned Mal's name since he was arrested." Angela glanced at her. "I've wondered how you felt."

"I think I've finally sorted it out. I was so physically attracted to Mal, it was hard to see him for what he was. More to the point, for what he wasn't, for what he lacked. The more time I spent with him, the farther I strayed from God. The more time I spend with José, the better I feel spiritually, the closer I feel to God."

"Makes sense." Angela nodded. "The struggle between the body and the spirit is like a clash between what you crave and what you need, like deciding between fudge brownies and spinach salad."

Maria gave a wry smile. "It's the difference between lust and love, desire and devotion."

Sunday after Mass, the four of them resumed their walks along the Mission Reach of the River Walk. This time, they followed the Acequia Trail's meandering paths, using low-water crossings to view the historic irrigation ditches and marshy swales. Then they finished by grilling out at the Acequia Park Pavilion.

Sitting across the picnic table from Angela, José caught her eye. "Have you seen Gabe recently?"

She shook her head. "Not since the Day of the Dead. I believe spirits are able to move on once they accomplish their missions. Maybe his task is complete."

"I hope so." José gave a thoughtful sigh.

"Gabe told me he needed a Christian burial on consecrated land and payback, but maybe getting you two together was his primary task." Angela smiled wistfully. "We don't always do things for the reasons we think. Sometimes we're unknowing agents of God, working out His plan, but for our own motives."

Kio called from the grill. "When's the big day?"

"December twenty-seventh," called Maria, grimacing, "two days after Christmas."

Angela glanced at her. "Why the long face?"

"I was hoping we could spend our first Christmas together as husband and wife." Maria gave José a wry grin. "But this was the first available date at the Mission."

"Small wait for a lifetime together." José took her hand in his. "Besides, we'll be able to spend New Year's together."

Kio brought over a plate of burgers. "Which Mission?"

José grinned. "San José, of course."

"And something I've always dreamt of," added Maria, her eyes sparkling, "a Mariachi wedding." Then she turned toward Angela. "Will you still be my maid of honor?"

"Count on it," she grinned.

"Then Kio, would you be my best man?"

"Wouldn't have it any other way."

Watching Maria and José together, Angela smiled. "I think the Holy Spirit's anointed you with another fruit of the Spirit: love."

"Anyone home?" called Angela, turning on the lights.

"Me," said a monotone voice.

Angela flinched, then realized it was Maria. "Why are you sitting in the dark?"

She shrugged.

"Daylight Savings time makes it dark so early. Just got off my afternoon shift at the Alamo."

Maria shrugged.

"Are you all right?" Moving closer, Angela saw the red eyes. "What's wrong?"

When Maria looked up, Angela saw the wet eyelashes. "I saw Mal today."

"Are you nuts?"

Maria sighed. "I had to see him."

Angela shook her head. "You're engaged to José, yet you risk that relationship to see a murderer, an addict. Why?"

She shrugged. "I don't know."

"What's his hold over you?"

Maria shrugged. "One minute, I hate him. I remember how he treated me when I told him I was pregnant. Then the next minute, I remember how it wasn't his fault. I start remembering . . . other things, and before I know it, I want to see him again."

"It's like an addiction, like you're trying to destroy yourself. Fine. Do what you want." Angela called over her shoulder as she walked toward her room. "You do, anyway. It doesn't seem to matter what I say. You don't listen. I'm through talking."

As she closed the door, her cell phone rang. "Hello."

"Angela?"

"Dev, how are you?" A smile came through her voice as she connected with her old roommate.

"Great, how 'bout you?"

"I'm fine," Angela paused, debating whether to share Maria's odd behavior.

"But . . . "

Angela summarized the situation and then sighed. "I don't know what's wrong with her. She needs help, but I'm not able to give it to her."

"My honest opinion is she's influenced."

"By what? Mal?"

"In a way," said Dev. "From what you've told me, he may be tormented by demons. Since Maria's been physically involved with him, they're spiritually connected, and if he's demonized, as I suspect—"

"You don't mean . . . " Snickering, Angela raised her eyebrow. Then she saw Gabe, silently watching, listening. Obviously glad to see him, No Name purred and rubbed against his legs. "You think Mal's demons may be influencing Maria's actions?"

"Yup." Dev's tone was convincing.

Gabe's raised eyebrow and nod confirmed it.

"I'm going to a healing conference this weekend," said Dev. "It's especially effective for people wrestling with demons and addictive habits. Why don't you and Maria join me?"

"Maybe that would help." Angela blinked as she thought it through.

"Can you talk her into it?"

"Somehow, I'll make sure we attend," Angela grinned ruefully, "come hell or high water."

It stormed nonstop Friday night. Saturday dawned late and gray because of the deluge.

"Nine inches of rain overnight. Weather reports say to keep off the roads. Highways are washed out, and underpasses are flooding." Maria lifted her eyebrow. "Are you sure it's safe to go to the conference?"

Angela looked from her to Gabe.

"Go," he said. "This is spiritual warfare."

"Yeah, I'm sure," said Angela.

An hour later, Dev met them at a suburban church. "You made it."

Angela gave her a wry smile. "I figured on the 'hell' part, but not the 'high water.'"

Dev chuckled as she linked arms with her and Maria.

"Ladies and Gentlemen," said the speaker over the PA system, "it's my privilege to introduce Dr. Alma Patterson, nationally known for her work with subjects suffering from demonization, dissociative identity disorder, and satanic ritual abuse. Additionally, Dr. Patterson has participated as an expert witness in criminal courts relating to the demonic and demonization issues."

Nodding her thanks, the white-haired speaker addressed them from the podium. "Who remembers Flip Wilson?" At a show of hands, the woman continued. "Remember his catchphrase, 'The devil made me do it'? How many of you believe it's possible for demons to influence your thoughts or actions?"

Sharing a wink and a nod, Angela whispered to Dev. "We're in the right place."

"From early childhood, we're taught there are no such things as spirits or demons," said Dr. Patterson. "If anyone says the devil made them do something, we think they're either crazy or trying to dodge responsibility for their own actions. We judge faith healers who claim to drive out demons as nothing but deluded fools." The speaker cocked her head as she stared out at the crowd. "Maybe it's time for a new worldview.

"The Bible takes the devil and demons very seriously. Dark angels plagued Jesus during His ministry. Two thousand years ago, Saint Paul wrote about knowing Lucifer's plans, yet today we question and even deny the devil's existence. People don't realize we're in a spiritual war. Though it's being fought all around us, we don't or can't acknowledge it.

"One of Satan's most powerful ploys is to keep us ignorant of both his reality and our power over him. Saint Luke wrote that Jesus gave his followers the authority to drive out demons. Saint John wrote, '. . . whoever believes in me will perform the same works as I do myself, and will perform even greater works, because I am going to the Father. Whatever you ask in my name, I will do, so that the Father may be glorified in the Son. If you ask me anything in my name, I will do it.'

"Demons are nothing but fallen angels, evil spirits. Saint Matthew wrote, 'When an unclean spirit goes out of a person it roams, then it brings back with itself seven other spirits eviler than itself, and they move in and dwell there.' Because they resent us, they want to inhabit us, inhibit us, demonize us.

"How does demonization take place? Satanic beings can enter us in many ways, through both conscious and unconscious invitation." The speaker smiled. "I see some of you wearing perplexed expressions. Unconscious invitation occurs when a person's been physically or emotionally abused and then holds on to their reactions of anger, hatred, fear, and bitterness.

"When a person's unable to let go of the negativity or forgive the abuser, the emotional baggage can lead to alcohol or drug abuse, bulimia, anorexia, sex addiction, pornography, or a host of other compulsive actions. Any one of those weakens the spiritual immune system, leaving that person vulnerable to roaming demons."

Angela watched Maria grow still and pale. Then Maria crossed her arms over her chest and grimaced. Finally, she turned toward Angela, her eyes dark. "What kind of claptrap crap is this, anyway?"

"It never hurts to broaden our perspectives." Shrugging, Angela whispered, "We might even learn something." She returned her attention to the spokeswoman.

"We're made up of five parts," said the speaker, "spirit, body, mind, emotions, and free will. Occasionally, when we're addicted or attracted to something that's harmful to us, something that makes no sense to us, we might want to look beyond our own intellect. Although God gave us free will, our emotions not only can lead us astray, they can open us up to demonization.

"I call it rubbish and rats. The emotional reactions that people cling to, wallow in, are the rubbish. The demons are the rats that feed on that rubbish." The leader grinned. "Without the emotional rubbish, there can be no rats. Cleansing your mind of all negativity—forgiving everyone who's ever hurt you—helps prevent any demon from entering you through unconscious invitation."

As the speaker continued, Angela glanced at Maria from time to time, trying to read her body language, guess her thoughts.

Finally, Dr. Patterson peered out over the audience. "But the evil one's cunning. Demons can enter an unsuspecting person in many other ways, for instance through family sins." She nodded. "Just as it sounds, it's sin that's connected to you or your partner and your or their family. Every sexual union you enter binds you to the inherited sins *or demons* of your partner and their ancestors. Keep in mind, this is not only for your lifetime, but for the lifetimes of your children and their children, to the third and fourth generations. Besides using deception, demons can enter innocent children, even babies through inheritance or generational curses."

Dr. Patterson checked her watch. "We'll delve into hereditary sin after lunch, but let's take a break and meet back here in an hour."

Scoffing, Maria turned toward Angela. "What's the name of this ridiculous conference?"

"Defeating Fallen Angels."

"Defeating Fallen Angels?" Maria sneered. "It should be *Defecating* Fallen Angels. I've never heard such shi—tripe." She stood up. "What a waste of time. What a waste of money."

"Try to stay open-minded." Whispering, Dev reached over and lightly placed a hand on her arm. "If not for your own sake, for your baby's."

Maria heaved a sigh. "I'll try."

"Come on. Let's discuss it over lunch." Angela gave her a wink as they hurried toward the cafeteria. "It'll give us food for thought."

As they joined the cafeteria line, Dev glanced at Maria. "Speaking of digesting subject matter," she grinned, "I know you think this conference is hard to swallow, but are you absorbing any of it?"

Maria took a deep breath. "I'm more than skeptical. When the speaker started talking about demonization, I thought she was some kind of con artist or weird kook." She shuddered. "And the topic's frightening. It's so dark." Rolling her eyes, sighing, she shook her head.

Angela's ears perked at Maria's changed tone, but she kept her thoughts to herself.

After lunch, Dr. Patterson welcomed them back with a prayer. Then she stared out at the audience. "Addictions, what's the essence of addictions? Is it a tendency, an obsession for certain chemicals or kicks, or is it something more fundamental?

"God created us to be loving beings able to give and receive love as naturally as we breathe. During the course of our lives, many of us were handled badly, rejected, abandoned. Deprived of love, we became damaged goods, unable to give what we did not have, and eventually became unable to accept. The cause of most addictive behavior is the want of love.

"This morning, I mentioned rats feed on rubbish. Spiritual rats, that is, demons, thrive on emotional baggage. Remove that negativity, that rodent-fodder, by forgiving everyone who's ever hurt you. This prevents demons from entering by unconscious invitation. Keep in mind, rats are only the secondary problem. The fundamental issue is always the rubbish.

"This afternoon, I'll show you how to remove that rubbish. Forgive those who've mistreated you, so you'll be free to accept and give love, as well as be free of addictive behavior that stems from a lack of love.

"For this exercise, I want you to close your eyes. Imagine going back in time to the moment of your conception. See the egg in one hand, and the sperm in the other. Mentally bring the sperm to the egg, and know, from the moment of conception, *you were wanted*. Whether your mother or father meant for you to be conceived, your Heavenly Father wanted your birth. God wanted you.

"Experts say memory begins prenatally. Some say fetal memories begin recording at thirty-two weeks, others say as early as eight weeks. Picture yourself month by month inside your mother's womb. Did you feel wanted, or were you 'an accident'? Were you conceived out of wedlock? Did your parents bicker or fight during your months of gestation? Were there tears, conflict?

"Tell your inner child that all will be well. Bless your parents. Forgive them. Jeremiah chapter one, verse five, 'Before I formed you in the womb I knew you.' God has always wanted you. Accept His love and embrace the excitement of your upcoming birth. Feel the deep peace as you replace fear and rejection with love and joy.

"Imagine your birth in your mind's eye. See God as He receives you and rejoices in your birth. Your Heavenly Father loves you.

"Now picture yourself holding this newborn baby in your own hands. How do you feel? Can you love this beautiful baby? Can you love *yourself*? Can you help this child overcome any feelings of rejection? Help this child develop into the loving being God intended.

"Next, search through your earliest childhood memories. Were you mistreated, abused? Forgive that person. Gradually progress through your early days, recalling any hurts or rebuffs. Forgive those people. Release the anger. Don't wallow in it. Don't give the rats anything to feed on. Forgive everyone and everything. Remove the negativity, the rodent-fodder.

"Continue through your adolescence, recalling any painful memories and forgiving the offenders. Absolve anyone and everyone from that era who may have hurt you. Then revisit early adulthood, forgiving, releasing. Bless the experiences and the people involved. Expel all the negativity that's festered throughout the years. Let go and let God."

At the end of the regression, the speaker discussed how demons can also enter unsuspecting people through inheritance, deception, and generational curses. Finally, Dr. Patterson closed the conference with a prayer.

"Now what do you think about the conference?" Dev peered at Maria.

"At first, I thought it was all psychobabble." Her eyes narrowed as she inhaled. "But then, as I started going through the regression, I began remembering things I hadn't consciously recalled before."

"Were you able to forgive the people involved?"

A faint smile crossed Maria's face as she nodded. "When the speaker talked about God receiving me in His hands at birth, I felt so wanted, so loved."

"What about when she asked you to pick up the baby? Were you able to love your newborn self?"

Maria glanced down, focusing on her belly. "No." Then lifting her head, she looked Angela in the eye. "I knew the life that baby had in front of it."

Wincing, Dev took Maria by the hand. "Come on. There's someone I want you to meet."

Angela slung her purse on her shoulder and hurried after.

Before the speaker left the stage, Dev caught up with her. "Alma, I'd like to introduce a special lady to you, Maria Ramirez." Then glancing at Maria, she said, "This is Dr. Alma Patterson, a woman who's met with and helped over two thousand demonized persons."

Maria frowned at Dev, then forced a smile. "Pleased to meet you." Her eyes never met the speaker's.

"Call me Alma," said the woman, holding out her hand. When Maria limply shook hands, Alma nodded. Then she glanced at Dev. "How can I be of assistance?"

"Our friend," Dev inhaled, seeming to choose her words, "shows signs of what appears to be obsession."

Maria tried to pull away, but Alma held on, still politely shaking hands. "What do you have to say about this?"

Shrugging, Maria slipped her hand from Alma's light grip. "Nothing." She swallowed. "There's nothing to say, nothing to tell. Nothing." Grimacing, she rolled her eyes.

"What about what happened last week?" Angela caught her eye. "You're engaged to José, yet you couldn't explain why you were compelled to visit Mal in jail."

Alma raised her eyebrow as she glanced at Dev. "Why don't we take this conversation to a less public place?" As she led them through a hallway, into a small conference room, she continued talking. "Compelled is a word that raises flags. Maria, would you say you simply wanted to see this . . . "

"Mal," said Maria, "Malachi Straub."

"Would you say you simply wanted to see him, or you couldn't stay away from him?"

"I . . . " Blinking, her forehead furrowing, Maria seemed unable to decide.

Alma nodded and gestured toward a group of chairs. When they were seated, she said, "Let's start our conversation with a prayer." Then she led them in the Our Father. "Maria, I'm not saying you're demonized, but in case any demons are present, I want to prevent them from disturbing this ministry. Do I have your permission to speak on your behalf?"

Maria nodded.

Declaring to the surroundings, Alma laid the ground rules. "In the authority of Jesus, God, and the Holy Spirit, I prohibit any violence, profanity, or nausea. I prohibit any actions that would embarrass this person." She listened silently for a moment. Then she looked at Maria. "If my suspicions are correct, a demon is present. Do I have your permission to test this theory?"

Maria licked her lips nervously, but again nodded.

"Then please close your eyes."

Maria gave an uneasy sigh but complied.

"Spirit, I challenge you in the names of Jesus, God, and the Holy Spirit. I demand that you come to attention."

Angela looked around the room. Nothing happened.

Again Alma said quietly, "Spirit, I challenge you in the names of Jesus, God, and the Holy Spirit. I demand that you come to attention."

Maria's hand began shaking.

"Spirit that's causing that shaking, come to attention." Alma's tone was conversational, yet she spoke with authority. "In the names of Jesus, God, and the Holy Spirit, I forbid you from exerting any control over this woman."

Maria's hand stopped shaking.

"Jesus, God, and the Holy Spirit," said Alma, "we ask that you assign angels to assist this ministry." She looked at Maria. "Do you see the angels?"

Eyes still closed, Maria nodded.

Angela raised her eyebrow as she glanced at Maria. For an instant, her shadow seemed to split from her. Angela swallowed.

Alma glanced at her. "Demons often come in groups, with each group having a lead demon. It saves time to discover the lead demon and then bind the lesser demons to him."

Trying to grasp Alma's reasoning, Angela wrinkled her brow.

"Spirit of Shame, I challenge you in the names of Jesus, God, and the Holy Spirit. I demand that you come to attention."

Maria opened her eyes and glared at Alma. "*Nein!*"

Angela and Dev glanced at each other.

"Spirit of Shame, in the names of Jesus, God, and the Holy Spirit, I order all the demons in your cluster to bind together: humiliation, incompetence, hopelessness, failure, guilt, dishonesty, duplicity, and any others."

"Nein!"

"Spirit of Shame, I command you to leave this woman."

"*Warum? Ich ihr nur felfen,*" said Maria's lips with a strong German accent. Again Maria's shadow momentarily seemed to separate from her.

"English, please," said Alma calmly.

"Why? I only help her," said Maria's lips but with a strong German accent.

Angela exhaled through her mouth.

"Spirit of Shame, I command you to leave this woman."

"I don't want to leave," said Maria in a German accent. "I won't hurt her."

"For the last time," said Alma, never raising her voice. "I command you to leave this woman."

Maria flinched. Then with a groan, she grimaced.

"What just happened?" asked Alma.

Maria's natural voice said, "I felt a pain in my stomach, as if something tried to rip my baby from me, and then I pictured two hands pulling the baby back."

Alma raised her eyebrow. "Spirit of Shame, is there another group of demons present in this woman?"

"*Ja,*" said Maria with a German accent.

"What is its name?"

"*Geist des Todes.*"

"English, please."

"Spirit of Death."

"Spirit of Death," said Alma, "I order all the demons in your cluster to bind together: abortion, murder, and any others. I command you to leave this woman."

Opening her eyes wide, Maria asked in her natural voice, "Are they gone?"

Alma nodded. "Maybe, but I noticed you clasped your baby when you said you'd felt a twinge in your stomach. Your baby may have inherited family spirits or generational demons." Changing from a soft, conversational tone to one of unyielding authority, Alma said, "In the names of Jesus, God, and the Holy Spirit, I order you to tell me if you have any grip on this child of God through inheritance."

"*Ja,*" said Maria with a German accent.

Alma glanced from Angela to Dev. "Demons that enter a baby at conception come through the bloodlines."

Angela cocked her head. "You mean demons can be passed down through the generations like genetic diseases?"

Alma nodded. "Exodus chapter thirty-four, verse seven, 'visiting the iniquity of the fathers upon the children and the children's children, to the third and the fourth generation.'"

Alma turned toward Maria. "Through the mother's or the father's bloodline?"

"*Der vater.*"

"English, please." Alma's tone was patient, polite, but authoritative.

"The father.

"How many generations ago?"

"*Drei.*"

"English—"

"Three."

"In the names of Jesus, God, and the Holy Spirit, I take authority over that ancestor three generations ago through the father's line and break your power in the third, second, and first generations. In the names of Jesus, God, and the Holy Spirit, I end any power you have over this baby through your connection with this family at the moment of this child's conception."

Her nostrils flaring, Maria inhaled a deep, cleansing breath. Then she groaned with relief as she sighed. "They're gone," said her natural voice.

Alma smiled. "Good, but you'll need to heal yourself by forgiving everyone in your past who's hurt you, including this baby's father, paternal grandparents, and great-grandparents." Alma glanced at Dev and Angela. "This afternoon, we went through the healing process to rid Maria of the rubbish. Now we've driven out the rats."

Maria's forehead puckered. "How can I be sure they 'stay' gone?"

"Forgive everyone who's wronged you," said Alma. "Heal your memories. Remove all your rubbish, so the rats have nothing to feed on, so they can't return."

"But how?" Wrinkling her brow, Maria twisted the dark, curly tendrils wisping at her temples.

Angela studied her long hair. *It's nearly grown back.*

"First, know the dark one," said Alma. "Ephesians chapter six, verse twelve, 'For it is not against human enemies that we have to struggle, but against the principalities and the ruling forces who are masters of the darkness in this world, the spirits of evil in the heavens.' You have to fight what you can't see. Through deliverance, the rats, the demons have been chased out of you, but the devil will try to reenter your mind through creeping doubts."

"How do I prevent that from happening?"

"Deliverance is a process. Today was only the start. Renew your commitment to God daily. Pray to Him. Listen to Him through spiritual music, through reading your Bible. Ask the Holy Spirit to reveal any areas that are hindering you. When He highlights them, confess your sins. Then remove any demons by demanding they leave in the names of Jesus, God, and the Holy Spirit.

"Finally, pray for God's help and protection in overcoming the devil's deceits and desires. Don't let him manipulate you back into old habits." Alma shook her head. "Ephesians chapter six, verses thirteen through seventeen, 'That is why you must take up all God's armor, or you will not be able to put up any resistance on the evil day, or stand your ground even though you exert yourselves to the full. And then you must take salvation as your helmet and the sword of the Spirit, that is, the word of God'.

"Last, but not least, pray for St. Michael the Archangel to protect you." Alma handed Maria a half piece of paper with the printed prayer. "Memorize this, so you can say it in moments of danger."

Maria looked from Alma to the paper. Then she read the prayer out loud.

"St. Michael the Archangel, defend us in battle. Be our defense against the wickedness and snares of the Devil. May God rebuke him, we humbly pray, and do thou, O Prince of the heavenly hosts, by the power of God, thrust into hell Satan, and all the evil spirits, who prowl about the world seeking the ruin of souls. Amen."

Driving home, Angela and Maria were quiet. When Angela finally spoke, Maria flinched.

"Sorry, I was lost in thought."

Angela smiled. "Understandably after what we've experienced today."

"Alma got me thinking. If I need to release all pent-up negativity, I'm going to have to come to terms with my parents."

Angela nodded.

"Maybe we could meet on neutral ground at my cousin Elizabeth's in the Hill Country."

Angela glanced at her. "And wouldn't Thanksgiving be a perfect time to introduce them to their future son-in-law?"

A week later, Maria joined Tulah and Angela at the breakfast table.

Coffee cup in midair, Tulah studied her. "What are you grinning about?"

"It's all set! Elizabeth just emailed that my parents 'would be happy' to join José and me at her house for Thanksgiving."

"I'm so glad." Angela hugged her. "It's the season to make peace."

Nodding, Maria looked from her to Tulah. "What will you two be doing?"

"My family and I are having an old-fashioned, country Thanksgiving near Friedrichsly." Tulah smiled warmly.

"I'll also be in the Hill Country. My mother and I are celebrating at home," said Angela.

"We'll each be with our families. I'm glad." Maria smiled at them. Then her eyes rested on the bud-vase centerpiece with a single rose. Pulling it toward her, she inhaled. "Lately, I've been dreaming of roses nearly every night. Wonder what that means?"

Tulah shrugged. "Google it."

"Is there anything else in the dream that might give you a clue?" Angela stirred granola into her yogurt.

Maria grimaced. "There is, but it's so misty, I can't make it out." Her frown turned into a hopeful smile. "Each night, though, it gets a little clearer."

The Wednesday before Thanksgiving, Maria caught Angela before she left for school. "I finally saw it."

Angela gave her a blank stare. "Saw what?"

"Every night I've had that recurring dream, the misty image became a little clearer, but last night it finally came into focus."

"What was it?"

"It looked like Our Lady of Guadalupe but surrounded by roses, not by sun rays."

Angela gazed inwardly as she recalled the stories of her birth and adoptive mothers. "I've always felt a special bond with Our Lady." Then she turned her attention on Maria. "Did she say anything, do anything?"

"I saw a beautiful scene where pink and yellow roses were blooming alongside cactus. Then she gave me a message. 'I want very much to have a little house built here for me,' she said, 'in which I will show Him, I will exalt Him and make Him manifest.'"

"'Here' . . . where was 'here'?"

Shrugging, Maria shook her head. "I don't know. I didn't recognize it." Her eyes took on a faraway glaze. "I just remember all the roses, dozens, hundreds of roses among the prickly-pear cactus." Then she peered at Angela. "What do you think it means?"

She chuckled. "Thorns are the first things that come to mind, roses with thorns, cactus with thorns." Now it was Angela's turn to shrug. "I don't know. What was your impression? How did that place make you feel? Maybe there's a hint in that."

Maria took a deep breath. Wearing a faraway look, she seemed to search her memory. Then her face relaxed as a peaceful smile played at her lips. "The only sensation I remember is feeling at home, like I'd finally come home."

"But it was nowhere you've ever been before?"

Maria shook her head. "I'm not even sure it's a real place. Maybe it was just a dream."

"Maybe," Angela gave her a mischievous grin, "and maybe not. You never know."

Thanksgiving morning, Angela and Judith went to Mass. The second reading was from first Corinthians. "I give thanks to my God always." Then the Gospel Acclamation was from first Thessalonians. "In all circumstances, give thanks, for this is the will of God for you in Christ Jesus . . . that you are not lacking in any spiritual gift . . . "

"Today's second reading is one the most beautiful chapters in the bible," said the priest. "The Corinthians had been torn by discord; various groups boasted their gift was better than another group's gift. Paul made it clear: There are many gifts but one Spirit. Each gift plays a role in building up the whole Body of Christ. We're many parts but all one body.

"Spiritual gifts are evidence God's filled us with His Spirit, but the Bible warns us they're temporary. This is where the gifts differ from the fruit of the Spirit. The fruit of faith, hope, and love remain long after the gifts have faded away. The gifts are God-given tools to inspire others to have faith, but to *live* your faith, you must bear fruit.

"If I speak without love, I am no more than a gong booming or a cymbal clashing. And though I have all the faith necessary to move mountains, if I am without love, I am nothing. Only these remain: faith, hope and love. Of the three of them, the greatest is love."

Nodding to herself, Angela thought of Maria and the fruits of the Holy Spirit as the priest finished his homily. Then her mind drifted back to Archbishop Garcia-Siller's sermon. "Meaning *thanksgiving*, the Eucharist is a sign of oneness. Pray for a spirited communion of women."

That Saturday, Kio picked up Angela at her mother's.

"We're going to the caverns." Angela smiled at her. "Would you like to come with us?"

"No, thank you." Judith gave a rueful chuckle. "Tripping over uneven walkways in dark caves isn't my idea of a good time. You two go on and have fun."

Angela kissed her cheek. "Okay, we should be back early." She waved as she stepped into the car.

Before he started the engine, Kio leaned over the center console and hugged her. "How was your Thanksgiving?"

"It was good, morning Mass followed by dinner. The best part was catching up with Mom," Angela gave him a wry grin, "which is ironic because she's definitely slowing down. She took so many naps these past two days, I finished my term paper a week ahead of schedule."

He chuckled.

She smiled to herself, remembering. "But I've enjoyed talking with her and watching old movies while we sipped cocoa in our pajamas. It's been like old times, cozy, low key." She turned toward him a warm smile. "How 'bout you? How was your Thanksgiving?"

"Not too different, except for watching stars through a telescope instead of watching television. You know. My father's an ardent stargazer."

Sunday night, Angela met Maria at their apartment door with a hug. "How did it go with your family?"

"They love José. He's the son they've always wanted." Maria gave a wry smile. "He's my ticket for getting along with my family. It's something like: love me; love my dog. Only in José's case, it's: love my fiancé; love me. In fact, things went so well, they want us to get married in Alpine instead of at Mission San José."

Angela raised her eyebrow. "Is that what you and José want?"

Maria sighed. "Both our families are from the Alpine area." Giving a lopsided smile, she shrugged. "It makes sense to have our wedding there instead of in San Antonio."

"But?"

"Whether it's because they want to make up for their actions last July or who knows what, they and José's family are insisting on throwing me a wedding shower."

Arching her eyebrow, Angela gave her a puzzled smile. "What's wrong with that?"

"The date is what's wrong. They want to hold it on the twenty-fifth."

"Christmas Day?"

Nodding slowly, Maria peered hard at her. "That would mean spending Christmas in Alpine with José's and my families instead of with your mother."

"Ah." Angela exhaled as the impact registered. "I see what you mean, although Mom had mentioned something about Ceren inviting her to spend Christmas in Houston." She winked. "Let me check."

"Great!" Maria's eyes sparkled. "Incidentally, I had another dream about Our Lady of Guadalupe and the roses."

"Any insights?"

"Possibly." First spreading her arms, she then brought her hands together. "From a wide-angled field of roses, the scene gradually shrank until it was a close-up of two, entwined roses, one pink and one yellow."

"What do you think that means?"

She chuckled. "I Googled their symbolism. A pink rose means 'love that's hopeful and expectant,' and a yellow rose means 'promise of a new beginning.' Two interlaced roses mean marriage."

"Don't forget the yellow rose of Texas." Angela grinned. "You can't work at the Alamo without that image entering into it."

Then Maria's eyes opened wide as she gasped. "I just remembered something else about the dream. Our Lady of Guadalupe repeated her words. 'I want very much to have a little house built here for me.'" Maria's eyes homed in on Angela's. "I can't help but feel she's giving me a message."

Angela smiled gently. "Maybe this gradual clarity of her intentions, these recurring dreams are providing you with another fruit of the Spirit: patience."

Her eyes shining, Maria nodded. "Maybe. if so, I'll have love, joy, peace, and now patience."

On the first Saturday of December, Angela and Maria joined the other employees at the Alamo. Wearing period costumes, they helped transform the grounds back to the 1830s through reenactments, special demonstrations, and craft-making exhibitions.

"As we travel back in time," said Maria, leading a group of tourists. "You'll learn about life in frontier Texas."

"This history talk sounds interesting," José said loudly for the onlookers' benefit. "Let's join it." He winked at Maria. Lowering his voice, he spoke to Kio and Angela. "Then let's catch Angela's corn husk doll demonstration."

"Actually, it's an activity." Angela grinned. "Rather than be by-standers, I want you each to make a corn husk doll. Lead by ex-ample."

Kio eyed the antique gun collection. "Just so long as we don't miss the flintlock rifle or live black-powder firing demonstrations."

"Or the reenactment story of the Alamo's siege and battle, the Battle of Béjar." José rubbernecked as he watched the actors set up.

Shaking her head, Angela chuckled. "Don't worry. You'll have time for it all before the *Fiesta de las Luminarias*. We don't close until five."

"Which is when the Béjar Fandango begins." José's eyes lit up.

"You'd mentioned that before." Angela glanced at him. "What is it again?"

"The Béjar Historical Society's living history interpreters are celebrating the 180th anniversary of the Texan victory at the Battle of Béjar with period dancing. The San Antonio Contra Dancers are providing live music and instruction starting at five, right here on the grounds of the Alamo."

"And sunset's at five-thirty-five." Kio winked at her. "Perfect timing for dinner along the River Walk when they light the six thousand luminarias."

At five, they heard the sound of fiddles coming from the Cavalry Courtyard. They hurried through the Alamo Gardens and arrived in time to see the musicians warming up. Men and women in el-egant period costumes mingled with people wearing tee shirts and jeans.

The emcee called from the stage. "Choose your partners. Gen-tlemen on the left. Ladies on the right."

A bewhiskered man in an old-fashioned, poor-boy cap, vest, and vintage poet shirt with gathered balloon sleeves held out his right elbow to Angela. "Ladies on the right."

Angela glanced at Kio, saw him grin, and shrugged. "Sure. Why not?" Laughing, she took the old man's arm as he led her in front of the stage.

Looking behind her, Angela saw that other historical reenactors had also picked partners from the bystanders. Although José took Maria as his partner, a woman dressed as the 'Yellow Rose of Texas' chose Kio as hers. They shared a grin as the emcee called instructions.

"Form long lines, with the men on the left and the women on the right. Now take three steps forward. Bow or curtsey, and then take three steps back. Take three steps forward and take your partner's left forearm. Turn completely around, let go, and take three steps back. Then allemande right."

They practiced slowly several times, and then the music began. The fiddlers began playing faster and faster. After a few minutes, the emcee added more instructions.

"In groups of four, take three steps forward. Bow or curtsey, and then take three steps back."

Angela found herself in a foursome with the bewhiskered man, Kio, and the 'Yellow Rose of Texas.' They followed the emcee's instructions as she added more intricate steps.

"Now put your right hands together and turn to the right, making a circle until you return to your starting point. Do the same with your left hands. Then pass through that couple, on to the next."

Changing partners, swinging from one hand to the next, they danced for a half hour until the fiddlers took a short break. As Angela caught her breath, she looked around the Cavalry Courtyard. It was dusk. Beyond the Alamo's stone walls, she saw the city putting on its Christmas night finery as the lights came on.

Kio glanced at his phone. "Time to go if we want to make our reservation."

Nodding, they said goodbye to their costumed dance partners, found José and Maria, and left through the Alamo Gardens. As they started toward the River Walk, Angela looked over her shoulder at the lighted Christmas tree contrasted against the illuminated Alamo. The moon slowly climbed above its limestone facade. "Oh, look."

Maria sighed. "The Alamo's so majestic at night."

"Especially when it's dressed for the holidays." Angela glanced at the Christmas tree's sports-motif decorations.

They took a shortcut to the River Walk through the stepped fountains of the Paseo Del Alamo and found a table beneath massive, twinkling trees. After they ordered drinks, they looked at the millions of colorful lights encrusting the trunks and branches of the ancient cypresses. More strings of colored lights streamed from the uppermost boughs, raining down light that doubled in the water's reflection. Even the graceful, arched bridges were decked out in string lights, their images creating mirrored ovals of illumination on the river.

They watched as the candles were lit in sand-filled paper bags. One by one, the luminarias began glowing until the banks of the San Antonio River were lined with light. Couples of all ages walked by, some hand in hand, some single file, some wearing what looked like tall chef's hats. Families pushing baby buggies strolled past them. Groups of uniformed men and women joined the *paseo*.

As they surveyed the leisurely parade of people, Maria turned to José. "What's the story of luminarias?"

"Some say the candlelit bags are meant to 'light the way' for reenactments of *Las Posadas* as the Holy Family searches for an inn. Others believe they're meant to guide the Christ child." José grinned. "Still others contend luminarias should be called *farolitos*, Spanish for 'little lanterns.'"

"Whatever the reason or name, their warm glow sure makes the River Walk inviting." Moving her chair closer to his, Maria leaned into him.

River boats decorated with colorful Christmas lights floated by. Each carried Christmas carolers, Latino ensembles, folk groups, or bell choirs from nearly two hundred school, church, and civic choral groups, ringing in the season. From the patios above, they heard visitors singing 'It's Beginning to Look a Lot Like Christmas.' Grinning at each other, they joined them in a spontaneous sing-a-long. When it ended, they cheered and raised their glasses in a mutual toast.

Angela watched the procession of boats and people. "Just like this promenade, life's a journey. Even our Mission Reach pilgrimage along the River Walk was a journey."

"And don't forget, Advent started last Sunday." Kio looked from the paseo to her. "Advent's a journey. Think of it: Joseph and Mary's journey to Bethlehem, the three wise men's search for the King, the shepherds' first seeking Jesus in the manger and then going out to spread the good news. Those were all journeys of faith."

"Besides a journey, Advent is waiting for the coming of the Christ child." Glancing at José, Maria added in a shy whisper, "Advent is waiting for the coming of our child."

Smiling, he took her hand in his. "It's a journey, but it's also a time of preparation and expectation."

Angela grinned. "Advent's an *advent*-ure."

"I heard of a prayer journey for Advent. A church in my neighborhood is holding it tomorrow night." José watched their expressions. "Would you like to go on a prayer journey?"

Glancing at each other, they nodded.

"It also happens to be the Feast Day of St. Nicholas." José grinned. "Afterwards, let's go to my place for home-made Christmas cookies and hot apple cider."

On December sixth, Angela and Maria attended a Mariachi Mass at Mission Concepción. The limestone chapel was brightly sunlit from the dome above. Enjoying the interplay of rustic and refined, Angela slowly scanned the sanctuary as they waited for Mass to begin. Vases of roses lined the altar's tiers. Incense smoldered, along with traces of sage, sweet grass, and copal. Taking a deep breath, she inhaled the fragrant air. The scents permeated the ancient chapel.

Alongside her, Maria leaned over to whisper. "After all my dreams about Our Lady of Guadalupe, I want to celebrate the Dance to Mary with the *Matachines*."

Angela cocked her head. "The what?"

"The *Matachines'* dance drama," said Maria. "Though it's rooted in Europe's Middle Ages, it's a traditional dance in the Hispanic Southwest."

"From the looks of this chapel, you're not the only one who wants to celebrate. It's standing room only." Angela glanced around the church. People were packed into the wooden pews. Folding chairs had been set up near the altar, and still people were standing three deep at the back.

One wizened woman caught her eye and smiled sweetly. Blinking, trying to recall her, Angela politely smiled back. *She looks familiar, but from where?*

Then the Mariachi musicians in their elaborate charro outfits began playing. Violins, base fiddles, guitars, mandolins, and trumpets announced Mass with a stylized entrance hymn, calling everyone to attention. Caught up in the pageantry, Angela forgot the woman.

After communion, Maria whispered, "I need some air."

"Are you all right?"

"I'm fine. The incense is just so strong, I can see it. I need a breath of fresh air."

Angela looked at the nearly blue air. "Want me to go—"

"No." She shook her head. "Stay till the end. I'll meet you out front."

As Mass let out, Angela left the chapel through the ancient, carved doors. Looking about the courtyard, she saw Maria talking to the small, wizened woman.

There's something familiar about her, but what?

Then the sun highlighted a gold armband encircling the woman's thin bicep. In its play of light, the serpentine armband seemed to wriggle.

Angela gasped as she recognized the old woman. *Toci.* She rushed across the crowded courtyard, but before she could reach them, the woman handed Maria something, turned, and with a smile to Angela, disappeared into the crowd of gathering dancers.

Maria held up a rosary as she approached. "Look what some lady gave me."

Angela looked around, but the woman was nowhere to be seen. "Did she tell you her name?"

"No." Smiling, Maria shrugged. "We just started a conversation while we were waiting for Mass to end."

"What did she have to say?"

"We were talking about the baby's due date. When I told her January 22nd, she gave me a knowing grin, winked, and handed me this rosary. 'What do doctors know?' she said. 'This is for the baby *whenever* he comes.' Then she placed her hands in front of my belly. 'Never forget, the womb is a sacred space. Have a safe delivery.'" Maria's lips lifted in a half smile. "I've gone from getting deliverance to receiving a delivery blessing."

Angela arched her eyebrow as she looked from Maria to the rosary. "This looks like an antique."

The Aves were frosty rose, vintage beads. Gold filigree capped the Pater beads swirling with gold and pink flame-worked roses. Instead of a crucifix, a medal of Our Lady of Guadalupe standing above a crescent moon hung from the end of the pendant.

"With all the roses and the image of Our Lady, it's a perfect gift to remember today and that sweet lady. In fact," Maria nodded, "I'll carry it with my bouquet at our wedding."

Angela smiled to herself as she thought aloud. "Toci is a sweet lady."

"Toci? Who's Toci?"

"Something tells me she was the woman who gave you this. She taught me all through my early childhood." Angela smiled to herself, fondly remembering. "Call it what you want—daydreams, angels, spirits—but until I was seven, Toci narrated 'videos' only I could see or hear."

Maria studied her. "Maybe this woman today just reminded you of . . . your narrator. Besides, how do you know you didn't dream those 'memories'?"

Angela raised her eyebrow. "You can't 'dream up' the knowledge she shared with me." Angela fondled the glass rosary. "Her lessons were just as tangible as these beads."

As she returned the prayer beads to Maria, she looked about the courtyard. Dancers were assembling in their separate groups. To her left, she saw religious performers in red outfits with the sequined emblems of Guadalupe printed on their black boleros. Dancers wearing blue costumes with the Aztec sun motif assembled near a troupe of yellow-and-red-costumed dancers. A group with hollow bone beads that rattled with each movement put the final touches on each other's regalia. Dancers with festive feather head-dresses practiced their steps as they stamped their feet and shook their gourd rattles. Spiritual dancers in red outfits with feathered diadems began warming up to the beat of their drummer.

A sprightly dancer wearing an old man's mask and a poncho began teasing and provoking the groups with his fancy footwork. Despite the various colors, shells, beads, feathers, and intricate needlework, each member of every group displayed a picture of Our Lady of Guadalupe. A group of barefoot children with long braids carried prayer candles and the letters PAZ festooned with red garlands. Mission Concepción's group of dancers with blue headdresses with pink, white, and gold feathers posed for a picture. To their delight, another person wearing an old man's mask and a costume of colorful but tattered strips of cloth comically sprawled on the grass in front of them.

Angela asked one of the bystanders, "Who's the masked person supposed to be?"

"He's one of the devils," said the woman. "At the end of the Danza to Mary, all the devils are destroyed."

Then a feather-costumed man blew into a conch shell. Angela thought it sounded like a cross between a trumpet and a foghorn. As people began lining up, she turned again to the woman. "What's happening now?"

"The curandero—"

"The what?" Angela glanced at her.

"The curandero, the shaman, just signaled the procession to begin."

Group by group, they lined up, each dancing stylized steps to the beat of their own drummer. Angela and Maria followed behind the woman's group, dancing along in triplet steps, imitating the troupe's moves as best they could.

Then Angela noticed another dancer in front of them. Remembering the stories Toci, Ceren, and her mother had told her, she whispered, "Look at his legs." Tattooed on the backs of his calves were Aztec symbols. Half-covering the tattoos, he wore white socks, each decorated with the picture of Our Lady of Guadalupe.

Maria glanced at them and, shrugging, looked to Angela for an explanation.

"The Guadalupe socks go on and come off." Angela smiled. "More than skin deep, the Aztec tattoos are a part of him. He dances for Guadalupe, but I suspect Tonantzin is rooted in his worldview."

As police monitored the traffic, they processed across Mission Road, taking the path alongside Theo Parkway. Across the street, people gathered outside their houses to watch. Cars pulled up and parked as the drivers and passengers gawked.

Then Angela noticed a man in a wide-brimmed Stetson, standing on the sidelines, not watching the parade so much as studying Maria. *What's he doing?* Angela moved to the outside of the sidewalk, protectively placing herself between the observer and Maria. From the tilt of his hat, Angela realized he had turned his head to glance at her. Though the hat shaded his features, she sensed his eyes on her.

Despite the sunny day and temperature in the low seventies, Angela shuddered. Tearing her eyes from him, she followed the procession to the San Antonio River, circling around Concepción Park to East Theo Avenue and then returning to the mission.

As the groups danced into the assembling throng of people in the courtyard, Angela heard a cacophony of drums, rattles, bells, jangling shells, a conch-shell horn, and all kinds of hand-made clacking instruments. Hundreds of costumed dancers wearing feathers, beads, shells, and bone reminded her of a Native American pow-wow but with a symbolism she recognized. The enthusiastic dancing was religious. They danced for the Virgin Mary, the mother of Jesus.

Angela and Maria found seats inside the church beside the woman. Group by group, each troupe step-step-sashayed up the aisle to the altar and zealously danced beneath the watchful gaze of Our Lady of Guadalupe's 1750s painting and the Immaculate Conception's 19th century painting.

Angela whispered to the woman. "What are they doing now?"

She leaned over to explain. "It's a *promesa*, a religious pilgrimage to thank God for answered prayers and a sacred dance to honor Our Lady. Tuesday is the feast day of the Immaculate Conception, and Saturday is the feast day of Our Lady of Guadalupe."

That evening, the four of them met in front of José's neighborhood church for the prayer journey. They studied the poster with the journey's route through the church's interior and read the explanation beneath.

To enrich your Advent journey and preparations for Christmas, stop at each station, participate in the activity, and reflect on the prayer. Please observe silence, and progress at your own pace. This is a personal journey.

As they stopped inside the church, they saw the first station with a sign. *What hopes, aspirations, or expectations do you have as Christmas approaches?*

They glanced at each other but kept silent.

Above a bowl of seeds, they saw the activity's instructions. *As a symbol of your hopes, take a seed and plant it in the tray of soil.*

Each pressed a tiny seed into the soil as they silently read the prayer. *From small beginnings come great things. From an acorn, an oak. From a drop of rain, a deluge. From a spark, a fire. From a seed, a harvest. From a step, a journey.*

One by one, they progressed to the second station's sign. *What burdens do you carry? What weighs heavily on your mind, on your heart?*

Above a basket of stones, they saw the activity's instructions. *Take a stone as a symbol of your burden, and give it to Jesus by placing it in the tray.*

Each picked up a stone. Angela held hers a moment as she recalled the worries she wanted to let go. She thought of Gabe's spirit and Mal's tortured soul. With a sigh, she gently placed her stone on top of the pile.

In their own time, each walked to the third station. Above a bare Jesse tree was a sign. *Who shares your journey?*

Beneath the tree were pencils and small papers shaped like leaves attached to strings. *Write the names of your loved ones on a leaf and hang it on the tree. These names will be remembered in prayers throughout the Advent season.*

Her pencil midair, Angela thought of her mother and birthmother, Ceren. Then Gabe, Maria, and José came to mind. When she glanced at Kio, she smiled, wrote on the paper leaf, and hung it from a branch. Before moving on, she read Saint Francis's prayer.

Lord, make me an instrument of Your peace;
Where there is hatred, let me sow love;
Where there is injury, pardon;
Where there is doubt, faith;
Where there is despair, hope;
Where there is darkness, light;
And where there is sadness, joy.
O Divine Master, grant that I may not so much seek to be con-
soled as to console;
To be understood as to understand;
To be loved, as to love;
For it is in giving that we receive;
It is in pardoning that we are pardoned;
And it is in dying that we are born to eternal life.

The fourth station was the altar. A large crèche was set up with Mary, Joseph, the angel Gabriel, shepherds, and wise men. Only the manger was empty in anticipation of the coming Christ child.

Spend time with God this Advent, read the sign. *Rest in His presence, in His strength.*

At the fifth station, Angela smiled to herself. Above a bowl of wrapped candies was a heart-shaped sign. *Know God's love for you, and take it with you.*

She helped herself to a heart-shaped mint and walked to the sixth station.

Below a light-bulb shaped sign was bowl of unlit votive candles. *Jesus lights our way. Take His light along your journey, and be a light in this world.*

Grinning to herself, Angela placed a tea-light votive candle in her jacket's pocket. Once outside, she turned to the others. "That last light-bulb shaped sign said it all, José. Great idea! I'm so glad you suggested it."

Smiling, he held up his tea light. "It's better to light one candle than curse the darkness." Grinning, he added, "Now for the St. Nicholas Christmas cookies and hot apple cider."

Chapter 9

*"Strategy without tactics is the slowest route to victory.
Tactics without strategy is the noise before defeat."*
— SUN TZU

"Do you hear that?" Her head cocked, Maria's ears perked.

"Hear what?" Angela listened.

"Glenn Frey's song, 'You Belong To the City.'" Taking a breath, Maria grimaced. "I don't know if I'm losing my mind or what, but I've been hearing that song all day."

"Maybe you've got the tune stuck in your head, and you only think you're hearing it."

Maria frowned. "I swear I've been hearing that song since we started work this morning."

Angela strained to listen. "Yeah, now that I know what I'm listening for, I do hear it faintly." She shrugged as she glanced around the Alamo's courtyard. "Maybe it's somebody's radio."

She shook her head. "I don't know, but it's creeping me out."

Angela looked at her narrowed eyes and worried brow. "Why?"

"That was Mal's song." Maria glanced around. "I can't shake the feeling that he's here, watching me."

Angela smiled. "Luckily, that's impossible. Mal's behind bars."

Shrugging, Maria ran her hand over the back of her neck. "I can't explain it. I just feel his presence, like he wants me to know he's here, yet he doesn't want me to see him."

Lifting her head, Angela took a deep breath. "Like he wants to control you."

"Exactly." Her eyes darting about the crowded courtyard, Maria glanced at each face, as if looking for Mal.

Forcing a chuckle, Angela tried to laugh it off. "Like I said, it's impossible. Mal's safely behind bars."

"Wish I could shake this feeling."

"It's only two hours till the Alamo closes. Focus on your next tour, and try to put it out of your mind."

"I suppose you're right." Nodding, Maria reached into her knapsack. "But I could use a sugar boost. Want one of José's Christmas cookies?"

"Sure."

Maria's expression changed as she felt inside her bag. Then she pulled out a CD. Turning it over, she read the label. "'You Belong To the City.'" Her eyes wide, she looked left and right. "He's here. Somehow, Mal got this into my bag."

"Wait a minute." Angela put her hand on Maria's shoulder. "Mal's in jail. He can't be here—"

"Then he's paid someone to watch me, sneak this into my bag . . . maybe follow me around, playing that song." Maria's eyes reflected sheer terror.

"Take a deep breath. You're surrounded by park rangers. You're safe here at the Alamo. Nobody can hurt you."

"But Mal's proved he can get to me here. Don't forget. He's got ties to that cartel."

"Obviously friends in low places." Angela grimaced. "It does seem he's trying to scare you, but that's all it is: scare tactics. Like I said, you're safe at the Alamo. Try to relax. No one can harm you here."

Shaking her head, Maria sighed. "I hope you're right, but . . . " She scowled.

"Your blood sugar's just low. Have a cookie. Sit down a minute, and catch your breath before your next tour."

Maria's phone rang. No ring tone. Blinking, she looked at Angela and gulped. "I don't recognize the number. What if it's him?"

Wearing a crooked grin, Angela tried to joke. "*He*. What if it's he?"

Maria looked at her with wounded eyes.

"Sorry." Chastened, Angela added, "Want me to answer it?"

With a woebegone expression, Maria nodded.

"Hello?" Angela grinned as she recognized the voice and handed Maria the phone. "It's José."

Taking the phone, relief flooded Maria's face. Her pinched eyes crinkled into smile lines. "Am I ever glad to hear from you, but I didn't recognize the number." Nodding, she whispered to Angela as she covered the speaker. "He's calling from work." Then as she listened, her smile drooped, and she turned pale. "I will, thanks." Her jaw slack, her eyes wide, she looked at Angela.

"What?"

"Detective Hadd just called José. Mal's escaped."

Tuesday, the four of them met for a picnic lunch in Mission Concepción's courtyard. Maria and Angela brought sandwiches. José brought Christmas cookies, and Kio brought tangerines and cool drinks.

"You've been talking about the illumination at Mission Concepción for the past week." Maria glanced from Kio to Angela and back to Kio. "What's so special about it?"

"Solar geometry." Kio pointed to the dome. "These mission churches were positioned so sunlight would stream through the windows and illuminate a certain feature, artwork, or tabernacle on a particular date, usually the feast day of a saint. Today's the Feast of the Immaculate Conception, this mission's namesake. Saturday's the Feast of the Virgin of Guadalupe."

Angela smiled at Kio before turning toward Maria. "We were here for the Feast of the Assumption, and the illumination was spectacular." She pointed at the mission. "The sunlight flowed through that round window above the door. It crawled across the flagstone floor, up the altar, illuminating Mary's face in a painting behind the altar and a starburst just above it. At the same time, another sunbeam shone through the sanctuary's dome and lit the floor in front of the altar, exactly at the center of this cross-shaped church."

"It's amazing the designers of Mission Concepción knew how to position the church and time the sunlight to this feast day." Maria's eyes traveled to the conical window above the front door. "Will the sun be coming in from the same window today?"

"No, this time it comes from the dome's south window. Then it crosses to the altar in the north transept." Kio pointed out the light's path with his hand. "On the winter solstice, the light crosses over the face and tabernacle to reach the top of the north altar. The docent called it the midwinter 'Resurrection' illumination."

"Remember, the sun was a heavenly metaphor for Christ, the Light of the World," said Angela. "*Christus Sol.*"

Kio nodded. "The winter solstice celebrates the end of darkness, the coming of light, the sun. It's a spiritual metaphor for the coming of Christ, the Resurrection, and salvation."

"What time does that happen?" José looked at them.

As Kio glanced at an app, his finger scrolled through the pages. "On the solstice, it happens at twelve forty-seven. On Saturday, the Feast of the Virgin of Guadalupe, it happens at twelve forty-two. And today the sun moves across the north altar at twelve forty."

"Yikes!" José glanced at his watch. "We'd better hurry if we want to see it."

They gobbled their sandwiches and hurried toward the entrance.

Just in front of church's heavy front door, Angela saw a woman selling shells on golden cords. "What are these?"

"These are symbols of the *Camino de las Misiónes*," said the woman. "With the World Heritage designation, San Antonio begins a new camino to honor the missions."

José nodded as he inspected the decal-decorated shell. "I've heard of these." He turned toward the group. "Just as the pilgrims wear seashells as they walk the *Camino de Santiago* in Spain to honor St. James the Apostle, we can wear these shells as we finish walking the Mission Trail."

"But why shells?" Maria took a closer look at the package in José's hands.

"It's a symbol of baptism. You'll see shell motifs all through Mission Concepción. I'll show you when we go inside." Then getting an idea, Angela spoke to the saleswoman. "I'll take four." Turning back to her friends, she grinned. "Consider this an early Christmas present."

Donning the shell pendants, they entered the church through the heavy wooden door. Angela led them into the baptistery, the room at the right, and pointed to the carved stone baptismal font.

"Here's an example of the shell motif."

Then they walked down the aisle just as the sun crossed the altar in the north transept.

Angela held Kio's hand while they watched. Smiling, she leaned close to whisper. "Our second illumination together."

He gave her hand a friendly squeeze as he returned her smile. "Who knows? Maybe this will shed more light on where we're headed."

Lifting her eyebrow, she pulled her head back to study him. "What do you mean?"

"Saturday I graduate," he whispered. "That'll leave only one of us in school. Maybe it's time to start thinking about our future."

She gave him a mischievous grin, then took a deep breath as if making up her mind. "Mmmmaybe."

As Angela drove them back to the Alamo for their afternoon shift, she told Maria about it.

Maria's eyes lit up. "Did Kio propose?"

"Not exactly," Angela gave her an impish grin as she turned into the parking lot, "but he sure was hinting."

An hour later, Maria rushed into the Alamo's gift shop.

One look at her red eyes told Angela something was wrong. "What's happened?"

Sobbing, catching her breath, Maria tried to speak but could not.

"Let's go where we can talk." Her arm around her shoulders, Angela guided her into the back room. "What's the matter?"

Sobbing, she said, "Mal."

"What about him?"

"He . . . he's here." She took a jagged breath.

"Here, at the Alamo?"

Maria nodded and then shook her head. "Not inside the grounds, but out front, by the Christmas tree."

"You saw him?"

"As I ended the tour, a man joined my group. I couldn't see his face. He kept his head down, hidden behind a wide-brimmed Stetson." She drew another jagged breath. "After everyone left, he pushed up the brim of his hat, and I recognized him."

Her shoulders slumping, Angela remembered the man in the hat from the parade's spectators. "What did you do?"

"I froze. I wanted to run, but I . . . I couldn't. I was in shock. It was like my muscles shut down, like in a nightmare. I couldn't move." Her eyes wide, she kept looking from Angela to the door, as if half-expecting to see Mal.

"Did he say anything? Do anything?"

She nodded. "He looked at my belly and sneered. 'You don't get off that easy,' he said. 'That baby you're carrying is mine. I'm going to be a part of his life and a part of your life till death do us part.'"

"Whoa." Angela quickly exhaled.

"Then he said, 'I've been watching you . . . *and* your boyfriend. I'll keep on watching you, but you won't know when. You won't know where, so don't even *think* of calling the cops. If you do . . .'" She choked back tears. "He said, 'Your boyfriend gets what *you* deserve.'" Tears streaming down her face, she looked at Angela. "What do I do?"

"Oh, Maria." Sighing, Angela put her arms around her. "We've got to call the police."

"No!" Maria's eyes opened wide. "We can't. Mal will kill José!"

"From what you've told me, he will if we *don't* bring in the authorities." Angela arched her eyebrow. "Why don't you call José, while I get our things? Tell him what's happened. Ask him to contact Detective Hadd but to keep everything quiet. We can't have any squad cars pulling up to the Alamo with sirens blaring."

Nodding, Maria brushed the tears from her face and dialed José.

As Angela gathered their belongings, she saw Gabe and did a double-take. He had changed so much, he looked exactly like José. Gone were the tattoos and sneer.

You know what's happened?

He nodded. "Don't worry. Just pass my information on to Charlie when he gets here. We'll catch Pretty Boy."

Is Mal still here?

"He's by the Christmas tree out front." Gabe grimaced. "My guess is he's waiting for Maria. When Charlie arrives, here's what you do."

Angela, Maria, José, Detective Hadd, and another detective huddled in the Alamo's storeroom.

Detective Hadd's expression was grim. "The plaza out front is thick with plainclothesmen. They have the suspect's description, and they know his whereabouts. Your only task is to draw him out in the open."

"Like a cockroach from the woodwork." Maria gave him a sour smile. "I'm the bug bait."

"Tell her to stand near the Christmas tree, pretend she's waiting for someone," said Gabe.

Angela relayed his message.

"Then what?" Maria's forehead crinkled.

"He'll come," said Gabe, "like a moth to the flame."

Again Angela relayed his message.

"I'll take the flame image over bug bait." Maria gave a cynical smile.

All business, Detective Hadd glanced at Angela. "Are we set?"

Angela looked at Gabe.

He nodded. "He's still there."

Angela bobbed her head. "It's time."

"Walk slowly, leisurely." Detective Hadd gave Maria last minute instructions. "Act like you're waiting for a ride, but you have some time to kill."

"Not the best choice of words." Her shoulders slumping, Maria grimaced.

José stifled a sigh as he reached for her hand.

"This should only take a few minutes," said Detective Hadd. "As soon as he makes contact with you, my men will surround him."

Maria nodded as she slipped the rosary over her head, wearing it like a necklace. Then she hugged José and started for the door.

Angela reached for her hand and whispered. "I think the Holy Spirit's anointed you with another fruit of the Spirit: self-control."

Maria squeezed her hand, took a deep breath, and then walked outside.

After a few minutes of silence, Angela turned toward Gabe. *What's happening?*

"Pretty Boy's watching her, but he hasn't made a move."

Then they heard Maria scream.

Angela turned to Gabe, but he was gone. Feeling helpless, she looked from Detective Hadd to José.

"I can't stand by and do nothing." José bolted out the door.

Angela hesitated only a moment before following. They ran through the exit in time to see Mal holding Maria like a human shield, her arm pinioned behind her back.

"Back off!" He warned the gathering crowd as he twisted her arm. Forced to comply, Maria winced with each step.

A car in the passing lane slowed and then stopped on the Alamo Plaza. When the passenger door opened, Mal began backing toward it. Never taking his eyes off the crowd, ignoring the traffic, he used Maria as a buffer.

Powerless, Angela and José watched from the sidelines. While Mal manhandled Maria, he continued backing toward the getaway car. He crossed a lane of moving traffic as a car sped toward them, apparently unaware of the drama.

A man shouted. "Watch out!"

At the last moment, Mal shoved Maria in front of the oncoming vehicle, jumped into the waiting car, and slammed the door as the getaway car peeled away.

The crowd gasped as she tumbled onto the street in front of the oncoming vehicle.

Closing one eye, Angela froze as she heard Maria scream.

The approaching car fishtailed, threatening to jump the curb, scattering onlookers in all directions. Burning rubber as its brakes grabbed hold, the car screeched to a stop in front of Maria's prone body.

The getaway car backfired, sounding like a gun shot. Onlookers ducked and took cover. The car then coughed and sputtered to a stop several feet down the road. Semi-automatics drawn, officers moved in on the car from all sides.

As the police apprehended the driver, Mal jumped out the passenger door. At gunpoint, he shoved a motor scooter driver off his vehicle and hopped on, speeding away between lanes of traffic.

José helped Maria to her feet. "Are you all right?"

She nodded as she wordlessly picked something up from the ground. Then hugging Jose, Maria fingered the rosary around her neck.

Gabe stood beside them, grinning mischievously as he caught Angela's eye.

What happened to the getaway car?

He grinned. "They just don't make fuel pumps the way they used to."

What about Mal? He's a threat to Maria and José while he's loose, and now he's escaped a second time.

"He's slippery, but his luck can't hold out forever. Be right back."

*Where are you go—*Angela realized he was gone.

Back at the apartment, Maria showed them what she had picked up.

Angela looked at the downy white feather. "You found this in the street?"

Her jaw slack, a look of wonder on her face, Maria nodded. "It's an angel's feather." Then her lip curled in loathing. "When Mal pushed me in front of the car, I thought that was the end."

José grimaced. "What went through your mind?"

"Besides my life flashing in front of my eyes?" Her smile was cynical. "I grabbed the rosary and said a quick prayer to Saint Michael to protect me."

José shook his head. "I should never have let them put you in danger."

"It's all right." Maria gently touched his shoulder as she glanced from him to Angela to the feather. "Either the Archangel Michael, or my guardian angel was with me."

He took a deep breath. "If anything had happened to you or the baby, I couldn't have forgiven myself."

"An angel was protecting me."

He gave her a wry smile. "How do you know that?"

"Though Mal pushed me, I didn't fall. I felt something catch me and gently lower me to the ground." She smiled. "Besides that, how else can you account for the way the oncoming car fishtailed and then stopped so suddenly? Or how the getaway car *didn't*? It had to be an angel."

Angela met Gabe's twinkling eyes. "It's as good an explanation as any."

"This is proof." Maria held up the feather as she recited, "When an angel's near, feathers appear."

"Can I see that a minute?" By twisting its tip, José twirled the feather between his fingers. "This looks like a Snowy Egret's tail feather."

"An egret?" Maria scoffed. "Egrets don't fly around San Antonio."

A smile tugged at the corner of his mouth. "Actually, they do. Though they're native to the coast, they show up just about anywhere between the gulf and San Antonio, wherever you see a river, creek, pond, marsh, or ditch."

Her eyes narrowing, Maria studied him. "You don't believe this is an angel's feather, do you?" Peeved, she pressed her lips together tightly. "Fine. You believe what you want, and I'll believe what I want. I'm convinced it was an angel that set me down gently, prevented the car from running me over, stopped the getaway car, and left this feather."

José and Angela chuckled good-naturedly.

"In fact, I'm going to hand-write our wedding invitations with the quill pen you gave me. But instead of the owl quill, I'll use this angel feather, so we have a heavenly wedding with angels for guests." Her eyes dancing, she gave them a defiant grin.

Gabe appeared just as José's cell phone rang. Angela watched as Gabe grimaced and slowly shook his head. "I was too late."

José read the caller ID and glanced at Maria. "It's Detective Hadd." He answered and nodded as he listened. At one point, he blinked, glanced again at Maria, and then looked away. "Yes, I will. Thanks for letting us know."

"What?" Maria's dark eyes studied him.

His Adam's apple bobbing, he swallowed.

"It's Mal, isn't it?" Gone was the sparkle in her eyes. "What's happened?"

José took a deep breath. "Detective Hadd said his men followed Mal to Interstate 35 and Loop 410. Mal was trying to exit I-35 and drive off the ramp when he lost control of his vehicle, plunged from the bridge, and landed upside down on Loop 410."

Barely a whisper, Maria asked, "How is he?"

José's voice was a monotone. "He was pronounced dead at the scene when EMS arrived."

Chapter 10

"Don't let small minds convince you that your dreams are too big."
– Anonymous

Saturday, Angela attended Kio's graduation ceremony, sitting with his parents in the Alamodome. Sunday morning, they met again for Mass.

Wearing rose-colored vestments, the priest began the homily with a beatific smile. "How many of you have tried Cherpumple?"

Amidst chuckles and grins, several people raised their hands.

"I tried it at my sister's house for Thanksgiving. Cherpumple's a conglomeration of three pies—cherry, pumpkin, and apple—baked into three different cakes: usually chocolate with the cherry, white with the apple, and spice with the pumpkin pie. Then the three layers are frosted and stacked on top of each other to make one towering dessert."

Grinning, he looked out over the congregation. "Does that sound mouthwatering? Let me see a show of hands."

A few raised their hands, but as Angela turned in her seat to view the response, she saw most people shaking their heads or turning up their noses.

"Or unappetizing? I have to admit. I'm not a proponent of Cherpumple. Some things weren't meant to be jumbled together into a hodgepodge of dueling flavors. Some ingredients were meant to be savored separately.

"Christmas and Advent are that way. I call it Chradvent, and the Chradvent season starts before Halloween, sometimes as early as August." He grinned. "Before yielding to the chaos of Chradvent, let's take a moment to celebrate what so many of us may have forgotten: Advent.

He gestured toward the oversized wreath. "We symbolize the season's four weeks with the Advent wreath, lighting one more candle each week, not lighting all four at once. We let the light gather and grow. During the first two weeks of Advent we lit purple candles, the colors symbolizing a time of prayer and reflection. Advent used to be called 'little Lent' because it's the time when we spiritually wait in darkness with hope for a promised redemption.

"Today, the third Sunday of Advent, is Gaudete Sunday. Our waiting for the birth of Jesus on Christmas is nearly over." He pointed to his vestments. "The color rose is a liturgical color meaning joy. We sing, 'O Come, O Come, Emmanuel.' We're captives waiting to be freed, waiting for the light. Jesus, the Light of the World, is coming, but until He comes, we wait and pray.

"Here's the thing. We shouldn't hurry it. Advent is the time for reevaluating, for making plans. It's a season of expectation. Dorothy Day compared Advent to a pregnant woman anticipating the birth of her child. 'She lives in such a garment of silence, listening to hear the stir of life within her.'

"Ask yourself, am I listening? Am I paying attention? Am I looking forward to Christmas? Why do children enjoy Christmas so much? The expectation, the anticipation, they wait, and they wait. If we plunge into the holiday season prematurely, we lose the anticipation. Without the expectation, the hope, when Christmas comes, it will be anti-climactic, just another day in a long litany of jangling bells and tinny elevator carols.

"Take a break from the fa-la-la-la-la and ho-ho-ho. Give yourself time to look within, to contemplate the One Who is coming. Ask Him what you can do to welcome Him into your life. If you shut out the jingle-jangle and wear a 'garment of silence,' you might be surprised to hear an answer.

"Cherpumple is overkill, overindulgence. So is Chradvent. To get the most out of each season, let's separate them and live each fully. Let's look forward to Christmas but first enjoy the anticipation during Advent. Christmas is the destination. Advent is the journey. Let's enjoy the ride."

Angela and Kio joined his parents for brunch in the King William District. After saying goodbyes, they arrived at the Institute of Texas Cultures just in time for José's interpretive tour. Waving hello as they walked past him, they joined Maria near the back of the group.

She gave Kio a hug. "Congratulations," Maria whispered. "I can say I actually know an astrophysicist."

Blushing, he shrugged. "Well, you know an out-of-work graduate. All I need now is a job."

Angela stifled a chuckle as she reached for his hand. "You'll get one."

"Welcome to the UTSA Institute of Texan Cultures' Winter Celebrations Around the World." Though José included everyone in his congenial smile, his eyes rested on Maria. "While you're here, you'll hear exchange students from around the world share their country's seasonal traditions. You'll find hands-on activities, such as coloring pages, paper lanterns, and piñatas. You'll see holiday displays from fifteen countries around the world, including Albania, Bosnia, Germany, Lebanon, Netherlands, Russia, and Tanzania"

One of the group raised his hand. "Where's the haunted hearse?"

José grinned. "You're talking about the Castroville exhibit." He turned toward the others. "For those of you who aren't familiar, the ITC night watchmen sometimes find the hearse's doors open. They shut the hearse doors, make their rounds, and then come back to find the doors open again."

"The news station ran a story of a ghost in the gift shop," said another tourist. "Have you ever seen it?"

Smiling, José shook his head. "Though I've seen the news clip, I've never seen the ghost. Maybe it's because I'm not here after hours, but many people believe the ITC's haunted. Several night employees have reported smelling tobacco smoke. They swear it's the same aromatic blend used by the former director, an avid pipe smoker. Another night watchman described hearing his name called, feeling his shirt pulled out from his trousers, and seeing the spirit of a Native American woman in the area known as 'the cave.'"

His eyes twinkling, José added, "Even if you don't see ghosts, I can guarantee you'll see demons and angels today. *Los Pastores,* a Tejano morality play about Mary and Joseph's journey to Bethlehem, is being presented. As the devils try to discourage the shepherds from visiting the baby Jesus, angels strike down the devils. Good wins over evil. Now if you'll follow me, I'll show you where they're performing the play.

"Incidentally, the Institute is always looking for volunteer docents. If you like dressing up in period costumes and enjoy being the spark that lights a passion for history in others, see me after the show." He grinned. "I'll get you started on the paperwork."

After they watched the morality play with its colorful costumes, they made the rounds of the Winter Celebrations. Then as they waited for José to finish his last tour, Maria noticed the gift shop.

"Still have some last-minute shopping to do."

Kio chuckled. "And I haven't begun my Christmas shopping. I'll join you." Then he glanced at Angela. "Why don't you wait out here?" He pointed at the oversized Texas state flag's neon representation. "In fact, why don't you stand over there?"

"Farther away, so I won't see what you buy?" Angela grinned as she stepped toward the neon flag.

Against the brightly lit flag, Angela watched a parade of figures and shadows that only she could see. Smoke wafted from a pipe-smoking profile reminiscent of Alfred Hitchcock's. A female apparition floated by, her long hair streaming behind.

Each carrying a bag, Maria and Kio left the gift shop just as José joined Angela.

"Where next?"

"We still haven't completed the last segment of the River Walk's Mission Reach." Angela fingered her pilgrim shell. "How 'bout we do that and then grab a bite to eat?"

José glanced at Maria. "Let's take two cars, park one at the Blue Star Arts Complex, and park the other at Roosevelt Park."

As they left the Institute, Angela looked up at the display of waving flags contrasted against the Texas blue sky and the Tower of the Americas.

Kio's eyes followed hers. "That observation tower has a revolving restaurant at the top. We should eat there during the Christmas season."

Angela shaded her eyes from the sun as she stared up. "It certainly must have a bird's eye view of the city."

José nodded. "At 750 feet, it should. It'd been the tallest observation tower in the United States between 1968, when it was built for the World's Hemisphere, and 1996, when Las Vegas built the Stratosphere Tower. It's still the tallest building in San Antonio and the tallest in Texas outside Dallas or Houston."

They caravanned to the Blue Star Arts Complex and drove Kio's car to Roosevelt Park, parking near the bicycle-sharing station.

"Let's loop south to Concepción Park, where Maria and I were last Sunday," said Angela. "Then we can head back to the car at the Blue Star Arts Complex. That will complete the entire River Walk, both the Museum Reach and Mission Reach."

José glanced at Maria and then back to Angela. "How far would that be?"

Angela checked the map. "It looks like a mile to Concepción Park, a mile back, and about two miles from here north to the Blue Star Arts Complex."

He and Maria exchanged a look. "Four miles might be too much for Maria. What if she and I rest here while you two hike to Concepción and back. Then the four of us can walk the rest of the way?"

Maria nodded. "I'd only slow you down, anyway."

Angela grinned as she looked to Kio. "Okay, we'll make this fast." Waving, she and Kio headed south along the wide cement path, keeping to the right to avoid cyclists.

Within a short time, they came to a chute.

"Is that a canoe chute or a fish ladder?" Kio scratched his head as he gazed at the steep series of steps built into the river's rocky drop.

Angela studied it. "I read they'd opened this part of the river to canoe and kayak paddling. Although I do recall something about SARA having to redesign the chutes to make them canoe friend-lier."

Several men were fly-casting in the river from a stepped em-bankment.

"What're you catching?" called Kio.

The angler cast and then turned toward Kio. "Bass."

They crossed a pedestrian bridge with brightly painted blocks of limestone.

Angela chuckled. "Don't those staggered stone blocks remind you of a castle's tower or the teeth of some fairytale dragon?"

He looked at the bridge, then at her, and shook his head. "No, not really."

"Where's your sense of imagination?" Shaking her head, she gave him a half-smile. "All work and no whimsy."

They crossed under I-10, listening to the whine of the traffic overhead.

"Except for near this bridge, we've only heard leaves rustling and birds calling." Kio reached for her hand. "You forget how close the Mission Reach is to downtown."

"And yet how far." She gave his hand a gentle squeeze as they walked in silence.

A few minutes later, Angela slowed her stride. Glancing about, she recognized the area. "We're at Concepción Park already?" She turned toward him with a grin. "Seems like we barely got started."

He hesitated, seeming lost in thought.

Her hand still in his, she looked up at him. "Want to start back?"

"In a bit." Looking around, he spotted a picnic table. "Want to sit down a minute?"

Blinking, she cocked her head to the side. "Why? What's up?"

He shrugged. "I just picked up a little something at the gift shop. Wondered what you . . . " He shrugged again, blushing. "Just wanted to give it to you while we're alone."

Narrowing her eyes, she studied him. "What have you got up your sleeve?"

"Nothing's up *my sleeve.*" He chuckled as he took a small package from his jacket's pocket.

Angela glanced at his face. Wearing a shy smile, he seemed unable to meet her eyes.

"What's gotten into you?"

"Nothing." Again he shrugged as he put the gift in her hands. "Here, open it."

Perplexed, she tried to read his expression, but he never looked directly at her. Finally, she undid the tissue paper and found a carved, wooden cat with a long, upright tail. She gave him a half-grin. "It looks like Frank and no-name. Thanks, so much, it's adorable." She leaned toward him to kiss him.

"It's more than that."

"What do you mean?"

"The tail's a ring holder." He met her eyes for only an instant before glancing away.

"But I don't wear rings." Wriggling her fingers, she held out her hands for him to see.

"I've been thinking about that."

As he raised his eyes to hers, she gasped, although deep down, she knew before asking. "You're hinting at something . . . what?"

He took a breath. Then, putting the carving on the picnic table, he took her hands in his and looked into her eyes.

"As you know, I graduated yesterday."

She nodded.

"That leaves only you in school." He took another deep breath. "Maybe it's time to start thinking of the future . . . our future."

Her pulse racing, Angela caught her breath.

"You graduate next December, don't you?"

She nodded. "Although, I've been thinking of taking summer school next year and graduating in August." She raised her eyebrow. "It would save a semester."

Kio's head bobbed as he thought it through. "Good idea." His eyes piercing hers, he moved closer. "What do you think of having a ring to hang on that cat's tail at night?"

Grinning, Angela felt herself flush. "What kind of ring?"

He cautiously met her eyes. "Hypothetically speaking, if I were to give you an engagement ring, what would you say?"

She swallowed a smile. "Hypothetically speaking?"

Grinning, he nodded.

"Honestly, until . . . if that moment should arrive, I'm not sure what I'd say."

Though smiling, he rolled his eyes. He ran his hand across his chin. Then he licked his lips. "Okay, if I were to propose to you before the end of the year, would you say yes?"

She gave him a playful grin, then took a deep breath as if making up her mind. "Mmmmaybe."

Giving a frustrated groan, he leaned over to kiss her. Then he helped her to her feet. "Come on. We'd better head back before José and Maria think we got lost."

She pulled him toward her in a lingering kiss, wrapping both arms around his waist. "If you were to propose . . . I don't think you'd be disappointed."

When they reached the pedestrian bridge, Angela saw the path continued on their side of the river, apparently paralleling the path they had taken to Concepción. "Let's take a slightly different route, not backtrack."

He gave her a skeptical half-smile. "It could dead-end, which would mean backtracking, anyway."

Angela grinned as she tugged at his hand. "Come on. It's an *ad-vent*-ure!"

A quarter mile from the bridge, they saw José and Maria sitting at a picnic table across the river. They shouted and signaled, but when that did not work, Angela called Maria on her cell.

"Hey, can you see us?" She waved wildly as she heard Maria's voice through the phone.

"Yup, how do you propose we meet each other?"

At the word 'propose,' Angela glanced at Kio. "Just start walking north on your side of the River Walk. The first bridge we come to, we'll cross over to you."

Hanging up, Angela and Kio began walking back toward the Blue Star Arts Complex as they kept pace with their friends across the river. Then they noticed an enormous but drained swimming pool.

"What is this?" Angela glanced at the broken windows of what appeared to have been a locker room.

"I think this land had all belonged to the Lone Star Brewery at one time." As they walked farther along, they came to a derelict industrial park. "Yup, there's the brewery."

"So no one owns it now?"

"I read that a San Marcos-based company wants to redevelop it into a mixed-use entertainment complex with a new micro-brewery, theater, and music venues."

Angela studied the derelict colossus through the chain link fence. "It's in an ideal location along the River Walk—in the city, yet removed."

He gave her wry smile. "Like being in the world, yet not of the world."

Then they saw a bridge on Lone Star Boulevard. Waving to José and Maria across the river to get their attention, Angela pointed to it.

Instead of waving back, José put his arms around Maria, seeming to comfort her.

"That's weird." Angela turned toward Kio.

"Wonder what's wrong?"

A few minutes later, they met up with their friends. One look at Maria, and Angela knew things were not right. "What's the matter?"

"I want to show you something." Her eyes red, her lashes wet, Maria motioned for them to cross Lone Star Boulevard with her. Then she pointed to the pylons beneath the bridge on the other side of the river. "I didn't recognize this area until I saw this bridge by the River Flood Control Tunnels outlet." She nodded toward the rounded, fan-shaped building across the river.

"It's a bridge." Angela hunched her shoulders. "What's so special about it?"

"See that ledge just below the arch?" Maria turned to face them. "That's where I slept those two nights before I met you."

Angela looked from her downturned eyes to the exposed perch. What a trap, no railing to have kept her from rolling over in her sleep and falling in the river, let along from being mugged or attacked. "I can't imagine how vulnerable you must have felt."

Maria took a jagged breath. "It was the worst time of my life." Her chin trembling, she pointed to the bus stop at the corner. "I had just enough money to take a bus to Parentage Incorporated. There was no way I would bring a baby into that kind of life."

"It's all behind you now." José put his arm around her. "You've moved on."

Nodding, she smiled at him through wet lashes. "Thanks to you and Angela."

He gave her a wry smile. "Thanks to God."

How different her life would have been if Dev and I hadn't been at Parentage Incorporated that morning. Angela glanced again at the crude protection the bridge offered. Taking a deep breath, she put on a bright smile and pointed at the River Walk.

"Speaking of moving on, come on, people. Our Mission Reach pilgrimage is nearly done. Let's celebrate completing our journey's last leg at the Blue Star Arts Complex. I'm starving!"

An hour later, they were seated at a rustic pizzeria, eating pepperoni and pulled-pork pizza. Angela glanced at the wall of stacked firewood within easy reach of the wood fired pizza oven. The brick wall behind the long bar boasted twenty taps of hand-crafted beer.

"To us," she said, raising her stein of stout, "for not only starting this pilgrimage, but for finishing it."

While Maria toasted with water, the others clinked their steins of ale against hers.

"Look how far our journey's taken us." Raising his stein again, José smiled at Maria. "To happy endings."

Maria returned his smile. "I'll drink to that."

"To new beginnings." Kio caught Angela's eye as he raised his stein.

Swallowing a grin, she clinked glasses. Then she glanced at each person seated around the small table. "We're all dressed for the third Sunday in Advent. Maria's wearing a scarf with pink roses. José's tie is fuchsia. Your shirt has a crimson tinge, and my blouse is a rosy pink."

"Next Sunday marks the last week of Advent." Kio lifted his mouth in a half smile. "Christmas is almost here."

"Two weeks from today is our wedding." Maria reached for José's hand.

"We know what we're doing that weekend." Grinning, Angela looked from face to face. "But what's on the agenda for next weekend?"

"There's the Dance Academy *Fiesta de Navidad: La Pastorela Folklórico* at the Guadalupe Theater Saturday." José glanced at each face. "How does that sound?"

Angela thought out loud. "Isn't that like the morality play we saw today, *Los Pastores?*"

"It's similar since it's the traditional Shepherds play, but they perform it to folklórico music with a flamenco flair." José shrugged. "It's gotten good reviews."

"Works for me." Angela smiled.

"That takes care of Saturday. What about Sunday?" Kio reached for another slice of pizza.

"They're holding *La Gran Posada* Sunday night." Angela glanced at them. "Are you up for another walk?"

"As long as it's not too long." Maria sprinkled pepper seeds on her pizza.

"It goes from Milam Park, through Market Square, past City Hall and the Courthouse, to the San Fernando Cathedral." Angela added, "It's one of the oldest Christmas traditions in Texas, dating back to the sixteenth century."

"It's been following the same processional route since colonial times." José scattered parmesan cheese on his slice.

Angela glanced at Kio. "How far is that?"

He shrugged. "About a mile and a half."

"That's not very far. Sounds like fun." Maria grinned. "Let's go to La Posada."

Kio nodded. "Count me in."

Saturday night, they met at the Guadalupe Theater in front of a large mosaic of the Virgin of Guadalupe.

Angela tilted back her head to stare up at it. "It looks like an oversized votive candle."

Kio gave a low whistle. "That's one tall candle."

"At forty feet, it's the largest mosaic of the Virgin Mary in the world." José pointed to the mosaics on either side of it. "Notice the eagle with a snake in its beak perched on a cactus."

They all nodded.

"It's from the story of the founding of Tenochtitlan."

"Mexico City," Angela grinned as she gazed at it. "I was born there."

When they walked inside the small theater, José led them to seats along the aisle of the side section.

"This had been a nineteen forties movie theater before they renovated it. The acoustics are great, but it was designed for looking up at a movie screen. The floor's slant is so shallow, it's hard to see the stage. These seats will give us the best view."

He and Maria sat in one row. Angela and Kio sat behind them. As they waited for the performers to come onstage, Kio tapped his shoulder.

"At the Institute, you'd said this was a morality play. Could you tell us a little more about it?"

José turned in his seat so they all could hear him. "When the Spanish missionaries came to the Americas to convert the native peoples to Christianity they had to overcome language and cultural differences. To bridge the gaps, the missionaries used mystery plays to teach the Bible stories. Basically, it's the story told in Luke about angels announcing Jesus' birth to the shepherds."

"You'd said La Posada follows the same processional route it's taken since the sixteenth century." Angela whispered, "Is La Pastorela still presented in the same way it had been originally?"

"New characters and events have been added over time. In fact, the play's become a comedy, where the Devil tries to sidetrack the dim-witted shepherds from their pilgrimage, and angels intervene to keep the them on course."

"Only this version is interpreted through music and movement," added Maria.

José nodded. "The adult dancers play the traditional parts of Mary, Joseph, the devil, and the archangel, while the younger performers play the roles of townspeople and shepherds." His eyes lit up as he chuckled. "It's the kids that steal the show."

As the music began, they watched the dancers come onstage. The men sported straw hats and white *guayabera* pants and shirts with red waist sashes. Twirling, lifting, and fluttering their multicolored hems, the women wore ranchero designed dresses with brightly colored ribbons and full, festive skirts.

After the performance, the four met for coffee and cake.

"Let me see if I've got this right. Tonight, we saw the story of Luke performed in La Pastorela, where the angels told the shepherds of Jesus' birth. Tomorrow, at La Posada, we'll reenact Mary and Joseph's search for an inn, for a place to give birth." Angela grinned. "We're certainly reliving the Christmas story."

The next night they met at Milam Park, where a volunteer pressed song sheets into their hands.

"This is the 'Canto Para Pedir Posada,' the traditional Christmas Posada music. Its title means 'Song to Ask for Shelter.'" José read over the lyrics and translated for them. "It's sung as a call and response, where the verses are sung alternately. First Joseph and the crowd outside the building ask to be let inside. 'In the name of heaven / I ask you for shelter / for my beloved wife / can go no farther.'

"Then the 'innkeeper' and choir inside respond, refusing them entry. 'This is not an inn / Get on with you / I cannot open the door / You might be a rogue.' The lyrics are different for each stop, but the result's always the same. Joseph and Mary are turned away."

A priest tapped the microphone for attention. "Join us in celebrating Los Posadas in song. Tonight we commemorate Mary and Joseph's steps when they sought shelter in Bethlehem."

The procession began as actors dressed like angels led the costumed Mary and Joseph, cathedral choir, and gathered crowd through the Market Square. Stopping first at *Mi Tierra*, then the Univision Studio, Spanish Governor's Palace, City Hall, and

County Courthouse, the people outside each building sang a verse asking to be let into each building. Those inside replied in song, turning them away.

Angela chuckled. "I feel like we're on another pilgrimage."

"We are." José nodded. "This is called a *caminata*, a short pilgrimage to remember Mary and Joseph's struggle to find lodging, and we're the *peregrinos*, pilgrims."

Finally, when they sang at the San Fernando Cathedral, the 'innkeepers' responded favorably. "Is that you Joseph? / Your wife is Mary? / Enter pilgrims / I didn't recognize you." Then the church opened its doors, and the group processed inside.

The priest addressed them from the podium. "You're all welcome here. The cathedral opens its doors to all pilgrims seeking God. As Luke wrote, 'A Savior has been born to you; he is Christ the Lord. And here is a sign for you: you will find a baby wrapped in swaddling clothes and lying in a manger.'

He pointed to the nativity scene near the altar. "When God came to earth, He didn't come in glory. He came as a helpless baby, born in a cave and cradled in a cattle trough. God made himself small, so we could understand Him, love Him. God gave Himself to us as a gift.

"Christmas began two thousand years ago with the gift of Jesus' birth and the gifts of the three wise men. In what's developed into a season of shopping and spending, remember God's original gift. This year, instead of wrapped presents, give of yourself. Give the gift of your time, both to God and each other. Holiday blues disappear, and joy is born. Have a merry Christmas!"

After they filed outside, they watched a group of children break open a piñata and scramble to find the scattered candies.

"Six more weeks, and we'll have a child of our own." José smiled at Maria.

She chuckled. "It might take a few years before he can swing at a piñata."

"Speaking of time, Christmas Eve is only four days away." Angela looked at them. "What's the game plan for the drive to Alpine?"

"I vote we take one car," said Kio

Angela nodded. "And get an early start."

"Since we'll be staying at my parents' house," said José, "why don't we take my car? I just had the oil changed, tires rotated, and a twenty-nine-point inspection yesterday. We should be good to go."

Tuesday after dinner, Angela was relaxing over dessert with Maria and Tulah when she glanced out the window. "It's dark already."

Maria followed her gaze. "Today's the solstice, the shortest day of the year."

"And tonight's the darkest night of the year." Tulah helped herself to a slice of pumpkin bread.

Maria shook her head. "You mean the longest night. The darkest was the night Mal died."

"You've never talked about him or how you've felt." Angela spoke softly as she studied her.

Her mouth turning down at the corners, Maria sneered. "You mean how I felt when he threatened to kill José, or how I felt when he shoved me in front of the oncoming car?"

Angela raised her eyebrow. "I mean how you felt about the death of your baby's father."

Maria took a deep breath. "If Mal hadn't threatened José or shoved me in front of a car, I might have grieved for him. As it is . . . " She pressed her lips together and exhaled through her nostrils. "I'm relieved. Now he can't interfere with the baby's life." She sighed as she stared at nothing. "I don't miss the person he'd become, but I do mourn the man he'd once been."

Just after sunrise December twenty-fourth, José and Kio picked them up at their apartment.

Three hours into the trip, Maria turned toward them. "Anyone besides me need a bio break?"

"I wouldn't mind stretching my legs." As she arched her back, Angela rotated her shoulders.

"We're roughly halfway to Alpine." Kio read from a brochure. "Why don't we stop in at the Caverns of Sonora, take the Crystal Palace Tour? It'll break up the drive."

José glanced at Maria. "Are you up for it?"

"After sitting all morning, it'll feel good to get some exercise."

"Yeah, but touring a cave?"

"It's no different walking below the earth than above it." She shrugged. "I've been walking every day. I'm used to it."

"What about climbing steps?" asked Kio. "The brochure says there are hundreds of them."

Maria turned toward him and Angela in the back seat. "As long as you don't mind going slowly and someone's in front and back of me in case I stumble, I'll be fine."

They arrived at the caverns in time for the first tour and began the descent. At the bottom of the stairs, the guide smiled. "We're a hundred and fifty-five feet below the surface, folks."

Maria chuckled breathlessly. "And there are three hundred and sixty steps. I counted them, *every one.*"

The tour guide led them through two miles of crystal corridors, pointing out the helictites and calcite crystal formations. At one formation, she turned toward them with a grin.

"This is one of the best show caves in the world. Its spectacle can't be exaggerated, even by Texan standards."

They stopped for lunch in Ozona and noticed a bas-relief, pink granite monument near the restaurant. Angela walked closer to read the inscription. "This is a statue of David Crockett."

"David Crockett?" Maria gave her a puzzled look. "Is that the same Davy Crockett who fought at the Alamo?"

"'Davy' was Walt Disney's invention." José smiled. "David Crockett was his real name."

They stopped for gas in Fort Stockton and saw the giant road-runner dressed in a festive Santa Claus hat and cape.

Maria chuckled. "I've never seen Paisano Pete sporting Christmas regalia before."

"Is he really the world's largest roadrunner?" Angela viewed him through the car window as they drove past.

"He used to be. That is, until New Mexico built a bigger version." José grinned. "Paisano Pete's twenty-two feet long and eleven feet tall, but the Las Cruces roadrunner is forty feet long and twenty feet tall."

Kio whistled. "That's one big bird. I wouldn't want him crossing my path."

As Angela watched the landscape change from flatlands to rolling hills to mountains, she became introspective. "José," she said from the back seat, "weren't you born in Alpine?"

Glancing at her in the rearview mirror, he nodded. "Why?"

"I was just thinking. You're not the first father-to-be traveling to his town of birth on Christmas Eve."

José laughed. "But my name's not Joseph."

"Close enough." Angela grinned at his reflection.

He grinned back. "And Mary's not riding a donkey."

"But Maria's riding in Jenny, which you say has a mule-like stubbornness."

Wrinkling his forehead, Kio wore a questioning look. "Jenny?"

Maria wore a sheepish grin. "It's what he calls this car."

"Why?"

José glanced at him through the rearview mirror. "Because she's as temperamental as a mule."

They arrived late afternoon at José's parents' home in Alpine, where his mother warmly welcomed them. Poinsettias decorated every niche, every inch of the front room. Two six-foot poinsettia 'trees' lined the front door. Another tower of round tiers filled with poinsettia plants created an eight-foot 'tree' in the family room. Pots of poinsettias graced every corner, every tabletop.

Glancing about, Angela took in the crimson and scarlet colors. "Your home's beautiful, Mrs. Aceves, so Christmassy."

"I love to decorate with poinsettias," she said, "and please call me Lupe." Then she pointed out the nativity scene beneath the Christmas tree. "*El nacimiento.*"

Angela opened her eyes wide. "This crèche is larger than I've seen in most churches."

José smiled. "My mother likes to celebrate Christmas."

Then she saw the manger, empty except for the straw. "Where's the baby Jesus?"

"We'll get the baby blessed at *medianoche Misa.*"

"At midnight Mass." Angela nodded.

After they got settled, José's mother brought them old-fashioned aprons that looped around the neck and tied in the back. "Now comes the fun part. We're going to make tamales."

"It's a Christmas tradition." His dark eyes sparkling, José chuckled. "Every Christmas Eve, we spend all day in the kitchen."

"All day?" Angela's voice rose on the last syllable. She glanced at the clock and grinned. "Maybe all afternoon."

Lupe put her hands on her son's shoulders and shooed him. "Now that I have a daughter and her friend to help me, go entertain Kio."

José chuckled. "Mama slow-cooked the pork this morning, so it won't take as long as usual. All we . . . " He glanced at his mother's raised eyebrow. "All *you* have to do is prepare the masa and make the tamales."

Angela grinned uneasily. "Okay, but you'll have to show me how. This is all new to me."

Lupe handed Angela a package of dried corn husks.

Her grin spreading, Angela stared at the husks. "What do I do with these?"

"Watch." Separating a husk from the package, Lupe placed it in a pot of simmering water.

"They have to simmer before they're soft enough to fold." Maria took a handful of husks and dropped them in the hot water, one by one. "Like this."

After all the husks were steaming, Lupe placed a large bowl, bag of *masa*, canola oil, chili powder, cumin, garlic powder, and salt on the table.

Angela looked from the bag to Maria and Lupe. "What's masa?"

"*Masa harina* is a kind of corn flour traditionally used to make tamales." Lupe opened the bag and poured a small amount on Angela's hands. "See?"

Angela ran her fingers through it, feeling its texture. "It's silky, like corn starch." When she wiped her hands on her jeans, she left behind tell-tale fingerprints.

Lupe laughed as she wiped her hands on her apron. "This is why we use these."

"Start kneading the flour and oil together like this." Maria demonstrated, while Lupe gradually added the spices. Then Maria turned to Angela. "Okay, your turn. I don't want to have all the 'fun.'"

Angela chuckled as she dug into the sticky dough. "Should it feel this tacky to the touch?"

Lupe shook her head as she gradually began adding more masa. "It should be the consistency of soft peanut butter. Maria, why don't you shred the pork and blend in the chili sauce?"

By the time the corn husks had softened, the masa was smooth and spongy, and the pork was shredded and seasoned.

Maria winked at Angela. "Now the fun part."

After they drained the corn husks and patted them dry, Lupe showed them how to make the fillings. "Smear two tablespoons of masa on the smooth side of each husk. Then spread a heaping tablespoon of pork in the middle. Pull the sides of the husk together and fold the tip up and over the sides, like this."

Taking a husk in one hand, Angela used the other to spread the masa with a knife. "It's like buttering bread."

When all the tamales were filled and folded, they stood them upright, packing them tightly together in the steamer.

Angela brushed the hair out of her eyes with the back of her hand. "Now what?"

"Now the tamales steam for about three hours," said Lupe.

"We're done?"

Maria smiled. "With the tamales? For now . . . "

"Uh-oh . . . what's next?"

"Pozole."

"Po . . . what?"

"Poh-SOH-lay," said Lupe. "It's a corn soup made with chicken, chili, and garlic. Then you garnish it with shredded lettuce, thinly sliced radishes, chopped avocado, fresh oregano, and lime wedges."

"Then are we done?" Angela gave a nervous chuckle.

"We've just begun." Lupe laughed. "After that, we'll make the *Sopa Seca*."

"What's that?"

"Basically it's angel-hair noodle nests simmered in tomato sauce." Then Maria turned toward Lupe. "What about the salad? If we slice and dice the vegetables now, we could toss them just before the party. It'd save time."

Lupe nodded. "Let's do that while the turkey's roasting and then make the *Buñuelos* and *Ponche Navideño*."

"After all that cooking, I'll be too tired to eat." Angela gave a dry laugh.

Wearing wide grins, they glanced at her and chuckled.

"I'm not joking."

"We can have a light supper and take a short siesta before midnight Mass."

Angela looked cautiously from Maria to Lupe. "What time does the party begin?"

"After *la Misa de Gallo*," said Lupe.

"After midnight Mass?" Angela's eyelids flew open. "I'll definitely need a siesta before then."

"In that case, let's get started chopping the veggies for the *Ensalada de Noche Buena*," said Maria. "The sooner we start, the sooner we finish."

Angela nodded. "What all goes into this special Christmas Eve salad?"

"It's the red and green colors that make it so festive. Beets and lettuce are the basics, but then we add whatever's on hand." Opening the refrigerator, Maria said, "I see apples, tangerines, jicama, pecans, and pomegranate seeds for a garnish."

"Sounds yummy."

Lupe started heating the shortening. "I'll get the buñuelos started."

"And buñuelos are what?" Angela looked up from the cutting board.

"They're crispy, fried treats sprinkled with sugar and cinnamon," said Lupe. "Something like sweet tostadas, they're delicious with Ponche Navideño."

"Christmas Punch, right?" Angela raised her eyebrow as she looked for confirmation.

Lupe nodded. "It's made from *tejocotes*."

"Mexican hawthorn's flavor is hard to describe," said Maria, "but it tastes like crabapples. It's simmered with finely chopped guavas and apples, cinnamon, brown sugar, and molasses and then served warm."

Angela grinned. "We'll feast tonight!"

They sat together at midnight Mass, Maria next to José, his parents, and her parents. Their extended families, Angela, and Kio sat in the rows behind them.

Directly behind her, Angela noticed Maria's gleaming, dark hair, even longer and curlier than it had been during the spring semester. *How fast it's grown. Pregnancy certainly agrees with her.* Then she saw how Maria sat close to José, always holding his hand or touching him, connecting with him.

When she glimpsed Maria lay her head on José's shoulder, Angela caught Kio's eye and gestured toward them with a subtle nod.

Leaning into her, Kio whispered. "Ever since Mal's grip on her was broken, those two have really bonded."

Angela nodded. "Now they're a pair, a team. One's never apart from the other," she chuckled, "except for this afternoon in the kitchen."

After Mass, it seemed half the congregation drove back to José's home. The house would have been jam-packed, but the night air was balmy. Everyone found a seat, inside or out.

Between eating, toasting, meeting the friends and family, and opening gifts, Maria, José, Kio, and Angela found only a few minutes to chat.

"Why don't we go for a walk tomorrow?" Angela glanced at them. "After eating all this food tonight, I could use some exercise."

"Good idea." Kio nodded. "Big Bend National Park isn't far, is it?"

"About an hour and half's drive," said José.

"Hiking, yes," Maria's hair bounced as she moved, "but climbing's a bit out of my range."

"Understandably." Angela grinned as she looked at her round figure.

"I think those steps today were more strenuous than we thought."

"You're carrying precious cargo." José leaned over to kiss Maria. "We'll keep to easy trails."

Chapter 11

"And When I Die"

— Blood, Sweat & Tears

They got a late start Christmas morning. While they ate a quick breakfast of coffee, tangerines, and reheated tamales, José gave them each a gift-wrapped present.

Angela started to get up from the table. "Let me get my gifts for—"

José shook his head. "These are just tokens, little symbols of the season, not the actual gifts. We can exchange those tonight with my family." Giving them a shy smile, he added, "I just want you to know how special you've each become in my life."

Kio opened his first. Raising his eyebrow, he gave José a skeptical grin. "Toothpaste and mouthwash? Are you trying to tell me something?"

José laughed. "No, no social commentary, just read the ingredients."

Angela opened hers next. "A bottle of hand lotion," she read the ingredients, "made with myrrh." Standing up, she gave José a hug. "Thank you. I think I'm seeing a trend."

Kio laughed. "Frankincense is in both the toothpaste and mouthwash. Thanks, *I think*, or are you accusing me of halitosis?"

"Nope, it's just a way to give you frankincense," José chuckled. "which is actually supposed to be good for oral hygiene."

"On that note, I'm brushing my teeth." Grinning, Kio got up and took his gifts to the bathroom. "I can take a hint."

"Just kidding," called José.

Maria grinned at him. "Let me think . . . Angela got myrrh, and Kio got frankincense. What Christmas gift could you possibly have gotten for me?" She unwrapped the box and found two gold angel earrings. Standing up, she kissed him. "Thank you. I love them."

"You're always talking about angels." He smiled gently. "Now you can carry them with you," he made quotation marks with his fingers, "'wear-ever' you go."

"'Wear-ever.'" Kissing him again, she mimicked his finger quotation marks. "I get it."

A half hour later, as they climbed into José's car, the engine sputtered and coughed before starting up. Giving the dashboard a light slap with his fingers, José scolded his car. "Jenny, quit acting up."

"Think it'll work?"

José shrugged. "Jenny's temperamental, but she's never let me down."

After a few miles of driving through monotonous desert, conversation tapered off. While Maria dozed in the passenger seat and Kio snored lightly beside her in the back, Angela watched as one range of mountains faded in the distance and another rose ahead. In between, for mile after mile, she saw flat, Chihuahuan desert. Then she sat up as she recognized the terrain.

"José, this area looks familiar. Is this near—"

"Good memory." He nodded toward a turnoff ahead. "This is the road to my great-grandfather's homestead."

"Did you say homestead?" Blinking, Maria lifted her head from José's shoulder.

He pointed to a road as they passed it. "That leads to my family's . . . well, until recently it was used as a hunting cabin."

"Oh, could we stop and see it?" Maria's head turned to watch it recede in the distance.

Angela saw him grimace through the rearview mirror.

"Maybe on the way back, if there's time."

Nodding, Maria again snuggled against José's shoulder. Angela leaned back and rested her eyes.

The next thing she heard was José saying, "We're here."

As she felt the car roll to a stop, she sat up. "Already?" Then she looked at her phone and chuckled. "Guess I dozed off, too. I thought that hour passed awfully quickly."

"This is the Grapevine Hills Trail. It follows a gravel wash until it climbs the last quarter mile into the boulders." José pointed to the trailhead and then gestured to the surrounding land. "This whole area was covered with volcanoes eons ago. Grapevine Hills is a laccolith, with giant, rounded boulders."

"Laccolith?" Maria wore a quizzical expression as she cocked her head.

"It's a dome formed from magma that was squeezed between a rock and a hard place." Grinning, José grabbed a backpack. "Incidentally, I've got water, protein bars, and even a first aid kit, if anyone needs them."

Stretching as they got out of the car, Maria chuckled. "You're like a boy scout."

"Always prepared?"

She smiled as she nodded. "Just like at our first walk along the Mission Trail."

"We've walked a few miles together since then." José reached for her hand.

"What range of mountains is that?" Angela pointed to the peaks north of them.

José grinned. "Christmas."

Angela gave him a puzzled stare. "Merry Christmas to you, too, but what range of mountains is that?"

Again he grinned. "Seriously, those are the Christmas Mountains."

Angela began chuckling. "The Christmas Mountains on Christmas Day."

José's eyes took on a faraway look. "My family's property is nestled in their foothills."

Angela caught his eye as they shared an empathetic smile. Then she glanced at Maria and Kio. *They don't know that's where we found Gabe. Maybe it's for the best.* Sighing, she grimaced.

José looked at them. "Everyone ready?"

They followed the trail through the gravel wash, and then began the slow incline to the boulders. On the last quarter mile, the path rose sharply.

"Take it slowly." His arm around Maria's waist, José helped her climb. "I didn't realize it was this steep, or I'd never have suggested this trail. Want to turn back?"

Breathless, she shook her head.

"Take your time." Angela turned to José as she glanced at Maria. "Got any water? I could use some."

Nodding, he turned around so his backpack faced her. "Upper left pocket." He glanced at Maria. "Why don't you take out a bottle for each of us, keep us hydrated."

A half hour later, they reached the top. Exhaling with a groan, Maria slumped on a flat rock. "Let me catch my breath."

"I hope this climb wasn't a strain." José's forehead puckered.

Smiling, Maria shook her head. "Give me a minute. I'll be fine." Then she pointed to the mountain peaks to the north. "Those peaks over there are the Christmas Mountains?"

José nodded.

"They look so rosy in this light."

"That's because the sun's starting to set." He grimaced. "Night falls quickly in the mountains."

"But they look so inviting." She looked up into his eyes. "Did you say your family's property is nestled in their foothills?"

Stifling a sigh, he nodded. "Yeah."

"Can we stop on the way back?"

Angela watched as he hid a grimace with a forced smile. "If you want."

"I'd like that." Her eyes sparkling, Maria grinned. "What a great place to visit today of all days."

Angela caught his eye as they shared a wry smile.

By the time they returned to the car, the shadows were long.

"It's nearly dark." José glanced at Maria. "Maybe we should just get back to my parents' house while it's still light. We can visit the old homestead another day."

"But today's Christmas." Cocking her head, she gave him a hopeful smile. "Seeing your family's place in the Christmas Mountains *on* Christmas would make it so much more meaningful. Can't we just stop a few minutes? Please?"

He gave her a grudging smile. "I suppose we can spare a few minutes, but seriously we should get back before my parents start to worry."

Maria shrugged her shoulders. "Can't we call them, tell them we'll be a few minutes late?"

He gave a rueful chuckle. "What do you think I've been trying to do all afternoon? There's no cell reception out here."

Maria sat up straight, absorbing the meaning. "This really is off the grid, isn't it?" Then, her eyes twinkling, she smiled. "Well, we can be a *few minutes* late. Let's just stop in for a quick look and then speed back to Alpine, okay?"

Shaking his head, José gave her a reluctant grin. "Five minutes, and then we're on our way."

In the back seat, Angela and Kio caught each other's eye shared a private smile.

On the hour, José turned the radio dial.

"At the top of the news, an eleventh video was released today exposing the latest scandal of Parentage, Incorporated. Captured on tape is an abortionist's sales pitch to peddle intact babies' heads. During a new interview with Lille Johnson," said the newscaster, "the CEO of Parentage Incorporated defended the abortion business's practice of selling aborted babies' organs. When confronted with the videos, Ms. Johnson claimed Parentage Incorporated had done nothing illegal. Listen to a taped interview with the CEO of Parentage Incorporated."

"Ms. Johnson," said the interviewer, "the video exposed the illegal practice of performing partial-birth abortions in Texas to late-term, unborn babies. Wasn't the purpose to obtain intact fetal heads for brain harvesting?"

"Tissue donation is perfectly legal as long as the abortion patient signs a donation consent form."

"As I recall, the sixth video depicted technicians harvesting fetal parts without patient consent."

"To my knowledge, every abortion patient signs a donation consent form."

"They're talking about the Texas Parentage Incorporated?" Maria's jaw slack, she looked down at her belly. Then she looked from José to Angela in the back. "That could have been my baby. That's what made me leave the clinic. I couldn't consent to them experimenting with it . . . with him."

Reaching for the dial, José tried to change the station.

"No, leave it on." The corners of Maria's mouth turned down in grim disgust. "I want to hear."

"What about the assertion," asked the interviewer, "that abortionists at Parentage Incorporated have used scissors to cut into living babies' faces to obtain intact fetal brains?"

"Assertions, nothing more," said Ms. Johnson.

"The videos divulged that Parentage Incorporated marketed aborted baby organs to biotech companies to create 'humanized' mice. What's your response?"

"Research," said Ms. Johnson. "It's all perfectly legal."

"Doesn't federal law prohibit the sale of aborted fetal body parts?"

Ms. Johnson scoffed. "Of course, the *sale* is prohibited. However, handling fees are perfectly legal."

"Although Ms. Johnson admitted to the transaction of aborted baby body parts," said the interviewer in a summarization, "she claimed it accounted for a 'tiny fraction' of the women's health services provided by Parentage Incorporated. When asked how she felt about the facilities delivering harvested baby parts to biotech companies, Johnson claimed she was 'proud' of Parentage Incorporated's ongoing contribution to women's health."

"Weather's next." Added the newscaster brightly, "Stay tuned."

Maria switched off the radio and sat in silence. Then mumbling under her breath, "But for the grace of God," she turned toward Angela. "If you and Develyn hadn't been at the clinic that day, my baby could have been cut apart for his organs." Swallowing, she slowly shook her head.

"But we were there." Angela was unsure what else to say.

José reached for her hand. "Angela and Develyn were there for you then, and I'm here for you now, forever."

Sighing, Maria gave him a wistful smile. "How different things could have been."

An hour later, as they approached the turn-off at the homestead, José tried one last time. "It's nearly sunset, and the electricity's been shut off. Once that sun dips below the horizon, it'll be pitch black out here." He forced a smile into his voice. "First thing tomorrow morning, I promise—"

"Ooh, just a quick look . . . please?" Maria looked up at him with large brown eyes.

He groaned but turned on the blinker and pulled off the highway. "Five minutes, seriously. Then we're headed back. The sun's nearly below the horizon."

"Thank you." She gave him a squeeze. "And just look at that sunset! It's spectacular . . . fiery golds and rosy reds." Maria took a deep breath, then sighed. "It's so beautiful out here with wide horizons, big skies, and majestic mountain backdrops." She took another deep breath, as if inhaling the color, the moment. Then she turned toward them. "Don't you get the feeling this is where God *meant* us to be?" She looked through the windshield, the side windows, and the rear, trying to see the entire sky. "*This* is what God wants us to see each evening, not brick walls or high rises."

Five minutes later, José parked in front of the ramshackle cabin. He hunched his shoulders and sneered. "This is it."

Angela stared at him. *Is he minimizing the land's beauty, so we leave the scene of his brother's murder?*

Opening the car door, Maria looked up at the sky. She uttered a sound between a sigh and a groan. Never taking her eyes from the heavens, she backed up, looking from horizon to horizon. "Oh, it's gorgeous. How could anyone not want to live here for the rest of eternity?"

José snickered. "For one thing, there's no electricity. For another, there's no water."

She glanced at him. "I thought you said the electricity was just turned off." Then she shrugged. "If there isn't already a well, I'm sure they could dig one or put in a cistern. You can always collect rainwater." She glanced at him again momentarily. Then with a sigh, she looked up at the expanse of sky. Hugging herself, she swirled as she gazed up at the sunset. "This is heaven. I don't know how anyone could ever have left this land. Its beauty's overwhelming." Closing her eyes, she took in another deep breath. Then she stopped and came to attention.

"Roses," she said. "I smell roses."

"They're by the cabin," José stiffened, "over here."

Following her nose, she started in the direction toward the gate and cattle guard. "The scent's coming from over here."

"No, not that way," shouted José. "It's getting dark. Come on. It's time to go back!"

"Just a minute," she called, her voice wafting on the breeze. "I smell roses."

Glancing from face to face, the three of them followed. When they caught up, Angela saw Maria standing in the exact location of Gabe's death.

"Look what I found!" The glee in her voice was unmistakable. "Roses, hundreds of pink and yellow roses, just like in my dreams. *This is it!* This is the place Our Lady of Guadalupe showed me in the dreams. This is where she wants to have a little house built." Maria's eyes homed in on Angela's. "I *knew* Our Lady was giving me a message, entrusting me with some mission, some task. This is it! This is the place!" Taking a deep breath, Maria looked around her, her eyes wide with awe.

"These are Wood's roses," said José, almost in a whisper. "My grandmother planted them many years ago."

Maria looked up at him and then stared at her engagement ring. "The same grandmother who wore this ring?"

Blinking, he nodded.

"And her roses continued to bloom out here after all these years, even with no one to care for them, water them." Maria shook her head in amazement. "And they bloomed on Christmas Day . . . in the Christmas Mountains." Again the joy in her voice was tangible. She looked up at José. "This is the best Christmas gift you could ever have given me."

Gulping, José tried to choke back tears.

Her smile dissolved as she put her arm around his waist. "What is it? What's wrong?"

Tears running down his face, he stared at the crime scene of his brother's murder. Then he glanced at Angela before turning to Maria. "This is where Gabe was murdered."

Maria's jaw fell slack. "This is where Mal killed . . . no . . . No!"

He nodded. "You're standing in the exact spot where Angela found Gabe's . . . where the roses are blooming."

"No, it can't be!" Maria cried out as she sagged, doubled over, and then crouched on the ground.

Blanching, José knelt beside her on one knee. "Maria, what's wrong?"

Wincing, speaking between stifled groans, she tried to smile. "I think . . . maybe the trail was a little steep."

"We've got to get you to the hospital." José put his arm around her. "Can you stand?"

Taking quick breaths, nearly panting, she nodded. "I . . . think so."

"Put your weight on me." José helped her to her feet.

Then with a groan, she sagged against him. She looked down at her legs and saw a gush of water pooling at her feet. "Oh, no!"

His eyes wide, José lifted her in his arms. "Hang on."

Maria winced as he picked her up. Then she threw her arms around his neck and pressed against him.

"Let's put Maria in the back seat." Angela opened the car door. "She can lay her head on my lap."

"I'll sit up front." Kio helped José lift Maria into the back seat and then hopped into the passenger seat.

"It's a half hour to Alpine." José jumped into the driver's seat and started the engine. "Hang on."

He stepped on the gas, but instead of taking off, the car lurched. Then they felt more than heard a thump, thump, thump.

José glanced at Kio. "I hope it's not what I think it is." Grimacing, he gave the dashboard a tap. "Jenny, don't let me down now."

They jumped out to check the tire. Grimacing, Kio poked his head in the open door.

"It's flat."

"No." Angela scratched her head. "While you two change it, I'm going to call 911, see if we can't get an ambulance out here. If Jenny's going to balk, we'll need a backup plan."

Kio nodded. "If one plan doesn't work, hopefully the other will."

When Angela moved, Maria winced. "Sorry, just need to reach my phone." She turned on her cell and saw one bar. Heaving a silent sigh, she tried dialing, but the call dropped before it connected. "Let me try to find a better spot for reception."

Again Maria groaned when she gingerly slipped out from under her head.

"Here, use this for a pillow." Angela gently lifted Maria's head and wedged her purse beneath her neck. "Be right back."

She walked around the property, testing the cell strength, but it never climbed above one bar. With an eye on the deepening shadows, she tried Kio's cell-phone reception. When that did not work, she tried José's.

Now nearly dark, Angela handed back José's phone. "No use. We're in a dead zone." As soon as she uttered the words, she wished she could have taken them back. Even in the twilight, she could see his eyes widen in fear.

"The lug nuts are loose. Just have to get the spare tire out of the back and jack up the car." José's eyes looked dark. "Maria will have to get out of the car while we jack it up. Can you stay with her?"

Angela nodded.

Kio came around from the back. "Is this your only spare?"

José gave him a puzzled look. "Why?"

Kio held it up. "It's flat."

"What?! The mechanic tested the spare just last week when he rotated the tires." Sighing, José put his hand to his forehead. He looked at the darkening sky, at his watch, and sighed again.

"José," called Maria. "José!"

The three rushed to the back seat and opened the door.

"There isn't time to get to the hospital."

His eyes wild, José's jaw dropped. "The baby's coming?" She nodded as he looked from her to his watch. "It can't be. You're not due till January twenty-second . . . not for another four weeks."

She shook her head. "Doesn't matter. It's coming."

"So soon? So quickly?" José swallowed. "I thought the doctor said labor should last six to twelve hours."

Maria hunched over and groaned. "I've got to lie down. Is there a bed inside the cabin?"

His eyes frantic, José reached for his keys. "I think I still have a key to this place. Let me check." He fumbled with his keychain, groaning in frustration. "It's too dark to see."

Angela reached through the driver's window and turned on the headlights. "Is that better?"

Nodding, José walked to the door and tried it. When it didn't fit, he tried another key. His chest heaving, he tried a third and fourth. Finally, it opened. "Can you drive Maria closer?"

Angela started the car and inched forward as the flat tire whapped against the caliche drive. Still pointing the headlights onto the porch and into the cabin, she turned off the motor.

"At least this will provide some light until we find a lamp or lantern." She grimaced, recalling the turned-off power.

José and Kio helped Maria out of the back seat, up the two steps onto the porch, and across the threshold. Angela vainly tried the wall light switch. Then she began looking in cupboards for a lamp. Finally, she started searching the drawers for candles.

"Just this." Shrugging, she held up a book of matches. Then she remembered the tea-light votive candle from the Advent Prayer Journey. "Just a minute. I've got an idea." She checked her jacket's pocket and found the tiny votive candle. "It's not much, but it's something."

José smiled. "Isn't it better to light one small candle than curse the darkness?"

When Kio saw it, he found a paper cup in the cupboard. "After it's lit, put it in here to make a mini luminaria."

José and Kio found a sleeper sofa, made it into a bed, and helped Maria onto it. Angela lit the candle, placed it in the cup, and set it on an upturned orange crate.

José's eyes flashed. "Maria's and my candles are in the glove compartment, and there's water and a first aid kit in my backpack. Be right back."

Angela gave Maria an encouraging smile. "It's going to be fine. Don't worry."

"I'm not." Maria's face looked calm, not anxious in the least. In her hands was the rosary.

A smile tugged at Angela's lips. "Toci hinted the baby would come early."

"She gave me this and her blessing." Maria took a deep breath. "It'll all work out." She looked around the sparse cabin. "Our Lady of Guadalupe led us here. This is where and when I'm supposed to have our baby."

Angela noticed Gabe standing beside the crude bed. He glanced from her to Maria. "She'll bear a son, and you're to name him Jesus."

Angela nodded.

"Where I took my last breath, her baby will take his first." Then Gabe half sang, half spoke The Blood, Sweat & Tears' lyrics to 'And When I Die.'

Angela smiled at the irony.

José returned with water, tea candles, a first aid kit, and hand sanitizer. "It's not much, but—"

"It's enough." A mantle of serenity seemed to envelope Maria as she smiled sweetly and reached for his hand. "It'll be fine."

Angela whispered, "I think God's given you another fruit of the Spirit: gentleness."

Maria nodded. Then her fingers tightened around José as her arm stiffened, and she braced her body against the contraction. A few moments later, her shoulders slumped, and she drew a deep breath as her body relaxed.

Kio came back with an armload of old towels. "I found these in a closet. Hope they'll do."

"They've got to." Angela gave him a wry smile as she took them from him. "Thanks."

Five minutes later, Maria's fingers again tightened around José's as her arm stiffened, and she braced her body against another contraction. Again her grip relaxed, and she drew a cleansing breath.

"I've got no experience with this," Maria's eyes swept their group, "but I think this is it." With that, she gave a scream.

"Okay, guys, out." Though scared herself, Angela didn't want Maria to feel self-conscious.

"No, I'm staying," said José.

Simultaneously, Maria said, "I want José here."

Kio pointed to the door. "Let me see if I can't flag down a car. The highway's only a mile or so from the house."

"Don't get run over. Here." José tossed Kio his backpack. "It's white, and it's got reflective material. You'll be more visible along the roads."

"Thanks." With a quick nod, Kio bolted from the cabin.

Angela and Maria shared a grin. Then, grunting, Maria braced herself for another contraction as José held her hands. In between contractions, he massaged her shoulders, while Angela lit more tea candles and arranged the towels, water, and first aid kit within reach.

Three contractions and ten minutes later, the baby was crowning. Scared, Angela glanced from the baby's head to José.

While he positioned himself to better see, his grip slipped from Maria's hand. She screamed his name as another contraction began.

"I'm right here." He clasped her hands tightly. "I'll be right here with you. I'm not leaving." He took a deep breath. "It's almost over. Our son's nearly here. Just keep doing what you're doing. You're doing great."

Maria tried to catch her breath between contractions, which began coming every minute. Another ten minutes and three pushes later, she brought the baby into the world. José's were the first hands to hold it. Shaking its tiny fists, the baby entered the world with a lusty cry.

They gave each other self-congratulatory smiles. Combining their scant knowledge and using the few tools at their disposal, they had delivered a baby that appeared healthy. Maria smiled when José placed the baby on her chest. She could not take her eyes off either of them, first looking at one and then the other.

José grinned at her. "Do you believe in love at first sight?"

Beaming, she nodded.

"What should we name him?"

Catching each other's eye, they simultaneously said, "Jesus."

Maria glanced away a moment and then added, "What about Jesus Gabriel?"

Tears welled up in José's eyes. Blinking them back, he gave a quick nod. "Gabe would like that." His bottom lip trembling, he ducked his chin. Then he looked up, staring into Maria's eyes. "Ever since Angela led me to Gabe's body, I've seen this land only as the crime scene of my brother's death, but now with our son's birth, you've changed that. I'm able to move on. Instead of death, this place means life . . . love."

"Rather than move on," Maria looked into José's eyes and took a deep breath. "What about building a new life right here. This is where Our Lady of Guadalupe led us. I have to think it's for a reason."

Smiling at the irony. Angela whispered, "Maria, I think you can add kindness and generosity to your list."

Then she saw Gabe standing beside his brother. After he lightly pressed his fingers to his lips, he touched them to the baby's head. With that, he faded into the night.

Turning toward Angela, Maria reached for her hand. "Thanks for all your help." Her forehead creased. "How did you know what to do?"

Angela shrugged. "Toci showed me many things. Can't say I consciously recall them, but I'm guessing this was one of the skills she taught me." Her shoulders slumping, Angela gave a sympathetic smile. "I'm exhausted. I can't begin to imagine how tired you must feel."

The baby lying on her chest, Maria grinned. "I feel high, higher than I've ever felt before. I think the endorphins are finally kicking in. The contractions came so quickly, my body didn't have time to release them until now."

Car lights flashed through the gaps of the boarded-up window, and they turned their heads.

"Who's that?" Angela and José glanced at each other and hurried to the door in time to see a four-wheel truck pull into the driveway.

"Help's here," shouted Kio's voice from the backseat window. When the truck rolled to a stop, he jumped out.

"Everything all right here?" asked a man's voice. He shined a flashlight into their eyes. Angela and José blinked and squinted.

"My . . . my wife just had a baby—"

"I'm a paramedic," said another man's voice. Then they heard the passenger door open, and a middle-aged man jumped out. "Where is she?"

"In here." Angela started leading him into the cabin.

"My wife and I live on the property next door," said a third man, climbing out of back seat. Two German shepherds followed him. "We saw lights and wondered if there was some trouble, hooligans, trespassers, or some such. Not long ago, a government agent was killed on this property."

"I know." José swallowed. "He was my brother."

"Oh." The man stopped in his tracks. "I'm sorry to hear that." Regaining his composure, he pointed to the two men. "These are my brothers, Peter and Matt, and I'm Jesse Wise."

Angela looked from one man to the other. Glancing at the two dogs, her shoulders began shaking. Though she tried to muffle it, her chuckling dissolved into laughter.

Wearing a perplexed half-smile, Jesse glanced from her to his brothers and then back to Angela. "What's so funny?"

Laughing, holding onto Kio for support, she struggled to get out the words as she pointed to the cabin. "Today is December twenty-fifth. José and Maria, inside, just had a baby boy they named Jesus." Still chucking, she pointed at the dogs. "Now shepherds and three Wise men show up." She burst into giggles. "It's the Christmas story all over again."

"The Wise men." Looking at each other, José, Kio, and the brothers snickered.

Ruffling the dogs' fur, Peter burst out in a new round of laughter. "And the shepherds."

Kio put his arms around her, and Angela felt his body quaking as he chuckled against her. Now that help was at hand, the nervous tension escaped through bursts of laughter. Slaphappy with relief, she laughed until she was weak.

Then catching his breath, Kio gazed up at the starry sky. "It's full moon tonight."

Jesse nodded. "The December Full Cold Moon."

"The stars seem so bright. I'd almost think we could see the Christmas star." Smiling, craning his neck, Kio peered from one end of the sky to the other. "The visibility's wonderful. I've rarely seen this many stars—especially on a full moon."

"The sky's usually clear out here in the desert," said Jesse. "In fact, McDonald Observatory's not far from here in Fort Davis."

Grinning, Angela turned toward Peter. "That's our cue to go in and see the baby. Don't get Kio started on anything astronomical."

Peter chuckled. "Or Jesse, for that matter. He works at the observatory." As they entered the cabin, Peter looked at the dilapidated conditions and crinkled his brow. "Kio told us about the flat tires and premature birth."

Angela grimaced. "Maria wasn't due for another four weeks. When we realized she was going into labor and discovered the flat tires, we tried calling, but—"

"No cell towers, no service." Peter nodded sympathetically. "It's a dead zone for cell reception out here." He gave her a reassuring smile. "I'll take a quick look, make sure they can be moved, and then let's get your friend and this Christmas baby to the hospital."

Fifteen minutes later, the eight of them and two shepherds piled into the truck and headed to Alpine. Jesse drove with Angela and Kio beside him in the front seat. José, Maria, and the baby sat in the back seat, while Peter, Matt, and the shepherds rode in the truck bed.

Through the closed windows, Kio kept staring at the clear skies. Jesse glanced at him. "You like stars, don't you?"

Kio nodded. "I come by it naturally. My father's an astronomer. I've been studying skies with him since I can remember."

"He just graduated with an MS in astrophysics," added Angela.

"That so?" Jesse gave him a second look, seeming to size him up. Then his expression softened. "There's an opening at the observatory for a telescope operator."

Kio's back straightened. "You mean for the Hobby Eberly Telescope?"

Jesse nodded. "Most of the work's from sunset to sunrise in front of a computer console, but if you're interested—"

"Yeah! What do I need to do?"

"The job's posted online." Jesse glanced at him. "Let me know if you apply. I'll put in a good word for you."

Kio gave a wary chuckle. "Thanks, but you don't know anything about me."

Jesse gave him and Angela a grin. "I know you risked life and limb flagging us down in the dark to help your friends. Aside from looking for help, I couldn't help noticing you were looking for the 'Star of Wonder.'" Then he spoke up, so José and Maria could hear him in the back. "Have you heard the latest Christmas-star theory put out by a Texan?"

They shook their heads. Angela murmured, "No."

"A fellow by the name of Rick Larson was researching old manuscripts and discovered the date of Herod's death had been off by three years. Long story short, he found there was a series of five conjunctions of Jupiter, Regulus, and Venus, which from the earth could have looked like one very bright star. Then Jupiter went into retrograde—"

"Which made it look like it had 'stopped,'" said Kio.

Nodding, Jesse caught Kio's and Angela's eyes as he grinned. "The interesting part about the three wise men was they weren't only astronomers. They were also astrologers. Regulus, the King star, is the brightest star in the constellation of Leo, the Lion. Israel's often called the 'Lion of Judah,' so the wise men knew something important was about to happen in that nation.

"Nine months following the first conjunction of Jupiter and Regulus was another conjunction of Jupiter and Venus in Leo. The wise men considered Jupiter the Father or the King planet and Venus, or Ishtar, the Mother. With those parental planets in conjunction, it's not a stretch for the Magi to have believed a king's birth was about to occur. This theory suggests if you were in Jerusalem looking toward Bethlehem on that December twenty-fifth, Jupiter would have been 'standing' in Virgo—"

"The constellation of the Virgin." Kio nodded. "What an interesting theory."

"I'd never heard that," said Angela. "Some people seem to think the Christmas star's just a story. Maybe there was a physical explanation for it actually happening." Then turning toward Jesse, Angela gave him a half smile. "Out of curiosity, what were you three 'wise men' doing driving around on Christmas night?"

Jesse chuckled. "Look in the glove compartment."

Angela opened the latch and took out three bundles. Carefully unwrapping one, she began laughing.

"Hold it up," said Jesse.

Smiling, she held up a figurine of one of the wise men riding a camel. "I'll bet there's a story connected."

Wearing a mischievous grin, Jesse nodded. "My wife collects camel figurines. The way some people collect pigs or horses, my wife collects camels."

Kio looked at him. "Why?"

"She's half Turkish."

Recalling her heritage, Angela spoke up. "I'm a quarter Turkish. My birth-mother's half. Her name's Ceren, Turkish for gazelle, but neither of us has ever felt any connection to camels."

Jesse shrugged. "I'm not sure what the fascination is, but ever since I've known her, she's collected camels. I'd wanted to get her a special Christmas present, and a friend of mine found these in an estate sale yesterday. Another long story short, we were just on our way back from picking these up. If it wasn't for these camels, we'd never have been out on the road tonight."

Shaking her head, Angela chuckled. "What timing."

"I'm beginning to think everything's timing." Maria's tone was reflective. "Everything happens in its time, in God's time."

José's cell phone rang. Answering, he said, "We're fine . . . all five of us." Muting the phone, he handed it to Maria. "It's my mother."

Grinning, she relayed the story. "We should be at the hospital in," she raised her voice. "How long?"

Jesse said, "About twenty minutes."

She repeated it for Lupe. "We'll meet you there."

At the hospital, they rushed the baby into the Maternity Ward, where the doctor weighed him, took his temperature, and measured the circumference of his head. She checked the baby's eyes, ears, mouth, heart, lungs, feet, spine, and hips. Then she gave Maria a thorough examination and pronounced them both healthy.

"However," said the doctor, "he'll have to stay here for observation."

Maria's face fell. "Why? If he's healthy, why can't I take him home?"

"He was born at thirty-six weeks. We need to monitor his breathing, weight, eating behavior, and a dozen other factors."

Her shoulders slumping, Maria frowned. "How long would he have to stay here?"

"There's no hard or fast rule. It all depends on how he thrives. It could be a day or two to a couple weeks. At a minimum, we need to determine whether he needs supplemental oxygen, can maintain his body temperature, has developed the swallowing reflex, and can eat on his own."

"Can Maria be discharged?" José's face looked drawn.

"For her health and the baby's, she should also stay a day or two. That way, she can breast feed and bond with him, as well as recuperate."

"What about the wedding?" Lupe's brow wrinkled. "Will she be strong enough to get married the day after tomorrow?"

Smiling, the doctor glanced at Maria. "That's up to you, but from my perspective, you're hale and hardy. Other than prescribing antibiotics to counteract the less-than-antiseptic birth conditions, I see no need for you to stay past a day or two. Anyone who can give birth under the circumstances you've described can certainly walk a few feet down the aisle."

Chapter 12

"Families are like fudge—mostly sweet, with a few nuts."
— ANONYMOUS

Saturday after breakfast, Kio got a call on his cell.

When he hung up, he had a look of wonder on his face. "Guess who that was."

Angela shrugged.

"Jesse."

"One of the 'Wise men'?" She grinned. "What'd he want?"

"He's picking me up on his way to the observatory."

She wrinkled her brow. "Why?"

"Apparently the hiring manager will be in the office today, and Jesse wants me to meet him."

"Wow." Her eyes opening wide, Angela grinned at him. "Who knows? You might be graduating to the working class." She kissed him. "For luck!" Then she turned toward Lupe. "Where's José?"

"He left early to visit Maria and the baby at the hospital."

At noon, José called. Lupe's eyes were round when she got off the phone. "She's coming home. They're releasing Maria and the baby tonight."

"Really? The baby's eating and gaining weight?"

Lupe nodded. "*And* the wedding's *on!* We've got so much to do!" Her eyes opened wider as she started listing the work on her fingers. "Call the family, have everyone bring food for the reception, bake the wedding cake, make the flower arrangements . . . "

She stopped so suddenly, Angela was alarmed. "What's wrong?"

"The dress, I need to take in the dress!" She blinked, processing. "First I need to call my sisters. Then . . . " She pulled potatoes, carrots, corn, onions, cilantro, and calabaza out of the fridge and handed Angela a paring knife. "Better start making the *caldo de pollo.*" At Angela's blank stare, she added, "Chicken soup."

People began arriving within the hour. Carrying trays or bags of food, relatives with party dresses carefully slung over arms, and suitcases, sleeping bags, and pillows in hand started ringing the doorbell or walking in and announcing themselves. Everyone congregated in the kitchen, where Lupe instructed each person about their tasks and sleeping arrangements in English and rapid Spanish.

Taking in the organized pandemonium, Angela grinned as she watched her in action. *The kitchen's headquarters, and Lupe's the commander in chief.*

Soon she found three relatives beside her, helping her peel and slice the vegetables, as more women squeezed into the kitchen to bake the wedding cake and prepare side dishes for the reception, as well as food for the evening meal.

Two hours later, Angela felt a bit overwhelmed by the orchestrated chaos. She snuck out of the kitchen and into the living room, hoping for a moment's escape. Twelve relatives squeezed around the dining room table, creating floral centerpieces for the wedding tables, boutonnières for the men in the wedding party, corsages for the bridesmaids, and pomander balls for the flower girls. Like a finely tuned assembly line, they turned out exquisite floral arrangements under the watchful gaze of one of the aunts.

Angela scratched her head as she looked at the mass of roses, floral tape, and greenery. "How many bridesmaids are there?"

"It's a small wedding." One of the cousins shrugged. "Counting you, only seven pairs of bridesmaids and groomsmen."

Another cousin looked up from her handiwork. "Don't forget the six ushers, two ring bearers, and four flower girls."

"And centerpieces for eighty tables," added a third woman with a wry chuckle.

Angela looked at the heaped flowers, the mountain of luggage stacked against the walls, the chattering clusters of ladies in the kitchen and dining room, and the boisterous males gathered around the television, watching a football game. "And you think we'll finish everything by tomorrow?"

"Of course, everyone knows their job and pitches in." The cousin grinned. "Even if we have to stay up all night, José and Maria will have a wedding to remember."

Just as the sun was setting, a group of grandnieces and nephews burst through the front door. "They're here! They're here!"

Chairs scraped and the chatter increased as everyone rose to greet José, Maria, and the new baby.

José politely tried to forge a path through the excited wall of well-wishers. Everyone wanted to peek at the baby, welcome Maria, and congratulate him.

Finally, Lupe took charge. "Maria needs her rest. Her only jobs tonight and tomorrow are to sleep, feed the baby, and get married."

As the group stepped aside, letting them pass, Lupe led her into the bedroom she shared with Angela.

Unsure what else to do, Angela followed behind, pausing at the sight. The room's floor was covered wall-to-wall with sleeping bags and air mattresses.

Just as dinner was starting, Kio walked in the open front door. He did a double-take as he glimpsed all the new faces. Then catching himself, he grinned, greeting everyone until he spotted Angela.

"What's going on?"

"Maria's home from the hospital, and the wedding's on! José's family is all here, helping make it a success." Then she noticed a glint in his eye. "How did the interview go?"

"Technically, it wasn't an interview," he grinned, "although, that's the way it worked out. I still have a lot of paperwork to submit," his eyes lit up, "but I just may get the job."

"Really? Congratulations!" Angela leaned over to kiss him.

"'May' is the operative word here, but I think I have a good chance at it. Say a prayer."

She nodded as she hugged him. "Always."

Everyone worked nonstop, going from one project to the next, as Lupe directed them. At two in the morning, Angela collapsed in bed, exhausted but chuckling from the camaraderie.

Just before she fell asleep, she smiled to herself. *So this is what a large family's like.*

She awoke to the mouthwatering aromas wafting from the back-yard smoker and grill. Then she peeked out the window to see the men combining ingredients for the dry rub, seasoning the chicken and brisket with the mixture, making a barbecue sauce, and smoking/grilling the meat.

Inside the house was synchronized mayhem. Somehow, everyone managed to shower and dress, as well as put finishing touches on the refrigerated flowers, towering wedding cake, reception's side dishes, and decorations. While Maria stayed in bed, the cousins fixed her hair, did her nails and makeup, and vied to hold the baby, while Lupe fitted her wedding dress with last minute alterations.

Maria grinned. "I feel like a princess, so pampered . . . so special."

That afternoon, Angela found herself following the two ring bearers, four flower girls, and six bridesmaids as she marched toward the altar to the beat of festive Mariachi music. She turned slightly to glimpse Maria behind her and saw her beaming in her newly tailored wedding gown. Lupe had used the excess material to create a ring sling for the baby, although it looked more like a matching sash across Maria's shoulder and chest. The tiny bundle within its folds barely made a bump.

José stood so tall and proud, the buttons on his shirt strained at their stiches. Kio beside him never took his eyes from Angela, and she found herself walking toward him as if this was their wedding day.

Maybe, some day, it'll be our turn.

Then, standing between José and Kio, she saw Gabe, looking like a mirror image of his brother, smiling, literally glowing.

Carrying only Toci's rosary in her hands, Maria began walking down the aisle as her father escorted her. At each pew, she accepted a de-thorned, long-stemmed rose from the person seated on the aisle. By the time she reached the altar, she carried a vibrant bridal bouquet of yellow and pink roses. Then with a kiss on her cheek and a handshake with her bridegroom, her father left her in José's care.

The readings were from Corinthians. "Love is always patient and kind . . . Love never comes to an end."

The words reminded Angela of the Thanksgiving Mass. Only these remain: faith, hope and love. Of the three of them, the greatest is love.

As the priest began the homily, he smiled at Maria and José. "What a beautiful season to enter into marriage. During Christmas, our minds turn to love, peace on earth, and goodwill to all. Yet two days after Christmas, we're beginning to see tinseled trees left at the curb and Valentine's Day decorations in the chain stores. Though return lines are still long, and post-holiday sales are thriving, for many, the Christmas season ended the day after Christmas.

"For believers, however, the Christmas season's festivities and traditions overflow into January. In fact, the Church observes eight days of celebrating Christmas. Starting on Christmas Day, the octave ends on January first, the Solemnity of Mary, Mother of God. During those days, we celebrate several Feasts, including today's Feast of the Holy Family." He glanced at José, Maria, and then at the baby cuddled against her. "What a perfect day to begin a marriage, begin as a family."

His smile faded. "Tomorrow we celebrate the Feast of the Holy Innocents, commemorating those children Herod massacred in Bethlehem as he tried to destroy the Christ Child." He touched the baby's head as it stretched its tiny arms and gently mewed. Then he looked out at the congregation. "This child is a testament to life, but we can't forget Herod's legacy. The slaughter of the innocents goes on today, but aborted babies aren't only slaughtered. Their internal organs are being harvested and sold for 'research,' experimentation."

Maria flinched at his words. Then she glanced at Angela as she protectively cuddled her baby against her chest and silently moved her lips. *Thank you.*

Angela nodded back, smiling, stifling a sigh. How different things could have been if Dev and I hadn't been outside the clinic that morning.

"Life is a gift," continued the priest, again wearing a cheerful smile. "And speaking of gifts, we celebrate Epiphany a week from today as we remember the three kings' gifts to the baby Jesus."

Angela caught Kio's eye and gave him a private smile as she thought of the Wise brothers and their German shepherds.

"The Christmas season is filled with exciting events and activities. The reason we have Christmas at all is because we're grateful Jesus was born to bring us salvation. The Christmas season officially ends with the Baptism of the Lord, two weeks from today. So leave up your Christmas trees until then. As Scrooge would say, keep Christmas in your hearts."

He beamed at Maria and José. "Christmas and marriage share parallels. Hold the love you feel for each other today throughout your lives. Just as the Christmas season is more than Christmas day, marriage is more than your wedding day. Cherish each other, and keep love in your hearts throughout your days to come."

When it came time to exchange the wedding rings, Angela watched Gabe hold Maria's hand as he guided José's hand. Recognizing the ring with two angels holding the stone in place, Angela recalled it as the first engagement ring José had given Maria. *How much has happened since the Guardian Angels' Feast Day.*

Clasping their hands in his, Gabe smiled. "Tell Maria she's received the final fruit of the Holy Spirit: faithfulness. *Now* I can move on." With that, he dissolved.

The following Thursday, Kio parked in front of the Tower of the Americas, and they walked through the glassed entry.

Holding her head back for a wider view, Angela surveyed him. "I thought you said we were going to dinner."

His eyes glowed. "We are."

"Yeah, but the revolving restaurant?" As she read the placards in the elevator, she lifted an eyebrow. "Can your student stipend afford it?"

Kio squeezed her hand. "Tonight's a special occasion."

She nodded. "It is New Year's Eve."

His eyes twinkled merrily as his face relaxed into a warm smile. "Has it been a good year?"

She thought of all the events: meeting Maria on 'Christmas in July'; taking the historical tours of San Antonio with José; and walking the Mission Trail Pilgrimage with their foursome. She recalled Mal's unwelcome entrance into their lives and his departure; the women's conference; and the Defeating Fallen Angels conference. *So much has happened.* She thought of the 'befores' and 'afters.' Gabe and his transformation; Maria and her change of heart; and Kio. She studied his face. *Has he changed, or has our relationship?*

He stared back wearing an amused grin. "What's going through your mind?"

She lifted a shoulder in a half shrug. "Just thinking about the changes, the shifts." She met his eyes. "Thinking about us."

"You are, huh?" He lifted his mouth in a mischievous smile. "What a coincidence. So am I." He reached for her hand as the elevator doors opened.

Angela glanced up at the foyer's glassed ceiling and then looked at the curved glass walls. Nearly tripping, she crossed from the stationary floor at the tower's center to the slowly rotating floor of its circular dining area.

The maître d' showed them to a table set for two alongside the glassed wall. Angela stared out as the city donned its evening finery. Lights began twinkling along the River Walk, the city's heart, as well as along the main arteries leading into the city. *San Antonio's alive. I can almost feel its pulse.* Then she glanced at Kio and felt her own pulse racing as a pleasant shudder slid down her back.

"It's—"

The waiter introduced himself and handed them menus as the water boy filled their glasses.

When they left, Angela tried again. "It's a lovely way to spend New Year's—alone with you."

"Is that as your best friend or your boyfriend?"

"Yes." Grinning, she lifted her water glass.

Kio touched his glass to hers. "To us."

The waiter stopped back at their table. "Would you like anything to drink?"

Wearing a sheepish grin, Kio glanced at the wine list and pointed to an item. "Yes, we'd like this bottle of champagne." Then he turned toward Angela. "Especially tonight, we need to toast each other in style."

"Water won't do?"

Grinning, he shook his head. "Not tonight."

The waiter returned with a bottle and an ice bucket. Then he filled their glasses. "Would you like to order now?"

"Could you give us a minute?" As the waiter left, Kio turned to her and raised his glass. "Let's try this again. As Dom Perignon, the father of champagne, said the first time he tasted it, 'Come quickly! I'm tasting stars!'"

Smiling, she clinked her fluted glass against his. "Leave it to an astronomer to work stars into everything, even a toast."

His eyes glittered. "I do have some star-spangled news—"

"The job?" She set down her glass and leaned across the table. "You got it?"

"Yup." Smiling, nodding, he lifted his glass in another toast.

"Congratulations! To your success!" Angela tapped her glass against his, sipped, and then set it down. "Something told me you'd get that job at the observatory." She sighed. "There was something magical in the air that night."

"It was certainly a Christmas I'll never forget."

They reminisced about Christmas, the baby, the wedding, and the year as they leisurely devoured their maple-glazed quail and coconut shrimp. After they had revolved around the city twice, Kio gazed at her, chin on hand.

Blinking, she grinned. "What?"

"Are you ready to go to a star party?"

"Tonight? New Year's Eve?"

He nodded. "Though we're 750 feet above the city, I thought you might want a closer look at the heavens."

"The planetarium's open tonight?"

Wearing a mischievous smile, he shrugged. "For us, it is."

An hour later, the planetarium's grinning night watchman let them onto the observation deck.

"Enjoy the view."

Kio fist-bumped him. "Thanks, Joe. I owe you one."

Their steps echoing in the hushed surroundings, Kio led her to the telescope. He pressed a button, and the dome opened to the night sky. The moon and a bright star shone through.

Kio glanced at her with a smile. "By Jove, that's Jupiter."

She chuckled. Then narrowing her eyes, she studied him. "You're acting very mysterious tonight, even for you. What are you up to?"

He took a deep breath. "I don't always tell you how I feel. Since I have a hard time expressing myself, I thought the stars might say it for me."

Cocking her head, she wrinkled her brow. "I'm not following."

"It's amazing what messages you can find in the heavens." He gave a nervous chuckle and moved toward the controls. "Let me adjust the lens. Then you can see for yourself." He fastened an eyepiece to the telescope. When he was satisfied with the focus, he stepped back. "Take a look. See if the heavens don't hold life's answers . . . or at least its questions."

Watching him warily from the corner of her eye, Angela walked hesitantly up the steps to the telescope. She closed one eye to focus through the eyepiece, and when the moon came into view, she gasped. Instead of seeing craters, outlined against the moon, she saw the words, 'Will you marry me?'

She turned around to see Kio on one knee, holding out a ring.

Squealing, her hands flew to her face. Then she felt tears running down her cheeks.

"You are my sun, my moon, and all my stars. I love you, Angela. I just didn't know how to tell you." He gave a shy smile. "Will you marry me?"

She floated down the steps in a daze, put her arms around him, and raised him up from his kneeling position. Staring into his eyes, she nodded. "Yes." She gave a nervous chuckle. "Does this make us officially boyfriend and girlfriend?"

He laughed. "More like fiancé and fiancée." Then he leaned down and kissed her.

Angela kissed him back, wondering at her depth of emotion. *Where'd that come from?* When they broke apart, she studied him. "How did you manage that?"

Wearing a grin, he shrugged. "I'd wanted to give you the moon and stars when I proposed, but on a grad student's stipend, I couldn't quite afford it. When I learned the observatory was going to toss this flawed lens, I got an idea. I took it to a gunsmith friend of mine, who makes custom reticles—"

"Reticles?"

"They're the etched cross-hairs for high-powered gun sights, and my friend engraved the words on the lens."

She glanced at the eyepiece. "It's so tiny. How could he fit it all on there?"

"It's only eight millimeters across," he grinned, "but that's nothing. In quantum physics, if you 'squeezed out' all the space between the protons, neutrons, and electrons, the world's entire human population, all seven billion of us, could fit inside a sugar cube."

"What?" Half closing one eye, she pulled back her head as she skeptically studied him.

"Sure, an atom's like a miniature solar system, with a million, billion times more space than matter—"

"I'm not questioning quantum theory." She sighed as she grinned at him. "Is this what marriage will be like with a star gazer? All science and no romance?"

Smiling, he took her in his arms. "Angela, I love you to the moon and back."

Tongue in cheek, she tried to stifle a smile. "Please don't tell me the distance."

"Four hundred and seventy-seven thousand, eight hundred miles, but who's counting?"

With a groan, she playfully punched his shoulder.

He drew her closer. "Seriously, when I look in your eyes, I see stars."

"You should." She kissed him. "You're the astronomer who put them there."

~The End~

ABOUT KAREN HULENE BARTELL

Author of the Sacred Journey and the Sacred Messenger series, as well as *Sovereignty of the Dragons, Christmas in Catalonia, Angels from Ashes, Untimely Partners,* and *Belize Navidad,* Karen is a best-selling author, motivational keynote speaker, IT technical editor, wife, and all-around pilgrim of life. She writes multicultural, offbeat love stories steeped in the supernatural that lift the spirit. Born to rolling-stone parents who moved annually, Bartell found her earliest playmates as fictional friends in books. Paperbacks became her portable pals. Ghost stories kept her up at night—reading feverishly. The paranormal was her passion. Wanderlust inherent, Karen enjoyed traveling, although loathed changing schools. Novels offered an imaginative escape. An only child, she began writing her first novel at the age of nine, learning the joy of creating her own happy endings. Professor emeritus of the University of Texas at Austin, Karen resides in the Hill Country with her husband Peter and her *mews*—five rescued cats.

CONNECT WITH KAREN

WEB SITE: WWW. KARENHULENEBARTELL.COM

FACEBOOK: KARENHULENEBARTELL

TWITTER: KARENHULENEBART

READING GROUP GUIDE FOR

Lone Star Christmas

Why is the title, *Lone Star Christmas*, significant? Why do/don't you like it? What would you have named *Lone Star Christmas?* Is the title a clue to the theme(s)?

Did you enjoy *Lone Star Christmas?* Why/why not?

What do you think *Lone Star Christmas* is essentially about? What is the main idea/theme of *Lone Star Christmas?*

What other themes or subplots did *Lone Star Christmas* explore? Were they effectively explored? Were they plausible? Were the plot/subplots animated by using clichés or were they lifelike?

Were any symbols used to reinforce the main ideas?

Did the main plot pull you in, engage you immediately, or did it take a chapter or two for you to 'get into it'?

Was *Lone Star Christmas* a 'page-turner,' where you couldn't put it down, or did you take your time as you read it?

What emotions did *Lone Star Christmas* elicit as you read it? Did you feel engrossed, distracted, entertained, disturbed, or a combination of emotions?

What did you think of the structure and style of the writing? Was it one continuous story or was it a series of vignettes within a story's framework?

What about the timeline? Was it chronological, or did flashbacks move from the present to the past and back again? Did that choice of timeline help/hinder the storyline?

Was there a single point of view or did it shift between several characters? Why would Karen Hulene Bartell have chosen this structure?

Did the plot's complications surprise you? Or could you predict the twists/turns?

What scene was the most pivotal for *Lone Star Christmas?* How do you think *Lone Star Christmas* would have changed had that scene not taken place?

What scene resounded most with you personally—either positively or negatively? Why?

Did any passage(s) seem insightful, even powerful?

Did you find the dialog humorous—did it make you laugh? Was the dialog thought-provoking or poignant—did it make you cry? Was there a particular passage that stated *Lone Star Christmas'* theme?

Did any of the characters' dialog 'speak' to you or provide any insight?

Have you ever experienced anything that was comparable to what occurred in *Lone Star Christmas?* How did you respond to it? How were you changed by it? Did you grow from the experience? Since it didn't kill you, how did it make you stronger?

What caught you off-guard? What shocked, surprised, or startled you about *Lone Star Christmas?*
Did you notice any cultural, traditional, gender, sexual, ethnic, or socioeconomic factors at play in *Lone Star Christmas?* If you did, how did it/they affect the characters?

How realistic were the characterizations?

Did any of the characters remind you of yourself or someone you know? How so?

Did the characters' actions seem plausible? Why/why not?

What motivated the characters' actions in *Lone Star Christmas*? What did the sub-characters want from the main character and what did the main character want with them?

What were the dynamics between the characters? How did that affect their interactions?

How did the way the characters envisioned themselves differ from the way others saw them? How did you see the various characters?

How did the 'roles' of the various characters influence their interactions as sister, coworker, wife, mother, aunt, daughter, lover, and professional?

Who was your favorite character? Why? Would you want to meet any of the characters? Which one(s)?

If you had a least-favorite character you loved to hate, who was it and why?

Was there a scene(s) or moment(s) where you disagreed with the choice(s) of any of the characters? What would you have done differently?
If one of the characters made a decision with moral connotations, would you have made the same choice? Why/why not?

Were the characters' actions justified? Did you admire or disapprove of their actions? Why?

Edwina and Jake both had moments where they struggled with their faith. When was the last time your faith faltered? What helped you get through that time?

What previous influence(s) in the characters' lives triggered their actions/reactions in *Lone Star Christmas*?

Did *Lone Star Christmas* end the way you had anticipated? Was the ending appropriate? Was it satisfying? If so, why? If not, why and what would you change?

Did the ending tie up any loose threads? If so, how?

Did the characters develop or mature by the end of the book? If so, how? If not, what would have helped them grow? Did you relate to any one (or more) of the characters?

Have you changed/reconsidered any views or broadened your perspective after reading *Lone Star Christmas?*

What do you think will happen next to the main characters? If you had a crystal ball, would you foresee a sequel to *Lone Star Christmas?*

Have you read any books that share similarities with this one? How does *Lone Star Christmas* hold up to them?

What did you take away from *Lone Star Christmas?* Have you learned anything new or been exposed to different ideas about people or a certain part of the world?
Did your opinion of *Lone Star Christmas* change as you read it? How? If you could ask Karen Hulene Bartell a question, what would you ask?

Would you recommend *Lone Star Christmas* to a friend?

The Recipes

"I love vitamin T: tacos, tortillas, tamales, tostadas."
— ANONYMOUS

SOPA SECA (DRY SOUP)

Prepare angel hair nests as you would rice pilaf. First brown the pasta in hot oil and then simmer in bouillon.

Ingredients

1 pound angel hair nests (or straight vermicelli broken into 3-inch-long segments)
1/2 cup olive oil
1 medium onion, peeled and chopped (about 1cup)
4 fresh tomatoes, peeled and chopped, or 1 cup crushed canned tomatoes
4 cups chicken bouillon
Salt and pepper, to taste

Directions

Fit the angel hair nests tightly in a single layer a large, covered sauté pan. Heat the oil until shimmering hot. Sautéing several at a time in the hot oil, brown the pasta angel hair nests on both sides and remove from the pan.

Sauté the chopped onions until soft, about 6-8 minutes. Stir in the chopped tomatoes and bouillon. Season to taste with salt and pepper.

Bring to a simmer. Tightly squeeze the browned angel hair nests in a single layer, turning once in the bouillon to moisten both sides. Simmer until the pasta has absorbed the liquid, about 6-8 minutes. Remove from heat. Turn nests over a second time and allow to rest for 4-6 minutes until all bouillon has been absorbed. Yields eight servings. To serve four, halve the recipe.

TAMALES — TRADITIONAL TEX-MEX CHRISTMAS EVE FARE

Tamale Meat Filling Ingredients
1 (3-pound) pork roast
1 medium yellow onion, peeled and chopped
6 gloves garlic, chopped, divided
Salt and pepper, to taste
1 teaspoon ground cumin, or to taste
1/2 cup chili powder, or to taste

Directions
Hint: If possible, prepare pork roast up to a day ahead of time.

Combine the pork roast, onion, and half the chopped garlic (3 cloves) in a large pot. Season with salt and pepper. Cover with water and simmer 2-3 hours, or until very tender. Using two forks, shred the meat and coarsely chop. Reserve the liquid.

Blend the shredded pork with the remaining garlic, cumin, and chili powder. Adjust seasonings. If dry, add a tablespoon or two of the liquid.

Tamale Ingredients

1 (8-ounce) package corn husks
2 1/2 pounds prepared masa
1 1/2 cups reserved liquid from roasted pork, warmed
1-2 tablespoons chili powder, to taste
1/2 heaping teaspoon ground cumin
8 ounces canola or vegetable oil
1/2 teaspoon garlic powder, or to taste
salt to taste

Directions

Hint: Find corn husks and masa in the ethnic food aisle of grocery stores.

Separate the corn husks and remove the strands of corn silk inside. Rinse and immerse them in a large pot of simmering water. If necessary, weigh them down with a saucer to keep them from floating. Softening can take from 1/2 to 3 hours.

Knead together the masa, liquid, chili powder, cumin, oil, garlic powder, and salt in a large bowl. Knead until the masa is smooth and has a spongy, light texture.

Drain the husks on paper towels and pat dry. Smear two tablespoons of masa on the smooth side of each husk. Then spread a heaping tablespoon of pork mixture in the middle. Pull the sides of the husk together and fold the tip up and over the sides. When all the tamales are filled and folded, stand them upright, packing them tightly together in the steamer. Cook over medium heat for about 3 hours, adding water as needed.

Serve warm with your favorite salsa. Yields ten dozen tamales. To yield five dozen tamales, halve the recipe.

Caldo de Pollo — Tex-Mex Chicken Soup
FOR A CROWD

Ingredients

4 -5 pounds chicken, cut into quarters
Water to cover
3 chicken bouillon cubes
5 fresh garlic cloves
2 medium onions, peeled, cut into large chunks
1 tablespoons salt, or to taste
1/2 cup fresh cilantro, chopped
3 pounds potatoes, peeled, cut into large chunks
4 ears corn, peeled, into 3 inch pieces
4 zucchinis, cut into 1-inch slices
1 calabaza, cut into 1-inch slices (yellow squash may be substituted)
3 stalks celery, cut into large chunks
1 cabbage, quartered

Directions

Place the chicken pieces in a soup pot with the water and bouillon cubes. Bring to a boil.

Add the garlic, onions, salt, and cilantro. Lower the flame and simmer 1 hour. Prepare the vegetables during this time.

Skin the chicken and skim the broth.

Add the potatoes and corn. Simmer for 20 minutes.

Add the zucchini, squash, and celery. Simmer for 10 minutes.

Add the cabbage. Simmer for 15 minutes or until the cabbage and squash are tender. Yields ten servings. Serve hot, ladled over Spanish Rice.

Spanish Rice for a Crowd

Ingredients

3 tablespoons vegetable oil
1 1/2 cups Long Grain Rice, uncooked
1/2 cup green sweet pepper, diced
1 sweet onion, diced
2 fresh garlic cloves, finely chopped
1 (10-ounce) can diced tomatoes and green chilies
1 (8-ounce) can tomato sauce
2 1/2 cups chicken bouillon
1 teaspoon ground black pepper, or to taste
1/2 teaspoon salt, or to taste
1/2 teaspoon cumin

Directions

Heat the oil in a large pan over medium-low heat.

Stir in the rice, pepper, onion, and garlic. Gently sauté all until rice is golden brown, stirring frequently.

Add the canned tomatoes, sauce, and bouillon, and bring to a boil.

Lower the heat. Sprinkle the spices over all. Cover and simmer (without stirring) until the rice absorbs the liquid (about 18-20 minutes). Yields ten servings. To serve, scoop the rice into individual bowls, and ladle steaming hot Caldo de Pollo over all.

Special Bonus!

FREE sample of Karen's other books in the Sacred Journey series, *Sacred Choices* and *Sacred Gift*

SACRED GIFT

Everyone is gifted, but some never open their package.

HAPPY READERS:

This is a beautiful story of survival – rich with redemption, forgiveness, and love! It visits two of the choices women have when faced with unexpected pregnancies. Abortions can leave the mothers with feelings of guilt, anger, and bitterness. Choosing adoption can leave the mother with a different sense of heartbreak and loss. Characters alternate in the spotlight, but Angela is the hub, with her spiritual connections playing key roles in the story. At times the story drags, feeling more like a history lesson touching on Religion, Art, Architecture, and Solar Geometry in connection to Franciscan friars and their design of Mission churches in Texas hill country . . . it's informative and entertaining, with a positive ending. Hats off to Karen Bartell for a job well done!
~ LORI LEGER AT *InD'TALE MAGAZINE*

Another grand slam for Karen Bartell. This story, set years later, gives us a glimpse into the life of the child from the first book, but also more back story on the three women from the first book. The story was woven like the strands of a tapestry. A tapestry I am anxious to know more about. Highly recommend.

~ MICHELE BREAUX-ROWLEY

EXCERPT FROM *SACRED GIFT*

Develyn's black-outlined eyes opened wide. Then she looked down, hiding what-ever slid through her mind. "I had a grandmother."

Angela smiled politely, thinking she was joking. "You mean your mother was older when she had you?" Nodding her head, she snickered. "I can relate."

"No, I mean I never knew my mother, never had a mother. My grandparents raised me." She sipped from her straw.

"Why's that?"

She grimaced. "My grandparents only gave me a sketchy summary, no details. Basically, they said she died giving birth to me." She grunted. "It was like this forbidden topic. Every time I brought it up, my grandmother got teary-eyed and left the room."

"Did your grandfather ever talk to you about it?"

Develyn scoffed. "He'd just shake his head, sigh, and mumble things like, 'maybe when you're older.'"

Angela raised her eyebrows. "And I thought I had it rough."

"Why?"

Angela sighed, and then licked her lips. "I knew I was adopted. It was an open adoption, for heaven's sake. I grew up with two...*three*... mothers, but recently my birth mother told me she almost aborted me."

"No." Stopping, Develyn grabbed Angela by the shoulder and turned her so they faced. "You're serious?"

"Yeah." Angela grimaced. "Talk about wondering if you were wanted—"

Her eyes big, Develyn said, "I'm a survivor."

"A survivor of what?" Angela snickered, again thinking she was joking. "The Titanic?"

"No," she started slowly, keeping her eyes on her cup. "Abortion."

"What do you mean?"

She looked Angela in the eye. "My mother tried to abort me. The abortion failed. She died, and I survived."

Angela's jaw dropped. "Ohmigosh." She blinked. "Are you sure? I mean, how could you know—"

Develyn's lip curled. "My darling cousin told me one day, laid it right between my eyes in no uncertain terms." She caught Angela's eye.

Grimacing, Angela shook her head slowly. "Sorry."

Develyn tried to shrug it off. "To quote the tee-shirts, it is what it is." She looked away.

In step, they turned and walked in silence, each sipping her coke, each lost in her thoughts. People passed them. Tour boats floated by.

Finally, Angela asked, "Have you ever...communicated with your mother?"

"Like in séances or Ouija boards?" Develyn held up her hands, shaking them as if she were scared, then abruptly dropped them and made a sour face. "What do you think?"

Angela heard the sarcasm. It was hard to misinterpret. She raised her eyebrows and was ready to back off. Then shoulders slumping, she groaned. Taking Develyn by the elbow, she stopped her.

"Look, whether you want to believe me or not, there's someone here who'd like to speak to you."

Develyn's left eyebrow and lip curled. "Yeah, right." She started off, but Angela again caught her elbow.

"I'm serious."

"And I'm Cleopatra." Develyn smirked.

"Fine, you don't want to listen, that's your business." Angela sighed. "I tried. I'm done," she said to the night.

"Who are you talking to?"

"Nobody." She sullenly sipped her coke. Then she threw back her head and groaned. "Okay, but this is the last try."

"Who the hell are you talking to?" asked Develyn.

"Ginny." Angela grimaced. "She's asking if the name Ginny means anything to you." When she was met with silence, she peered at Develyn. "Does it?"

Develyn's eyes reminded Angela of an owl's. "You're not kidding, are you?"

"Who's Ginny?"

Develyn shook her head. "Ginny only to her family, Virginia was her name."

"All right, who is she?"

"My mother."

FIND IT AT YOUR FAVORITE BOOKSELLER OR AT
www.Pen-L.com/SacredGift.html

SACRED CHOICES

An inspirational love story

HAPPY READERS:

This was a really great story. The characters are confronted with important life-changing choices that the average person hears about all the time. Anyone can relate to the conflict that each character is facing. But each one makes their choice with the knowledge they have at the time. The characters and their stories have stayed with me and I look forward to hearing more about them in future work.

The story brings in a study of history and culture, which can be relevant at any time and is certainly relevant today. Along with that is the differences in viewpoint from one generation to another. But ultimately it shows that in many ways, we are all alike and are only different because of the choices we make.

~DIANE MUELLER, MSLIS

Thought provoking story revolving around a controversial topic. Story crosses generations, ancient religions and modern day Catholicism, paternity and maternity, to name a few topics. The main characters counterbalance each other, some being rational and others more defined by emotion. Intrigued by possibilities for a sequel.

~DIANE CMEREK GORCHS

EXCERPT FROM *SACRED CHOICES*

The woman shrugged as the air emitted a crackling or frying sound that seemed to run up and down the musical scales.

"It...it almost sounds like singing." Ceren looked around, wondering who would be singing at a time like this. Following the contours of the angel's wing, her eyes were drawn upward. At the wing's crest, violet-blue tufts of flame flashed and arced to the crown of the angel's head and gradually dropped, tracing along the blade of its sword.

"What is that?" Ceren stepped back, partially to get a better view, and partly to move away.

The high-pitched, musical hissing crackled louder as the short, tufted flames followed the sword's edge down through the serpent's stony profile. Then the violet-blue tufts leapt to the angel's leg, and began a slow descent along its periphery, gradually creeping closer. Frozen now with fascination, Ceren stood riveted, unable to recoil or retreat. Only her eyes moved as they tracked the flames' descent.

Nearer and nearer they edged toward the statue's feet until the violet flames blazed inches from her and the old woman.

Bound in wonder, Ceren watched the impossible happen. The flames jumped from the statue's toe tips to the old woman's metal armband, seeming to shoot out from her jewelry's serpentine head and tail. Ceren blinked. The armband seemed to wriggle around the old woman's withered bicep as the flames inched down her arm to her fingertips. Her nails began glowing violet-blue like tiny jets of flame.

The old woman looked at her fingers, looked at Ceren, and then cackled as if she had thought of something amusing. Never taking her eyes from Ceren's, she reached over, and touched Ceren's hand, igniting her fingertips.

"Passing the torch," she hissed against the wind.

Ceren watched in horror and fascination. Her fingertips sparked and flickered with violet-blue flames. Other than a slight shock when the old woman had touched her, she felt nothing. No pain, it wasn't consuming her. It wasn't fire, at least as she knew it. She watched the tiny hairs rise on her arms and shuddered as the hair rose on the back of her neck.

Tickled, laughing with relief, she said, "It's static electricity on steroids."

Again she felt a drop of rain, but this time it gave off a mild shock as it touched her. It reminded her of the time she had visited a farm as a child. She had held onto the electric fence, almost enjoying the tingling sensation of the slowly pulsating, electric current.

Another drop and then another sprinkled them, each drop generating milder and milder shocks, diminishing the flames' intensity, until their fingertip flames went out. Ceren checked her hands, but the flames had left no trace, other than their memory. She looked at the sky and watched the squall line move on, leaving only cirrus clouds in its wake. As quickly as the storm had blown up, it blew away, leaving the air refreshed.

Ceren breathed deeply. The peculiar experience left her feeling like a child who had gone out to play in the rain. She felt cleansed, carefree, cheered, until she remembered her appointment.

Again, she checked her watch. Thanks to the traffic and crowds, it had taken longer than expected to reach the chapel. It would take at least as long to return. She sighed, hating to leave Tepeyac, loathing her next destination.

She turned to say goodbye to the old woman, but she was gone. Ceren looked in all directions, checked the chapel's courtyard, but, except for a couple standing on the steps, she was alone.

ALSO BY KAREN HULENE BARTELL:

CHRISTMAS IN CATALONIA

A simple trek through Spain becomes a life-changing journey through fear and hope.

On an obligatory walk along Spain's Camino de Santiago before her marriage day, Gwen Alton's trek becomes a life-changing journey through ghosts, fear, and hope, and the beginning of a life-long pilgrimage.

BELIZE NAVIDAD

Follow your star or follow the crowd?

Belize Navidad is Christmas magic in a tropical-isle setting. This one warms the heart as it chills the spine, with nods to *A Christmas Carol* and *The Gift of the Magi*.

ANGELS FROM ASHES: HOUR OF THE WOLF

True love is like a ghost. Many believe in it, but few encounter it.

Chloe Clark stumbles on both but, burned by romance and riddled with low self-esteem, she's unable to recognize true love when it finds her. Agreeing to care for her great-aunt Edwina, she travels to Door County, Wisconsin. There she meets Hud, a charismatic Menominee Indian man, who initiates her in sunset cruises on Lake Michigan, the aurora borealis, his tribe's Wolf clan, and the importance of faith, family, and love.

At her great-aunt's antiquated house, Chloe learns of her family's roles in the tragic Peshtigo Fire of 1871 and the miracles at the Our

Lady of Good Help Shrine. Things get frightening when she accidentally summons the spirits of two restless relatives who begin manipu-
lating her emotions.

Faced with the still-unsolved murder of her great-aunt's sister at
age fourteen, an ongoing family feud from six decades before, and
a vengeful phantom, Chloe must help her ancestors find peace to
be freed of their grasp. Can she realize that peace and find true love
with Hud?

Find it at your favorite bookseller or at
www.Pen-L.com/AngelsFromAshes.html

Dear Readers,
   If you enjoyed this book enough to review it for Goodreads, B&N, or Amazon.com, I'd appreciate it!
                    Thanks, Karen

Find more great reads at
Pen-L.com

www.ingramcontent.com/pod-product-compliance
Lightning Source LLC
Chambersburg PA
CBHW071233250626
47163CB00001B/157